FREEING SHADOWS

L.L. KOMBE

Book Design by Undertable Studio
ISBN
978-0-9958086-0-7

"When it is dark enough, you can see the stars."
Ralph Waldo Emerson

For Emma
and Sam—my home

"She dared to dream for herself and her sister. One day they would find their own happiness, and she prayed that Catherine would be fiercely loved, as she loved her."

CHAPTER ONE

THE ACCIDENT

Present—1953, London
Rita

Rita tried to open her eyes but the simple effort produced a stabbing pain. Everything appeared blurred; still, she could make out the shape of her hands. She squinted for a clearer look and saw they were covered in an odd shade of red. The sudden realization that she wasn't alone shook her violently out of her daze. As she struggled to turn, an excruciating pain shot from her lower back and she could strain only her neck to look to her side. She saw nothing—he was not here.

The car was eerily quiet except for the smoke that hissed threateningly from the rear. Her eyes searched frantically for any sign of Kurt. *He was sitting right here with me when it happened. Where has he gone?* She couldn't bring herself to look outside because she knew he must be out there if not trapped in here with her. She would brave the pain. *The injuries can't be that bad.* She tried to reassure herself as she struggled with her seatbelt until the clasp broke free. Its dampness urged her not to think about blood.

In the dark, her hands trembled as they clutched and pulled at the handle to open the door. It stayed jammed shut. She attempted to move her legs and sighed with relief when she realized they were not broken. Clenching her teeth, she moved to the passenger's seat where Kurt had been sitting moments ago and kicked the door free. She felt little strength left and sat still to catch her breath. *Could this be a dream?*

She looked down at her crimson-red hands then smelled the leak of gas and knew this was no dream and that she must move faster. She crawled out of the car on her hands and saw him as soon as she reached the ground. He was not moving but appeared to be breathing. She never knew she could withstand so much pain. The sight of Kurt lying bloodied on the ground was more than she had ever suffered, even now. She ran towards him and knelt beside him. He gasped for air and tried to speak and she bent forward, placing her ear beside his moving lips.

"Marie."

Rita felt her heart sink.

§

Wartime—1944, Rouen
Kurt

Kurt was running, although he felt like he was flying, not in a free sort of way, but in flight from something—darkness, death, the ultimate ending. He was gasping for air, his heartbeat vigorous and alarmingly fast. But he couldn't order his legs to stop. They were moving uncontrollably, and he believed he could make it—just a few more miles. He could already hear the bullet rounds and people screaming.

That sounded like François. They had played cards back at camp just last night and laughed hysterically about things he couldn't call to mind now. He must focus—where is he running to? Rita. He was running back to her; if he could survive this war, he would fly home to her.

A rifle shot—it wasn't far from where he ran. Who are they aiming for? Are they chasing him? When did he get separated from his group? He had thought he was between François and a group of five maquisards. Their disorganized group consisted mostly of young Frenchmen, inexperienced and clueless with respect to warfare strategies, whose sole determination derived from their desire to avenge their deceased families so brutally killed by the Germans. La Résistance, as they were known, was meant to be a crucial addition to their team in France, but Kurt had felt skeptical from the beginning. He had little faith to count on them to rescue him from this German-occupied territory.

§

When the war broke out in Britain, Kurt had been one of the first in his class to enlist. He was unattached to anyone at the time and had preferred it that way, having focused most of his time and energy in college to advance in his engineering studies—a path that his father had methodically planned out for him. But when war was declared on his country, it lit in him an unfamiliar, almost exotic desire he never suspected existed. Since childhood, he was not the kind to volunteer for any remotely risky tasks. In retrospect, it could be that his parents so fiercely shielded him from the enticing thrills of danger—a well-intentioned protection— that would later charm him into making drastically different decisions for himself. But no one, not even his parents, could have shielded him from war. And now, he was free to make decisions of his own. Why not be part of something greater than himself, bigger than his own ambitions that were apparently not his own to begin with?

And so it began. He went through grueling training with boys hardly older than seventeen; others were closer to his age. He unexpectedly came to love this newfound companionship, a kind of brotherhood seldom found elsewhere, even among his closest classmates. He had a sister back home, but he couldn't equate her with someone close to him. So there he found himself, among friends, close confidantes, and brothers.

When he was selected to focus on operating radios, a sense of relief came over him. He knew he wasn't the brave, hardened soldier he strived to be; but as that burden lifted from him, he was simultaneously overcome by guilt. Why shouldn't he want to be amidst the brothers he had come to respect and love and fight beside valiantly for his country? And then, as if life had decided to give him a second chance to make things right, after a few weeks into his training, he received from Milton Hall a letter with vague content, lacking all the important details soldiers should know before committing to a specific operation. Without much thought, he left for Milton Hall. After a few days of interrogation, mostly regarding his skills as the top radio operator of his regiment and his fluency in French, which he had studied since grammar school, he was approved and transferred into the British Special Operations Executive (SOE).

There, he was taught to shed his previous notions on being a dignified soldier of war, adhering to the common rules that would dictate his integrity, even when facing the enemy—and take on a wholly new and foreign perspective as an agent for a clandestine operation named Operation Jedburgh, excelling in sabotage schemes such as cutting radio lines and destroying railroads and bombing bridges to pave way for the Allies' troops into Normandy.

When the Americans arrived at Milton Hall, they were then separated into groups of mostly three, consisting of one commander, an executive officer, and a radio operator. He soon found himself in Group Luke, the name of the commander who would lead their team. They were to land before the Allied invasion, parachuting into Normandy and making their way up through the Rouen forest, where they would meet up with groups of maquisards from the surrounding villages and begin training for the eventual assault on Cherbourg.

When they first dropped into Normandy, it took them about a week to get things organized. Other than training the overzealous and inexperienced maquis, they were given the task of filtering out the undercover Vichy government spies who would foil their entire mission. It was a precisely detailed operation, and Kurt was beginning to have his first taste of what the other agents called "guerilla warfare". He felt himself drawn to the dangers of such an exclusive and clandestine operation.

Perhaps he would have a chance to prove himself yet. Luke led the mission, or at the very least, tried to. It was obvious to almost everyone but Luke that he wasn't quite equipped for the role. He was too inexperienced and young.

But who was he to judge? Kurt smiled when he thought of himself in comparison with Luke. He was twenty-one and had barely held a rifle. He left home because, well, everyone did, and who didn't want to be in a victorious war against a failing enemy? Today, though, he didn't feel as confident as he once did, and he thought this may well be his last day on Earth.

A twig snapped. Kurt thought he heard Germans in the distance, and he stopped in his tracks to listen intently for any kind of movement. This had been taught in training. What were they supposed to do when they came across a troop of German soldiers while separated from the group—alone with no ammunition? He closed his eyes, but all that appeared were flashes of Rita and him laughing under the stars as they made a promise to each other. What was that promise? Reaching into his pocket, he pulled out a worn-out picture and tried to steady his hand to get a clearer glimpse of her.

They had met right before he left for Milton Hall. She was an unexpected attachment he had been trying to avoid throughout his college years. But as fate would have it, she entered his life with such intensity that he couldn't help but reciprocate her affections. Long before he knew it, this mutual fondness had transformed into a loving commitment he had no willpower over. A smiling, happy Rita—he squinted at the sight of her, not knowing whether it was from the sweat beads forming on his forehead or his tears. He looked at the picture a second time, not knowing where he would be in the next minute. For a short, fleeting moment, he tried to muffle out the sounds of rifles and the rushed, chaotic movements of his friends and enemies surrounding him. He took in the whole image—Rita with her straight, lustrous brown hair, her large blue eyes saddened by his leaving her so soon after their engagement. What had she said when they exchanged good-byes at the train station? He cursed himself when he couldn't remember anything, not even her voice.

Another rifle shot.

His legs started to move again. He wasn't going to stop this time. The grass was soft and wet with morning dew under his worn-out boots. He imagined for a brief instant that he was running away from his brother, who loved to chase him in the yard after the first snowfall of the year. There was not a cloud in the sky, and the sun shone down on him, burning his back and blinding him like an unwanted spotlight. He wasn't sure how much longer he could run, and he wondered how many of them were scattered throughout the city, fleeing from the Germans with no clear destination. He suddenly realized he was running in a forest with tall pine trees surrounding him, trees that reminded him of Christmas back home. He could almost smell the baked turkey and hear the clinking of wine glass and the laughter of his family.

This is not the end. Please, let this not be the end.

It happened with no warning. He heard the sharp sound of a bullet shot into the air, and he could determine to the second when he felt it pierce his left knee. He leapt high, almost gracefully, like a choreographed dancer, before he crashed unceremoniously to the ground.

It felt like a lifetime before he was able to open his eyes, but all he can see was darkness. *Is this the end?*

He heard bodies shifting, and people whispering above him. He tried to squint, hoping to recover his vision. He wasn't going to die in German hands. His hands were trembling but he managed to bring one into his left pocket in the frantic search for a grenade. He was going to end this, right here, right now.

"*Papa, Papa! Il bouge!*"

It was a woman's voice, clear as the bells that hung on his family's Christmas tree by the fireplace. The voice sounded sweet enough to relieve him from the pain shooting through his left leg. His fingers loosened the grenade in his hand. He let out a sigh of relief and thanked God that he recognized the French words she whispered like a lullaby before he did anything foolish. He tried to move his head towards her voice, but he was fading out again, and he wondered how complete darkness could get darker.

"Rita," he heard himself mutter before he let the darkness swallow him whole.

§

Present—1953, Paris
Catherine

It was a small, cramped room that smelled of old library books—the kind that no one cared enough to even flip through. She could barely see the walls in the enclosed space as it was filled with boxes piled atop one another. The sense of entrapment felt familiar.

"Mlle Aumont?" A middle-aged man with a hastily groomed beard and beady eyes stared from behind thick-framed glasses and greeted her with an apologetic smile. She could tell that he knew who she was; his recognition was apparent, although he tried to hide it. This was an odd place for her to be—a renowned, world-class ballerina sitting in a cramped interrogation room.

"Bonjour." Catherine nodded nonchalantly, and reached into her bag in search of her much needed cigarettes. She had control of the situation, or at least that was what she tried to convince herself from the moment she stepped into the foul-smelling room.

There was very little information divulged to her when she received the phone call requesting her to pay the detective a mandatory visit. Slowly, her eyes scanned the board that hung on the wall. Several pictures were pinned up haphazardly, and below each of them was a brief paragraph describing who the subjects were and what atrocities they had committed. The handwriting was small and almost incomprehensible, but she could make out the words as she skimmed through them. Years of torture summed up in a few sentences. She winced at the thought of her darkest hours—the ones she spent underground—out of sight and out of harm's way.

"Mlle Aumont, I'm Pierre Duprès." The detective extended his hand as he stared at her in admiration. "I've asked you here to inquire about . . . uh . . . how shall I put this . . ."

The detective lowered his gaze, exposing his embarrassment about the meeting.

"Please, continue." Catherine looked directly at the man designated to intimidate her. She felt empowered by his hesitation to interrogate her.

"Mlle Aumont, we have been informed by someone that you are, or have been, a Nazi sympathizer."

The uncertainty lingered in his eyes, and he let the pause go on for too long. He shifted uncomfortably in his seat and cleared his throat. He needed to start anew to reassert himself before the great Catherine Aumont.

"To be frank, we are still searching for a few high-ranking officers that were stationed in Rouen where you were . . . lived . . . what I mean is—if you have any information pertaining to the . . . " His voice trailed off and Catherine felt sorry for him.

"Monsieur Duprès, I do not have any information on any ex-Nazi officers." Her voice was graciously firm with a hint of refined arrogance. She was not going to stay here another minute. Calmly, she slid her hands into her fine leather gloves and stood up to face the detective. Before opening the door, she tilted her head slightly towards him, her eyes cold and unforgiving, as if addressing a lowly servant who had no place in her parlor.

"I don't suppose you can tell me, Monsieur Duprès, who it was that gave you this information?"

§

Present—1953, Paris
Catherine

She sat on her bed, waiting for her him to come home—an exhausting game that Luke had forced her into for the past few months. A waiting game. It had surfaced unexpectedly—this drunken, unpleasant side of Luke that she wasn't familiar with until now. A loud noise in the hallway announced his return.

Luke staggered forward, and when his legs felt the hardness of the bedframe, he let himself collapse onto the bed. Even in his drunken state, he knew his side of the bed. He was dressed in full tuxedo, with his bowtie still in perfect place, although his hair looked disheveled. She subconsciously ran her fingers through its thick curls, an affectionate gesture she had grown accustomed to despite the anger she felt for his behavior.

"Marie."

It used to hurt her when he would say the name in his sleep, or in a drunken state, or when he thought she wasn't there—as though saying it would bring Marie back to life. Catherine felt almost nothing because she was stronger now—and indifferent. Still, she winced whenever she heard her sister's name. But today, perhaps due to the awkward meeting with Detective Duprès, overwhelming memories rushed back. Her eyes filled with tears, and she felt surprised by how bitter they tasted as they rolled down her cheeks into the corners of her pursed lips.

She was always the brave one in the family. Marie had her strengths, too, but they shone through a different light. For nine years now, Catherine tried not to think about her, but her shadow seemed to be lurking everywhere—in Caroline's journal, in her childhood memories, in her own reflection. Neither she nor Marie would ever admit it, but they did shared similarities. And try as she might, Catherine couldn't pinpoint what they were. Marie was shorter, with straight, flaxen hair and her bright hazel reflected her sweet, loving disposition. Taking more after her mother, Catherine inherited her blond curls, distinctive ocean-blue eyes, and a character "as stubborn as a yew," according to her father.

It was difficult not to love Marie, her younger, gentle-spirited sister who, to her, was almost flawless save for her unintelligibly messy handwriting. There was little they disagreed on, and one of the few things they fought about was whether to bring a wounded soldier into their cave. She remembered that day, and replayed it in her head as a reminder of her beloved sister.

It was 1944.

§

Wartime—1943-1944, Rouen
Catherine

She usually sat at the table with Marie, and they would read all day. It didn't matter what they read, as long as they could keep their minds focused elsewhere. Not here—not in the middle of this ongoing war. Maman kept herself constantly busy, preparing dinner—and dinner meant any variation of potato recipe her genius Maman could conjure up. A "rich" meal meant potatoes and beans with a small portion of meat they had saved up since last week when Catherine spotted a rabbit near the door of the cave. One day, Catherine had to venture outside to capture it so that they might eat something else for dinner. Maman came close reprimanding her for going without her permission. Catherine could tell by her eyes as they changed from a soft kindness to a fiery rage that shone whenever she got furious at Catherine's shenanigans. But that day Maman didn't say a word. Catherine knew that even Maman longed for an uplifting change in their mundane meals, and any kind of meat would mean a feast.

She could still taste the stale bread that was their most common meal and recalled how her stomach churned painfully whenever that was the first food she tasted after two days. She didn't miss that part, but she ached for her family and wondered if she would mind being back in the cave again, just to be together with them for one more day.

Seeing the cave for the first time had been one of the most depressing days in her life. She remembered being led down by Papa, her hand clenching his so tightly that day. She didn't want to let go until he hugged her tightly and reassured her with kisses on her forehead. The cave was dark, cool, and empty, and she couldn't imagine this being their home for the next few weeks or perhaps longer. Maman's eyes were sullen but not cast down; she looked determined to survive these evil times.

"Come, girls," Maman's cheerful tone tried to brighten the darkness that enclosed them.

She led Marie and Catherine by the hand, and they knelt together for *berakhot*, a prayer to ask God for blessing. To this day, Catherine could not decipher whether it was to thank God for the cave or to ask him to somehow bless the dark hole that was going to be their refuge, their new home.

Papa didn't join them as he was not a believer of spoken prayers. He preferred to keep to himself and mouth silent prayers to God.

"Can we pray for Philippe too?"

Marie's request surprised them all. It was the first time someone had spoken his name since he died the year before. The family huddled in a hastily formed circle around the last of their luggage that had been moved from their home aboveground.

Maman's eyes shone with overwhelming love and sadness, and she was thankful still because her two daughters were spared from the wrath God had thrown at her family. She nodded softly to Marie and squeezed her hand gently. It was a gesture that best showed her affections when she couldn't find words.

"Certainly, we'll say a prayer for Philippe."

As the family prayed in the cave that would be their home, they couldn't know that it would be another sixty-seven days before another person arrived and shared in their darkness.

Catherine recalled the events of that day just like it was yesterday.

There was a loud thump above them, and they froze in the midst of their actions. Papa, who was reading old newspapers, all from before the war to refresh his memories of better times, titled his head sharply upward towards the source of the noise. He clumsily steadied his glasses and waited for the next movement. Or gunshot.

Maman had been sewing an old, worn-out skirt. The needle fell out of her hand, and Catherine was certain that she heard it drop to the ground. Marie was drawing, practicing her knowledge of human anatomy from memory as she had forgotten to bring her biology books when they had moved into the cave.

Naïve and inexperienced with war, they thought they would have a second chance to bring their cherished photo albums, clothes, or favorite books from their home, but returning to their house was not an option once the Germans occupied the town. Before then, they had heard stories told as if they were tales from a distant land. No one believed the war would ever affect them. They heard when the German soldiers had slaughtered a family including five children, the youngest not yet five years old. Each family member sobbed and begged while they waited for their own execution.

One day, when Papa returned from a short walk in the forest looking for firewood, he was astonished to see so many roofs lit up like torches. Shaken at the horrific sight of their beloved town, he had entered the cave with little to say other than "it is gone. . . just gone." Since that day, Marie and Catherine stopped asking when they might return home to rescue Mignon, the family dog. They just prayed that she got away. After all, Germans couldn't tell which dogs were Jewish.

Marie stopped studying the meticulously complex details of the heart organ as soon as she heard the daunting thump. She glanced silently at Catherine and stayed motionless, as if any movement would betray their presence. Marie had indisputably the most beautiful hazel-green eyes Catherine had ever seen, but on that day they were filled with dread and silent screams.

Catherine continued peeling potatoes for dinner after hearing the strange sound. Maman cast an angry glance her way and glared at the potatoes as if the very sound of peeling would give them away. Catherine rolled her eyes. What harm could her peeling potatoes do?

With a quiet, swift movement, Marie surprised them all by standing up abruptly and scurrying towards the "door" of the cave. It was not much of a door, rather more of a small opening hidden by branches and leaves that Papa re-arranged every morning and night. Maman watched in horror as Marie slowly climbed up the wooden ladder leading towards the opening. Catherine turned to Papa, who also looked dismayed.

She found herself captivated by Marie's sudden bravery, and her eyes followed carefully until Marie disappeared from sight. A sob came from Maman, and as soon as she heard it herself, she stifled it but couldn't stop her tears as she stood shaking uncontrollably. Papa hurried towards the ladder and hesitated for a few seconds before starting to climb.

Catherine was now in the cave alone with her mother. Her heart pounded so fast hard against her chest she thought she might vomit. *Why aren't they coming back?*

Marie's voice punctured the overwhelming silence and Catherine's heart almost leapt out of her chest. She gasped for air, and started to choke.

"Catherine! Maman! It's a wounded soldier!"

Maman steadied herself against the table. She looked pale and fragile and still beautiful in her mid-forties.

Catherine remembered that moment. Maman had looked like a frozen rose about to crumble in the harshest of winters.

"He's not German," Papa whispered as he popped his head back in. He glanced reassuringly at Maman.

Mama sighed in relief, her eyes still angry. She glared accusingly at her husband. He should have announced this news sooner.

"For goodness sakes, you two, get back down here!" Maman's voice trembled. "Don't make me go up there." She sounded slightly steadier now, but Catherine instinctively knew that Maman was bluffing. She hadn't moved an inch from where she stood.

"Papa! Papa! *Il bouge!*" Marie was almost shrieking. Catherine couldn't withstand the suspense. She ran towards the ladder, ignoring Maman's furious whispers ordering her to come back.

She wasn't prepared for the blinding sunlight and had to shield her eyes with both hands, almost forgot she was on the ladder. She steadied herself and heard her mother sigh with relief. They usually emerged during late afternoons or evenings and rarely in broad daylight. Catherine climbed out of the cave clumsily and while she knew that the area was clear, she still crouched, and her eyes darted back and forth to check for suspicious movements.

Then she saw him. A wounded young man dressed like a maquisard. His eyes were closed and he looked so peaceful and still as he lay on the ground. The grass below his left knee was covered in dark crimson red. She couldn't take her eyes off the blood that flowed out of his knee.

"We have to move him." Marie took off her coat to cover him and started to inspect his breathing, acting like the nurse she was meant to become if not for the brutal interruptions of war.

Papa could only stare back blankly at Marie. He wasn't ready to take another person into the cave, let alone an injured one. He was a compassionate man, but in a time of war, desperation, and hunger, he couldn't be sure he was able to care for someone outside his family. He thought about how many potatoes might be left in the cave, and how many more times he could venture outside to hunt for meat.

His heart told him that he should while he knew fully well that he couldn't.

Catherine watched the blood drain from his face and she thought he would faint. She took his hand in hers and felt him jump at her touch. He quickly wiped away the tears that he thought were falling down his cheeks but soon realized that his eyes were dry. He looked up and saw the lingering morning dew on the branches of the apple tree by their cave. The sun was strong and it hurt his eyes to look directly at it. How many more times would he be able to see the daylight before being dragged from their cave by German soldiers?

Death, it seemed, was inevitable—and he felt it more closely as he watched the young man struggling to breathe, his life slipping away as quietly as he had imagined his own death.

"Marie, he's not going to live down there." Catherine thought about Philippe, and how he struggled and fought to stay alive on that fateful day.

Why hadn't anyone helped Philippe? And why should they help this man now? Her heart stung a little, but she kept her eyes stern and steady. She had to protect her family who was still alive and well.

Marie said nothing and didn't look at Catherine. Instead, she tore the seams of her skirt and vigorously tied the soldier's badly injured knee. Catherine turned her face away. She knew that Marie was training to be a nurse one day but she didn't know how her shy, inexperienced sister was brave enough to withstand such gruesome war injuries.

"He reminds me of Philippe," Marie muttered, not expecting anyone to hear her, but they all did—every word.

Papa took a few cautious steps forward and looked for himself, his eyebrows raised, still suspicious of whether this young man was spy for the despicable Germans. His serious face softened after a closer look. The man did resemble Philippe with his dark brown hair and long nose—a few more years and Philippe would've been about the same age and height.

Catherine didn't want to look at the stranger laying on the ground, as if the resemblance alone would prompt them to rescue him. But then he coughed, causing him to wince and let out a soft groan. Hearing him, she realized that he wasn't Philippe, but he was still full of life.

"Papa, Catherine, help me!" Marie grunted as she lifted the man's arms. Her breath was visible in the air, her nose red with the biting cold, but her eyes were incandescent and burned with hope. Was this her way of bringing Philippe back to them?

Catherine and Papa, as if under a spell, heeded Marie's orders and began to lift the man's legs. It was then that Catherine felt the full weight of the war, the heartbreaking atrocities following endlessly violent battles, and the goodness that struggles to push through every horror and bring a glimpse of hope into every darkened cave.

§

CHAPTER TWO

THE MEETING

1943-1953
Rita

She recalled being lifted onto a stretcher after the accident and the unbearably loud sirens of an ambulance. She had turned her head, feeling the deepening soreness of her neck and seeing Kurt lying still on the ground. There were people surrounding him and ambulance workers shouting orders. Rita hadn't been on a battlefield but she reckoned that this was a close enough portrayal of one. She didn't know if he would survive, but she couldn't keep her eyes open and let them close.

Darkness came and she willfully let it swallow her whole as she craved a deep sleep. She woke up in a hospital bed. She smelled fresh flowers and knew there had been visitors. It couldn't possibly have been Kurt who brought the flowers. She felt too terrified to open her eyes and see him lying in his own blood. She tried to chase the image from her mind but her resistance seemed only to evoke the horrifying scenes of the accident. Maybe it was all a bad dream. She opened her eyes slowly, praying that there would be nobody lying on the ground. The room was dark; when she saw her bandaged feet, the familiar dread swarmed over her. She recognized that her dream was, in fact, reality: she and Kurt had been in a car accident.

There was no one in the room with her and she failed to understand why. Which hospital was she in, and why was she left alone? She started to cry, and when she tried to wipe her tears, she saw that her left hand had been thickly bandaged and she couldn't move her fingers. With her free hand, she reached for the tissue box on the nightstand but knocked down a glass of water on the bedside table. Footsteps rushed along the hall, and she thanked God that someone was coming.

"Ms. Collins! Ms. Collins!" The young nurse rushed to her bedside and adjusted the catheter Rita hadn't seen on her left arm.

She was about to correct the anxious nurse then realized she and Kurt had not been married. Her last name was still Freidman. The accident had occurred the night before their wedding. Distractedly, she turned her engagement ring around her finger.

"Where . . . where is he?" She began to panic and felt a stab of pain in her arm having moved too quickly.

The nurse didn't know who Rita was asking for but nevertheless tried to calm her patient with fake promises while adjusting her catheter.

"He'll be here soon, dear. He'll be here soon."

A flurry of footsteps could be heard in the hallway. Someone else was coming. Rita immediately recognized the scent of her mother's perfume as she entered the room. It was a subtle blend of roses and lilies.

"Oh, Rita, you're awake."

Her mother took her hands and gently kissed her bruised knuckles.

She saw her mother's painted nails, and she remembered. They had agreed on soft pink for the wedding. The bride and her mother would have matching fingernail color. The white bed sheets she lay on reminded her of her wedding dress, which had been made from the silk parachute

Kurt brought back from the war. She had sewn it herself with freshwater pearls and sparkling white beads at the seams and waistband. She had purchased a handful of crystals for the sleeves. It was a beautiful dress, and she looked radiant and happy when she first tried it on. Kurt hadn't seen it, but Rita kept picturing his face when he saw her for the first time walking down the aisle. It would be an epic moment, a wedding to be remembered and talked about for the next few years among all her friends. A brave American war hero who survived Normandy against all odds and returned safely to marry the love of his life. But the truth was, no matter how happy she was that he had come back to her unharmed, her joy had been dampened by a quiet, sad stranger who looked an awful lot like Kurt.

She tried to recall the details of how they first met. A simple encounter that lacked all the sensational details that would make a good story, but it was one she secretly cherished. A handsome stranger had chivalrously given up his seat for her on the train. A faint smile and a friendly nod. It did not take long for them to fall in love, as with most of her friends during the war. Life was short, and the time spent together was fleeting, making every moment worthwhile. He was not timid in showing his affection and Rita did not shy away from him as she previously had done with other suitors. It was a strange time, and people behaved differently and boldly. They deliberately stepped out of their daily routines and danced with the possibility of a brand-new tomorrow if it ever came. Soon after their fateful meeting, she found out he had been called to join an operation different from the one where he was stationed —one he could not speak to her freely about. All she knew was that he was expected to draft a will before he left in the event he didn't return. That was the extent of her knowledge about the operation.

At first, Rita thought him to be a quiet, reserved young man, but in the three months they had spent together, she discovered a different, wilder side to him that she found curiously desirable. He was a young man who dared to dream, and it hadn't occurred to him that he may not survive the war. His infectiously daring attitude in life drew her to him, and soon they were engaged to be married.

Unlike other couples during the war, they did not rush their wedding.

In defiance against all possible outcomes, they chose to wait until after Kurt returned and now their marriage was indefinitely postponed. But Rita felt confident, although she didn't understand where her unwavering belief came from. She wasn't as religious as her parents; still, she somehow held on to a hope that remained beyond her understanding. Kurt would come back. And when he did, they would flaunt their happiness in the face of death, whose grip did not succeed in tearing them apart.

But when he did come back to her, it was as though life had something even grimmer in mind for them. The joy and ambitious drive that once fueled Kurt's every smile and movement had been somehow stripped away from him during the war. He seldom spoke to her, and when he did, he would tell her about some of the hardships he had endured but never in a coherent manner, preventing her from fully understanding the extent of his suffering.

The weeks leading to their wedding were painfully different than what Rita had imagined. It had already been postponed for more than six months. She found out from reading the newspapers that most of the men in his battalion were severely injured, had been tortured, or had died from their wounds. She gave him time and space then tried to re-enter his life again as subtly as she could with extreme patience and unconditional love.

With the damning realization that the change within Kurt was too complex to fathom, she was left bitter and unwilling to tolerate the silences forced upon their strained conversations.

On the night of the accident, they were driving to her parents' estate for the rehearsal dinner. She wore a crimson red dress, Kurt's favorite color on her but which did not seem to please him anymore. He had stopped noticing the way she dressed and no longer showered her with compliments. He was meticulously dressed in a gray suit and a bright yellow tie dotted with white doves with freely spread wings.

Chained down by the memories of the war, he felt anything but free and continued to refuse Rita's affection.

They had been fighting about something insignificant. She was familiar with the painful routine and knew his satisfaction came only when his words drove her to tears. She had shouted harsh words that she couldn't imagine uttering earlier, while his placid expression stayed as unresponsive as on the day he had stepped off the plane a war hero. She shouted in an unrecognizably shrill, coarse voice.

A familiar song, "I'll Never Smile Again" came on the radio. Frank Sinatra crooned in the background, assuaging the tension in the air. They had danced under the stars to the song only days before he left. He had whispered something sweet and she cried, not knowing if they were tears of happiness or sadness. She had felt their love blossoming and yet so close to ending.

She stopped shouting and allowed herself to surrender to the swaying melody and the crooning voice. When the song ended, she felt tired of fighting the stubborn pride that refused to be tamed. She wanted him to come back to her and was willing to give it another try. She gently caressed Kurt's hand, and they sat quietly, allowing the silence to transform into a healing mediator and no longer a weapon of spite.

Seconds before the crash into an oncoming truck, he turned to her and opened his mouth to speak. The words became inaudible as the sound of the collision and glass shattering swallowed their voices and unsparingly tore through their bodies.

What did he say? What were those last words that she couldn't hear?

When Rita shifted in her bed again, she felt the sheets underneath her body. The thought of being somewhere other than in the debris of the car frightened her. She didn't want to be alone.

"Where's Kurt?"

Her mother's expression was difficult to read. Her lips were pursed but her eyes showed no devastation—nothing to suggest death of her future son-in-law.

"He's here, Rita." Her eyes darted to the left. "In the next room."

Rita heard the sirens again, and she held her breath, contemplating the worst.

"Is he alright? Why didn't they put us in the same room?"

She watched her mother's face and knew the next piece of news wouldn't be good.

"It's just that . . . he hasn't woken up yet. And he's been talking loudly in his sleep."

Her mother reached over to hold her hands now clenched into fists.

Rita remembered why her chest was hurting and why she had difficulty breathing. She had escaped from the damaged car and had run to Kurt. He had muttered something . . . someone else's name.

"Marie," she whispered.

Her mother's eyes flashed a sign of recognition and she looked away, fixing her eyes instead on the beautiful, fresh flowers that were not from Kurt.

§

Present—1953, Paris
Rita

The road outside looked empty, with only a few taxis waiting by the stand. Grim and gray, the skies announced no good news; rain would inexorably arrive. Rita, with her one suitcase, hesitated before stepping out of the airport. She had no idea where she was going, and she didn't know a single soul in Paris. How did she even get here?

A sharp screech from behind awakened her from her thoughts. She was at the airport, standing in front of the exit door. She turned back and saw an elderly couple pushing their luggage cart together. Did they travel often? Did they make a promise to each other to see the world together? She glanced at her hand, clutching the handle of her small suitcase.

She pushed through the door and the autumn breeze caressed her cheeks. She still needed to figure out where she wanted to go. Her hands searched inside her purse until she found the single clue she had brought with her and pulled it out. A portrait of a beautiful young girl, her hair in a single braid spilling down to her chest, appeared to smile at the artist painting her. She looked happy, like nothing in the world could make her unhappy in that captured moment. She leaned against a tree trunk, her arms behind her back and her legs crossed flirtatiously. Her clothes weren't drawn with much detail—a simple blouse with a plaid skirt reaching to her knees. Her dimpled smile made Rita think they resembled each other. She turned the paper over and felt her heart break a little more.

"Marie, 1943. France." The writing had already faded, but she could still make out the words. It didn't quite look like Kurt's handwriting, but the picture was in his possession.

She found it when her mother handed over the things that the paramedics had collected at the scene of the accident. It was folded neatly and tucked away in Kurt's wallet like a secret that was meant to be kept, not meant for anyone but himself. She   could tell by the way it had been purposely slipped into an inner pocket. She first thought it was a portrait of her, although she didn't know him to be an artist—let alone a fine artist—and this was very meticulous work. Only when she saw the other side did she realize it was the same person Kurt had longed for: a girl named Marie.

"Marie." She spoke the name aloud—a pretty name—very fitting for a beautiful and mysterious French girl. She wanted to see her for herself, talk to her, and ask her questions. Who was she? How had she met Kurt? How did she make him fall in love with her? How did she make him forget her? She didn't want to hear any of these answers but felt compelled to do so. In order to save whatever might be left between Kurt and her, she needed to hear everything.

She looked out the taxi window at the bustling crowd on the Champ-Élyssées, and her eyes searched for anyone resembling the girl in the portrait.

§

Present—1953, Paris
Luke

The sun shone on his face. That familiar light announcing every morning that it was new day, a new beginning. Luke loathed mornings, preferring it to be night, complete darkness, all the time. He tried to push himself up, his arms too weak to sustain the weight of his body, and he let go abruptly. Falling back onto his mattress, he felt a longing for someone next to him—Catherine maybe. He glanced over to his left, and found nothing. No surprise there. She was rarely around these days—or maybe she was. He was always too drunk to remember whether she was there when he fell into bed every night for the past two months.

He heard movement in the hallway. The bedroom door was opened, and he half-heartedly looked for any sign of Catherine, unsure of whether he wanted to see her.

She appeared out of the blue; her black dress blending with the darkness of the hallway. She slipped in without glancing at him, but he knew she was aware that he was awake and staring at her. He wanted to say something—anything. He had kept quiet for the past few weeks, mumbling yes and no to her questions, never giving her the satisfaction of a full sentence—a punishment he was convinced she deserved.

He stared at her silently. He had always liked the way she looked: tall, slim, blessed with perfectly balanced curves. She had broad shoulders, long arms, and a beautiful pair of straight legs with toned muscular calves that reminded him of a Greek sculpture. She was, after all, a kind of a goddess. As a much-revered ballet dancer, Catherine was graceful in all of her movements—the way she walked, how she drank her tea in the afternoon, and the manner in which she undressed at night. She naturally possessed the air of a dancer—altogether graceful with a hint of arrogance about her.

She stood near the dresser, opening letters with her hair pin. Her dark, lush eyelashes shielded her deep blue eyes, but he could see that she was eyeing him discreetly.

"I see you're awake. What did you drink last night, the whole bar?" Her English still retained that French accent he found so sexy. It was hard to resist her in the beginning whenever their subtle disagreement intensified into a fight. It sounded as though she was trying to seduce him, and it always managed to excite him when she was in a fury.

Her eyes were on him with his disheveled hair, shirt half undone with a wine stain near the third button, and a messy tie.

"No." Luke rested his back on the pillow, his hand half shielding his face and his legs crossed awkwardly.

Catherine saw that he wore his shoes to bed, a habit she never got him to change.

"Luke, you have to explain. What are we doing here? You haven't spoken to me in days. Is it something I did?"

There was no room for apology in her voice, although she sounded sincere, yearning to know the reason for his silence.

Luke arched his eyebrow, intrigued by her interrogation. He crawled towards her, still without the strength to stand. He admired her dress and its sensual, low-cut back, and even without her heels, her willowy legs moved gracefully. He felt an urge to put his hand on her bare shoulder but restrained himself.

He wanted to tell her. Let the truth engulf them both. But that would mean they would have to confront the reason why they got together in the first place. It was a subject they averted at every turn for many years, going on about their lives as if it hadn't affected them. Today, however, it could no longer be suppressed. The truth was bursting at the seams of the walls they had built.

"We'll talk later." He couldn't bring himself to say it yet. Not until he had mustered up the courage to break her. Calmly and indifferently, he watched her stunning face twist into disheartened dejection. As if she fully grasped the horror of the plans he had for her, she turned and exited as quietly as she had entered.

When did his love for her begin to falter? From the hallway through the half-closed door, he watched her solemnly pick out a black coat as if she were leaving to attend a funeral. He felt overrun with melancholy and compelled to record the point in time when they began to fall apart, their bond breaking like old paint flaking off a canvas. This was the end of their union. He felt sadness, but a trace of suppressed relief escaped from his mourning. Guilt began to seep in. Perhaps he had expected this all along.

He watched her standing in front of her mirror. It captured her intimidating beauty as she reached into her jewelry box. Yes, the evidence of her betrayal. A deep, engulfing satisfaction overtook him and he graciously allowed the guilt to evaporate from his being. He was not the culprit—Catherine was.

On nights when he felt her stirring in her sleep, he sometimes would awaken and remain perfectly still while observing her. More often than not, she rose and walked to the shelf where her jewelry box was kept. She would open the drawer as quietly as she could, stirring his growing suspicions. There was something in there that she kept secret, and on the night of discovery, he found himself imagining it into something more darkly insidious than it may have represented.

An insignia of the SS, discreetly placed under Catherine's strings of white pearls, countless pendants, and a cluster of rings. It was meant to be hidden well—a small, defenseless badge that could fit into the palm of his hand. He had held it once, feeling the feather-like weight of the despicable sign that embodied all the world's evils. And it belonged to his wife. He couldn't bring himself to immediately ask how she had come to possess it.

He had offered an anonymous tip to the police, hoping that she would be publicly humiliated and confess to him. But she disclosed nothing. He would have to interrogate her himself. He allowed himself one last glance at Catherine and took in a slow, deep breath. The stormy confrontation could wait another day. He slammed the door, shutting her out of his vision.

§

Present—1953, Paris
Catherine

She watched him leave, and wondered for the hundredth time if he had ever really loved her. She had pretended for the past three years that she knew the answer. As a distraction from self-pity, she picked up Luke's coat and dusted it lightly with her hands. She felt his wallet in the pocket and opened it, knowing exactly what she was going to find.

She pulled out a hastily drawn portrait of a younger Catherine, and her sister, Marie. The drawing looked as though the artist had hastened to finish before he forgot what they looked like. She felt a sudden urge to cry, and this time she allowed herself to fall apart. Without Luke, she would have to brave lonely nights, relive the dreadful memories alone without a shoulder to wake up on, or arms to wrap tightly around her so that she wouldn't feel utterly abandoned again. She let herself go and gave into her overpowering tears, the drawing still clutched in her hands.

§

Pre-war—1940-1942, Rouen
Catherine

Before the war, Papa was a well-respected tailor in Rouen. He ran a small shop in town, a family business inherited from his father. A hardworking man who had little ambition other than to provide for his family, he earned a modest living and did well within the given circumstances.

As the eldest daughter of a wealthy jeweler, Maman was endowed with a large sum of money, and much to Papa's relief, she deliberately kept it out of his sight, honorably guarding her husband's pride. She kept it as savings for their three children. Her bourgeois upbringing had been strict and she had little tolerance for Catherine's tantrums and constant demands for new dresses. Maman kept a diligent eye on her daughter who, in her opinion, was too susceptible to worldliness.

Catherine's passion for dance was apparent from a young age. She was given the rare advantage of enrolling in a ballet school in town, performing with such ease and grace that her teachers vehemently convinced her parents to keep her in the school despite the tuition fees Maman initially deemed extravagant and wasteful. With little willpower over his paternal desire to indulge his children, Papa was Catherine's loyal supporter from the beginning and actively lobbied for her to continue her ballet classes.

Marie, who was one year younger than Catherine, had a fragile, shorter frame in comparison. Frail health made her susceptible to colds. Papa and Maman continuously worried about her and incessantly fussed over her meals and clothing. Maman was especially protective, always making sure that Marie had more red meat and vegetable than any of them at dinner time.

Catherine didn't mind the extra attention and care given to her sister, but she was convinced that Marie was stronger than her appearance suggested. She believed that Marie purposefully hid her true self under a cleverly concocted disguise. Marie liked to wear her hair in a bun, as if intentionally concealing her shiny flaxen hair from the public eye, and her shy green eyes would masterfully avert strangers' gazes when they were seen together. Maman was fiercely diligent in reminding them that true beauty came from within, and they should be more focused on how their hearts affected others rather than on their appearance. Catherine didn't mind the advice, but she also didn't pay it much heed.

She also understood from an early age how to utilize her beauty to her own advantages. At only six, she had cunningly begged a shopkeeper for more candies, ignoring her mother who stood transfixed and watched as the owner offered Catherine three more lollipops as if rewarding her charms. She greatly enjoyed the compliments continual reminders of her captivating beauty and confidence.

Her mother worried about her boldness and the reactions of others around her. Catherine was born to be admired with her deep blue, doe-like eyes and long, blond hair that fell to her waist in soft curls. She must be carefully guarded lest she grow up too fast and become vulnerable to the praise that would inevitably come her way.

And as Maman had predicted, Catherine relished the lavish attention, and as a prominent dancer in her class, she was acutely aware of how important her stage presence meant to her success as a performer. Impatient and prematurely ambitious, she felt ready to take the world by storm, with her perfect lines and beautifully arched feet.

As Catherine grew into a headstrong child who feared no one with the exception of Maman, she enjoyed the authority of ordering her other siblings around, though she did so with kindness as she wholeheartedly adored Marie and Philippe.

At school, Catherine was openly admired by several boys of her age, but she never reciprocated any of their affection. Boys her age were uncouth, immature, and she had no time to trifle with them. She held her regard for the older students, sometimes even shooting flirtatious glances towards college students on her bike. Though young and inexperienced, she felt more than ready for her chance at romance.

Her head filled with endless daydreams about kissing and cuddling with a handsome, older boy. They would lie on the grass on their backs, his fingers trailing down her dress, and she would pretend to ask him to stop while secretly hoping he would not. He would take her face into his hands, gazing with affection into her eyes, and they would kiss for a long time before he put his hands under her dress. She could think of nothing else for days other than her fantasized lover, and her thoughts would drift so far that she was unable to concentrate on her dancing.

When they still had lived in their old house, a large country cottage with an old, tired porch swing in the front yard, Marie and Catherine accompanied each other to and from school. It was more than a daily routine; it was a time reserved for them, without the annoying, younger Philippe by their side, begging them to buy him sweets.

Marie spent her time studying at the nearby bookshop and waiting until Catherine was done with her ballet lessons. They danced a few stops along the way as they headed home. They always saw something new: Mme Proulx, the bookshop cashier, stealing books when she thought no one was looking, or Benoit, the boy who delivered the morning newspaper, who pretended to do his job as he followed them home. They never found out which of them he was actually stalking. Catherine didn't care for younger boys, so she couldn't be bothered to add him to the list of her admirers.

Then there was Mlle LaCroix, a famous lady in town who owned a bread shop. It was a quaint, small building with a red roof, and every morning, the scent of fresh-baked bread and pastries oozed from the half-opened windows. Everyday, the floor would be meticulously mopped, until each tiles shone and brightened up the entire shop. Rows of glass jars were placed behind the counter, each one with colorful candies that filled up to the rim. Freshly baked bread and pastries were stacked neatly in baskets—enticing to both children and adults alike. For every day of the week, beautifully crafted cakes of all kinds would be on display, strategically placed on tiered dessert pedestals for the whole of Rouen to see and admire. Mlle LaCroix was a perfectionist to the core, not only with her own immaculate appearance, but her shop was akin to a spectacular creation. Small portions of meringues, madeleine cakes, and chocolates were always generously placed in a basket for her clients to sample and fall deeper in love with her shop.

Ironically, the patissier wasn't known only for her delicious sweets. People flocked to her shop as if her bread were the only ones worth buying, as if her goods contained mysterious, magical ingredients that lured them to her. But everyone also knew that her customers, ranging from young boys to elderly men, lined up for her bread to get a good glimpse of her angelic face and full breasts carelessly covered by tight shirts and an even tighter apron. It was a scandal all the women in town liked to gossip about but never confronted at home. No wives in Rouen were ready to admit their husbands were all helplessly in love with Mlle LaCroix.

There was a strange pride in the women of Rouen, reflecting the confidence their men could not be tempted by lust and beauty. But almost every man in town who had been to Mlle LaCroix's bread shop faithfully returned to her, day after day, to buy bread for their families.

"What was so special about Mlle LaCroix?" Catherine recalled Maman asking the question aloud one evening at the dinner table. Word must have spread that Papa had occasionally visited the celebrated bread shop, and Maman felt highly indignant about this rumor.

Papa could only clear his throat. His cheeks turned slightly red and he continued reading his newspaper. It wasn't long afterward that Maman forbade him to buy bread from Mlle LaCroix. However, because she did have the best, and less expensive, bread and pastry sweets in town, and since Philippe would consistently beg for them, Maman gave the task of frequenting Mlle LaCroix's shop to her young daughters.

Even on days when they weren't asked to bring bread home, Catherine managed to persuade Marie to accompany her to Mlle LacCoix's shop. They bought nothing as they weren't given any money, but Catherine would sit by the door and observe the men gathering around the Rouen beauty and wished she might learn Mlle LaCroix's secret ways. Every once in a while, she would come over to the girls and chat with them. She seldom stayed long as her customers kept her busy, but she would always give them a small slice of her pound cake or leftover of her famous chocolate biscuits. She would wink at them, like this act of kindness was forbidden and not meant to be discovered. Catherine found that she was most irresistible at such moments, and she secretly longed to learn the infamously seductive ways of Mlle LaCroix. Perhaps she would work in the shop with her one day and they would both become the talk of the town.

One day, as part of their weekly routine, they stopped by the shop. Mlle LaCroix was speaking with a handsome young man no more than twenty, and she was smitten with him. The sisters sat outside, unable to hear the conversation, but she looked pleased with whatever he was saying to her. The beautiful patissier leaned over the counter, her arms stretched across, almost close enough to touch the hands of the man who stood across from her. Marie was as intrigued as Catherine, her head slightly tilted towards the small opening of the door. Mlle LaCroix and her customer were now conversing in whispers.

"What do you think he's saying to her?" Catherine's eyes shone excitedly.

"I don't know, but doesn't she look happy?"

Catherine felt it was something more than happiness. This wasn't the same jolly expression Mlle LaCroix wore when she greeted her other customers. Her eyes had taken on a different kind of brightness. The young man reached out and grabbed Mlle LaCroix's hands and he drew her closer to him, their foreheads almost touching. He whispered something into her ear and she started to giggle. Dark, curly hair framed his handsome face. A worn-out, brown leather jacket was slung over his shoulder, a neatly folded blue and white handkerchief protruding from his left pocket. Catherine wondered what it would be like to be grabbed by him and her thoughts wandered off again. At sixteen and fifteen, respectively, the sisters were closely watched by their mother, shielded from young men, and consequently inexperienced and oblivious to the power they would one day yield over the opposite sex.

Mlle LaCroix suddenly realized there were unwanted spectators outside her shop, and she jumped back, bashfully fixing her curly strands behind her ears.

Catherine heard the young man clear his throat. He turned back quickly to see if anyone were behind him, and for a brief moment, his eyes locked with Catherine's as he leaned towards Mlle LaCroix to give her a quick kiss. Catherine didn't look away, but Marie gasped and turned back immediately, as if she knew they were in the wrong, witnesses to this secret, scandalous kiss.

Mlle LaCroix said something to him and handed him a brown bag with her best professional smile, as if he were any other one of her regular customers. Catherine and Marie watched him approach the door, and before long, he was standing before them, a handsome, tall young man, towering over them. He looked down at the sisters with their cheeks slightly blushed and smiled at them—a harmless, polite kind of smile, and handed the brown bag to Catherine.

"For you." He pointed at Mlle LaCroix and waved to the girls in a nonchalant manner, as if dismissing them from the shop. From behind her counter, she smiled at them, and Catherine stood up, pulling Marie along.

"Thank you!" Marie blurted out, before following her sister who was already running home.

That day, Catherine learned there were some things adults kept as secrets and that she was deemed too young and inexperienced to be allowed into their sacred world. She felt shamefully inadequate, a feeling she would never forget. She was being treated like a child when she wanted to be treated as an equal. Her body had already begun to change, her breasts were fuller, and she had lost the fat on her cheeks that she dreaded so much. Just the other day while staring into her own reflection, she realized she may one day be Mlle LaCroix's competition. She left Mlle Lacroix's shop not because she was angry but because she understood her. Mlle LaCroix wanted time alone with this man, someone who was special to her, and Catherine was ready to find something similar.

Later in the week, Catherine approached Antoine, a boy in her class who stared at her persistently. Most of the time she pretended not to notice, but she found the attention to be amusing, and with no other admirers in sight, she turned to Antoine and smile back. Unwilling to give any boy the complete satisfaction of her affection or attention, she would hold back a little, always leaving them wanting more. It was a habit she had subconsciously picked up from observing Mlle LaCroix. As the list of her admirers grew longer, she knew she had mastered the trick. When she tapped Antoine on the shoulder, he almost fell to the ground when he turned to find Catherine standing next to him. It was after school, and she asked him casually if he wanted to accompany her to her ballet class. He swallowed hard and couldn't answer right away but duly followed her as if he were under a spell.

They left school together and walked side by side on the road, their hands almost touching, and Catherine could sense that this subtle contact was driving him mad. When they approached the ballet school building, she turned quickly at a nearby corner and led Antoine into a narrow alleyway behind a wine shop. The empty wine boxes were stacked haphazardly, but Catherine climbed on top of them effortlessly and giggled as she invited Antoine to join her. They sat together and she could feel his leg pressing against hers. She has never done this before but had seen it in movies forbidden by Maman. She had snuck into the theater with her friends and watched older men and women boldly displaying their passion onscreen.

As in the movie scene, she threw her head back and tried to reposition her body as she lay on her left side, her elbow supporting her weight. She realized how silly she may have looked to Antoine, who hadn't take his eyes off of her since they left school. He surely must have thought she had done this before because he seemed to expect her to take the lead. The lust in his eyes was apparent, and Catherine knew that she had the control of the situation, and she reveled in this newfound power.

She took his hand in hers and guided him to her chest. She had expected him to be as timid as before, but as soon as his hands found their place on her breasts, they went wild. He quickly unbuttoned her shirt and impatiently lifted her bra as his hands fondled her breasts with a force she hadn't imagine he possessed.

She sat passively, almost bored, watching him lust after her with his inexperienced hands. He awkwardly planted kisses on her cheeks and neck, and she found it difficult to reciprocate. Her mind wandered off and she thought of the handsome young man who had visited Mlle LaCroix at her shop, how he had looked at her with such irresistible charm. Her imagination took hold of her, and she began to pant at Antoine's touch. She found herself enjoying her first moments of physical intimacy with a boy she barely knew. It didn't take him long to reach up her skirt and pull at her underwear, an act that she hadn't expected she would have to fight off. As she attempted to pull away, he forcibly held down her arms and a sense of panic overtook her. She saw a lust in Antoine's eyes that she no longer recognized.

A box tipped over, and the sound of a wine bottle breaking startled them. Catherine sat up straight in one motion. A cat jumped from the fallen box and landed landed on her uncovered thigh. It looked at Antoine's stunned face and scurried away, leaving them sitting like two guilty children caught stealing from the candy jar. Catherine stood up first, and after smoothing her skirt with both hands, she calmly buttoned her white linen shirt and adjusted the collar. She turned to Antoine and said as nonchalantly as she could, "Thank you for walking me. I'll see you in class tomorrow."

She was aware of the danger she had found herself in moments before, but she felt as though she had conquered something significant. Seduction? Desire? Whatever it was, she now had a firmer grasp of this newfound power, and she knew how to wield it better. In high spirits, she danced out of the alleyway in elaborate pirouettes and made the decision to skip ballet class as she ran to Mlle LaCroix's shop, eager to see her face to face.

§

Present—1953, Paris
Rita

Rita wasn't quite equipped for this. She came to Paris with her luggage filled with all the weather-appropriate clothes, but she knew she was bound to be missing something once she arrived. On this morning, she walked the city streets in search of a map. The rain began without any warning. She hadn't seen a single cloud was in the sky when the violent downpour started, suppressed for too long in the heavens. By the time she was able to escape into a store from the heavy rain, her woolen coat was soaked through and she felt cold and shivered from head to toe, recognizing how alone she was in a foreign city.

Without a concrete plan in mind, she didn't know where to begin. There were some clues from the drawing and its unique landscape. The hand that drew the picture was indeed swift, as the lines of the scenery appeared rushed, as though it didn't have time for secondary imagery. The artist's subject absorbed all his focus and skill. But Rita had studied the picture closely. She had had time to do so while resting at the hospital alone with the portrait of her fiançe's lover. The landscape consisted of rows of unruly hills with red-roofed houses scattered in the background. It was a long shot, but Rita felt determined and adventurous to the point where she almost forgot the purpose of her being here—until the moment she stood alone, wet and cold, without a map to guide her through the ambitious mission she set for herself.

§

As she stood by the traffic lights impatiently waiting for her turn to cross, a man rushed out from behind, attempting to cross before her. From the corner of her eye, she caught sight of a taxi approaching at full speed and instinctively pulled the man back by his sleeve. They fell onto the rain-drenched ground, his umbrella dropping out of his hand and striking Rita's forehead. Dazed from the shock, she felt no pain at first. As her hand touched where the umbrella had fallen, nausea surged through her at the sight of her blood-tainted fingers.

"*Je suis vraiment désolé...*" the man reached into his suit pocket, fumbling to find his handkerchief and dabbing clumsily on Rita's bleeding forehead. Luke needed only one glance at the young woman shivering in his arms to freeze in the moment. He stood looking baffled, his eyes locked on her familiar face. She was holding his handkerchief over her forehead and he felt his face shift from boyish embarrassment to bewilderment.

His expression reminded Rita of Kurt when he awoke from one of his nightmares, screaming about things that had happened to him in France.

"I'm sorry, sir. Are you alright?"

She felt irritated since he was the one who had caused the accident, and he should have been inquiring after her injury. A small crowd began to form, curious and whispering among themselves. A middle-aged woman stepped forward, pushing away the others, and she began to examine Rita's wound with a motherly care. She spoke in French to Luke, her voice coarse and unpleasant, but he seemed unaffected by her words and sat listlessly on the ground, watching Rita with an inexplicable anguish.

§

Present—1953, Paris
Luke

Luke tried to wake up from this dream but couldn't shake himself out of it. It was her—it *was* Marie, wasn't it? Granted, he was still drunk from the half bottle of whiskey he indulged in directly after breakfast. But sober or not, he could still recognize her in any state of mind. He's had countless dreams of her in all kinds of scenarios. Now she was as real as ever—the same penetratingly inquisitive eyes as he remembered. But they were green, weren't they? Or were they a light shade of blue, like the ones he was staring into now?

He ran his hand over his wet hair, still dripping from the rain, to look more presentable before her—this unexpected apparition. He could hear her asking if he was alright, but he couldn't bring himself to answer, or speak her name, because he knew that this familiar, beautiful creature in front of him would deny the name ever belonged to her.

He blinked, and at once, Marie instantly faded and a young woman bearing an uncanny resemblance to her stepped into her shadow. His perfect dream was shattered again by the cruelness of reality. It was as he feared—she was someone else. He felt a spasm of pain; the old scar had not completely healed, and someone was tugging at it, attempting to tear it apart and reveal the rotting flesh underneath. He took a step forward and attempted to speak, but the words in his head stayed muted, and he was defeated again by the weight of the past. He thought of Catherine and how he had left things with her. He had chased her away and felt a pang of regret in his chest.

He felt the alcohol running through his veins like poison, and while he anticipated and welcomed death every day of his life following the war, he struggled now to fight the encroaching darkness. He wished to see her again, even if it were not really her. He was falling into the abyss, and as he willingly let himself go, he felt his head hit the ground, and the doors to his most dreaded nightmares swung open.

§

Wartime—1944, Rouen
Luke

It was after dark, and Luke was starting to get nervous. Their mission had gone just as planned. With his team and a small group of maquis, they succeeded in blowing up a bridge in a nearby village to delay the arrival of German troops from the South. But he still had one man unaccounted for. François and a few maquis got separated from Kurt during an unexpected ambush, and there had been no opportunity since to return to the scene. The teenage group that went out with him and Kurt and François returned with minor injuries and complained about the shrapnel wounds on their arms and legs, while the older members quietly kept to themselves, solemnly bandaging their own cuts.

No one wanted to believe that Kurt was a lost cause, and Luke hated the thought of leaving any of his men behind. Especially on the first mission he led. A life of a Jed agent may not mean much to the Résistance, but it would do harm to the morale to his team, as small as it was. They received instructions to go ahead from the shadow bosses earlier that morning, and while they fully understood the danger of this mission, it was nonetheless an exciting event after weeks of training. Luke knew that some were itching for an attack, for their chance to avenge their lost loved ones. The village was quiet with no signs of German presence, and Luke thought it the perfect opportunity to lead his team towards their objective.

He wasn't ready and would always doubt himself. He was a good soldier, perhaps one of the best in the military school at which he trained. But he didn't aspire to be remembered as an army man. His hands weren't created to kill but to bring his imagination to life. Sitting on a sack of old potatoes in the farmhouse they were stationed in, he stared at his hands.

Dirt was trapped underneath his fingernails and he regarded them in disgust. Slowly, he watched his hands begin to shake. They know— Luke nodded to himself, acknowledging the obvious truth: they were not the hands of a soldier but those of a painter. This was not their place.

§

Before the war, he had engaged in talks with a few art galleries about exhibiting his paintings. He was a confident artist, almost arrogantly so. People's eyes lit up with excitement and admiration whenever they came across his work. He was good, and he could have been better. He threw his half-smoked cigarette on the ground and immediately picked it up when he remembered that a pack of cigarette was considered luxury goods in war-torn France. They shouldn't be wasted. Like how he would waste his talent if he were killed in action. Kurt's face came to mind again. Shit. He didn't know Kurt very well, but it hurt him to lose one of his men. *I'll look for him when it's light out.*

He could hear one of the men stirring in his sleep. Only a few of them snored; it wasn't so bad. He started to get to know his men only a few days ago. He liked François, a talkative twenty-one-year-old from Bordeaux with a damn good sense of humor. An aspiring writer, he jotted down notes at night, gathering materials for his book. Luke wondered if any of them would appear in his story. Perhaps the ones who don't survive the war—they always make for good heroic tales. *That's one consolation. If I don't make it, at least I'll be remembered in a book.*

§

Present—1953, Paris
Luke

He was running again, with a rifle in his hand, making his way from the Seine River back to his base. But where were his men? Was he in this alone? He couldn't remember bringing Kurt or François along with him on this mission. Did they get lost along the way? Should he turn back to look for them? He couldn't think straight with this throbbing headache. He hastened to get back to his base. As he got closer, the road became covered by a thick mist that appeared out of nowhere, and he realized he was lost.

"Marie!"

Why was he screaming her name? Was she his mission? He stood—not only lost—but desperately broken, knowing he had failed her when she died in front of him so many years ago. But why was he still screaming her name?

"Monsieur… Monsieur!"

A voice he had not heard before woke him from his recurring nightmare. He opened his eyes slowly; they felt heavy—probably due to the excess amount of whiskey he had drunk earlier. He followed the voice and at first thought he recognized the woman in white—yes, the young woman he met earlier today. He must have scared her when he mistook her for Marie. He recognized the nurse's uniform and realized that he was lying in a hospital bed. He tried to sit up and the nurse leaned in to help him.

"Where is she?" Looking distraughtly at the nurse, he thought she should know who he meant. The girl who bore such striking resemblance to Marie. She had stood right in front of him before he had lost consciousness. How could he let her slip away?

The nurse didn't answer immediately. She pursed her lips and her eyes held his with the reprimanding look a mother displayed when scolding her mischievous child.

"The young lady who brought you in, Sir?" She addressed him in English, as if to distance herself from him. "She left very quickly." She looked away from him and at someone else who was in the room.

"But someone else is here to see you."

"Luke!"

Catherine's low voice called out to him familiarly, and he was glad that she was there. But when he turned to face her, he saw no compassion or love in her cold, blue eyes. The nurse left quietly without saying anything. Her swift and urgent footsteps betrayed her anticipation to exit the room in the heat of unrelenting marital tension.

Catherine stood beside his bed with her arms crossed. She wore a perfectly fitted dark blue dress that reached her ankles, and her hair had been braided and pinned in an extravagant up-do. Her appearance was so perfect, and from a distant she looked as though she was onstage, just like that fateful night when their paths crossed again after the war. Though Luke hasn't touched her in a long while, he remembered how smooth her skin felt underneath her glamorous clothes, and how she liked to lie close to him after they made love. As much as he resented her now, he missed the times when they had needed and wanted each other like it was the last thing on earth that could keep them sane.

She felt his eyes on her but defiantly refused to look at him, graciously allowing the silence to take over as she pondered why she had bothered to show up today.

"The hospital notified me that you were in an accident."

There was little concern in her voice and her hands fiddled with a speck of lint she picked from her dress.

"I see." Luke sat up on the bed, and he winced from the headache that still lingered. He attempted to straighten his shirt collar to make himself more presentable before her, the great Catherine Aumont. "Well, as you can see, "I'm fine."

"I will stay here," Catherine said. "The nurse wants to keep you overnight in case you have a concussion."

She moved towards the chair beside his bed and sat down without meeting his gaze. He may not want her there, but as indifferent as she may appear to him, she was worried and still cared for him.

Luke watched her settle beside him and shrugged at her insistence. "Suit yourself, Catherine."

"I've packed some of my things." She enunciated her words carefully, wanting him to understand that she was serious. It was her final bluff before she succumbed to the reality that they were, in fact, broken.

"I see." And that was all. It was more than enough to wake her from the self-pity she disdained.

She stood quietly by him until he fell asleep. Knowing what was to come, she picked up her coat and purse and headed for the door. She wanted to leave before hearing that familiar name called out in agony during another one of his nightmares from the past.

§

Present—1953, Paris
Catherine

Instead of going to her dance rehearsal, she decided to take a long stroll by the riverbanks. There was no regret leaving Luke, but she now felt a growing emptiness in her heart. Luke was the bridge to her past and he enabled her to step back into history whenever she felt like doing so. He was there for her as a reminder of who she once had been, and she realized only now that they were separated that they had stayed together for the same reason. They had used each other as a shield from reality, living in one another's shadows, comforted by the fact they had existed at one time in the imperfect, treasured world of the past.

She arrived back at her hotel room, her temporary home, and she hadn't the energy to remove her coat after her long, tiring walk. A good amount of wine would help her sleep well tonight. She generously poured herself a full glass of red wine and trudged out to the balcony. She stared into the starry sky, endeavoring to count the stars. This was something she used to do with Marie and Philippe when they couldn't come up with a new game and when it became too dangerous to wander outside their house. She continued to count the stars, pointing to each one.

It was on the swings in the yard, the ones that Papa built for them, where they sat trying desperately to count them all. She giggled, remembering how she and Marie purposely counted out loud so that Philippe would lose his current number.

She forgot where she was for the moment and leaned on the metal handle of the balcony, pushing all her weight forward. The silky fabric of her dress caused her arms to slip, and she watched as her wine glass, still half-full, dropped to the ground. It shattered with a finality that left her feeling a bewildering sadness.

Her hands clutched the balcony railing as she tried to get a closer look at the carnage. She wondered if she should let go and fall to ground so that whoever might find her would grieve for her just as she had mourned her broken wine glass.

§

CHAPTER THREE

THE ROUEN SISTERS

Pre-war to Wartime–1940-1943, Rouen
Catherine

"Careful!"

Catherine didn't realize she was walking on the sidewalk again, and while she was thankful Marie had pulled her back to the road they were meant to follow, her heart stung from deep bitterness. People walking by avoided their eyes. They knew these two girls. It was a small town, and Catherine and Marie didn't need to wear the Star of David to distinguish themselves, as many did in other towns. Everyone knew who was Jewish and who was not, and for the first time in her life, Catherine wished that she was anything but Jewish. She wasn't used to being slighted. It was her calling to be in the spotlight as a prodigy dancer and not singled out and scorned for her Jewish blood. The stage had been within her reach only the year before.

She had been selected to star in the school's year-end ballet performance. Then one afternoon after practice, she was asked to stay behind and Madame Lafayette delivered the unfortunate news. She would to be cut from the dance list. Tears welled up in her teacher's eyes as she coolly contained her sadness. Whether it was in defiance, refusal to give in, or denying herself the pity that had become all too common around her, she withheld her tears.

For Papa, the official measures adopted by the Vichy government meant a direct blow to his business and the family's income. The yellow placards in the storefront window of his shop had been replaced by the more noticeable and threatening red placards, deterring customers and attracting unwanted spectators.

Furious with their circumstances, Maman had taken down the placards several times, only to have Papa remind her of the consequences only too clearly spelled out in the newspapers.

§

Today, the sisters walked quietly side by side towards Mlle LaCroix's shop to buy the loaf of bread their mother had asked for this morning. Before they entered, Marie pulled her sister back for the second time and signaled for her to wait; a German soldier was speaking with Mlle LaCroix inside the shop.

Catherine couldn't get a good glimpse of him before Marie pleaded with her to sit down. They had ended their habit of lingering in town since the German troops moved into Rouen. They were not completely aware of the politics of war, but as girls of a sensitive age, they could detect the unfriendliness rising around them like an encroaching wall, ready to fall and wipe them off the face of the earth. She turned to her sister and saw that her soft, thin hands were trembling.

"Marie."

Her sister kept quiet, and Catherine suspected that it had something to do with the man in the uniform speaking with Mlle LaCroix. Neither of them had had any confrontation with German troops, but they had heard about the little boy shot in the Bois-Guillaume forest because he didn't stop at the order of German soldiers.

Marie's eyes were downcast and she sat as still as she could. Catherine could feel her sister's heart pounding, resounding next to her own.

"Marie, it's alright, we're going home right after this."

Her sister said nothing, a sign that she was frightened to her core. Ever since war was declared in France, fear lurked everywhere, waiting for the right moment to pounce. During this time, Catherine began to pick up on different signs that each of her family members would give away when they felt afraid. Philip was too young to understand the vulgarity of war, and neither Maman nor Papa had the heart to explain the sinister predicament they found themselves in. Marie's silence always preceded her tears, and Maman's hands would tremble uncontrollably when she heard of the death of friends and family from all over France.

Papa, who seldom let his sorrows show, would let a deep crease form between his graying brows, a subtle sign that only Catherine noticed and understood. Now, with Marie by her side, she felt her sister's fear, and they both sat without exchanging words until the German soldier walked out with a bag of pastries. Fearing the rumored and unpredictable wrath of German soldiers, they held their breath as he walked past them, hoping they could render themselves invisible. They didn't dare look up and waited until they could no longer hear his heavy boots on the cement ground.

Catherine stood up and prompted Marie to follow her. They trod towards the doorstep. What used to be the most casual errand of the day had turned into a kind of mysterious mission to be undertaken with the utmost secrecy.

"My girls, it's been so long since I've seen you here!"

There was a hint of surprise in Mlle LaCroix's voice, but they all knew why Catherine and Marie and other Jewish customers hadn't been seen in her shop the past few months.

Catherine wasn't sure whether Mlle LaCroix lied out of kindness, as a way to shield the truth from the teenaged girls who, at their age, clearly understood the abhorrent segregation, or if she lied because she had nothing kind to say about the situation. There were no words that could act as a remedy to their pain. Everybody suffered under the German occupation, even the non-Jewish French, but there remained an advantage for not being of Jewish heritage. Otherwise, the blood running through Jewish veins mercilessly exposed one as an individual who is rightfully and legally scorned by everyone else.

Marie smiled sweetly, her dimples creasing, at the beautiful Mlle LaCroix in her signature red dress that shamelessly showcased her cleavage and desirable curves. Her hair was newly permed and she was moving her freshly baked croissants from the tray to the glass tiered dessert platters in a buoyant mood. Not wanting to linger for too long in town, Marie said they were here for two loaves of bread and some pastries for Philippe, who had an incurable weakness for mille-feuilles, especially hers.

"Yes, of course!" There was too much enthusiasm in Mlle LaCroix's voice, like she was attempting to disguise an underlying sadness. As she gathered Marie's order, Catherine watched her wipe a tear from her cheek. Perhaps it was a fly she had swatted away—it all happened too quickly.

They paid her with the exact change that Maman entrusted to them. She always knew how much everything cost in Mlle LaCroix's shop. But when Mlle LaCroix handed the bag to Marie, she gave back a few francs and clutched Marie's hand tightly in hers as if it contained all the luck she wished them.

The girls returned home and gave the remaining change to Maman. There was an unreadable expression on her face that Catherine couldn't interpret until she was older and had experienced heartbreaks of her own. Maman had blushed when Marie showed her the change they received from Mlle LaCroix. But back then the prices for everything fluctuated every day. Maman had grasped the money in her hands and her eyes clouded. A sorrowful look crossed her face and she muttered to herself as she turned away.

"What a kind woman she is, Mlle LaCroix."

A week later, the girls were sent grocery shopping again, but this time they were specifically instructed to go to a different bakery shop. They didn't think much of it, but Catherine felt disappointed that she wouldn't see Mlle LaCroix. She wanted to be just like her when she was older—except that she wasn't going to own a bakery shop. She would be the best ballet dancer there had ever existed in France.

Obediently, the two girls hurried past the shop, but Catherine's footsteps came to a halt when she inhaled a familiar aroma that lingered in the air, luring her to its source. Spellbound by the scent of freshly baked cookies, she forgot where she stood. Her eyes closed and she tried to remember the taste of Mlle LaCroix's chocolate cookies. She almost felt the sweet, dark chocolate melting on the tip of her tongue, and the softness of the cookies as they crumbled in her mouth.

She basked in her fantasy until she collided into someone whose scent was exactly like Mlle LaCroix's.

"Monsieur, we are so sorry!"

Marie was picking up items that had spilled from the German soldier's bag—the same soldier they had seen yesterday. He stood in front of them, appearing taller and stronger than she remembered. His grocery bag lay on the ground; apples, ham, bread, and a few cookies scattered alongside it. She tried to act calmly, but her distraught, watery eyes betrayed her pretense of bravery in front of a man who could hand out their death sentence with one word.

Catherine quickly followed her sister and knelt on the ground, scrambling to reach the fallen items. A chocolate cookie, broken in half, lay near her feet. She picked it up and felt its warmth and knew it was fresh from the oven. The soldier's boots, still shiny in their first stroll of the day, were straight ahead of her. She and Marie had ruined his morning. Her hands were stained with chocolate and she felt stupid and inept. She could barely move, and although she could not see him with her head bowed as though she were a slave, she could feel his eyes on her. Was he deciding whether she would live or die for this trifling misconduct?

"Keep it." As he walked away, his voice was low and authoritative, with a hint of a German accent in his French.

The girls, in apprehension, kept their eyes down until the sound of his boots sounded far enough from where they knelt. Catherine looked up. He didn't take anything at all, not even the bag he dropped.

"Is it...is it for us to keep?" Marie's eyes were fearful but held a glimmer of hope. Maybe—just maybe—he left everything on purpose for them.

Catherine giggled and they began throwing the items back into the bag, laughing as it became fuller and fuller, with cookie crumbs falling to the ground like fairy dust.

On this particular day, they decided to venture down an unknown path—a shortcut. They wanted to rush home and share the unexpected gift. They would have to hide the true identity of the generous donor from their parents and make up a believable tale about finding the bag deserted on the ground, possibly left by a benevolent stranger. They weren't starving yet, but having sweets and ham in the house was something they hadn't had for a long time. This would be a special treat for poor Philippe and his insatiable appetite for sweets.

Marie walked in front of Catherine, skipping in her steps. In that moment, Catherine believed, with sixteen-year-old naivety, that they would miraculously lessen their parents' burden by presenting them with this bag of goods. Kindness was now a rare thing, and because it was so rare—especially from a German soldier—she took it to heart and felt that her world was finally being pieced back together. People were good again and there is still hope in their shattered lives.

A group of teenage boys, wearing smiles that disguised their intentions, were fast approaching them in a subtly menacing manner, like dark clouds announcing a heavy thunderstorm. Marie halted her steps and turned back to her sister, her eyes searching for assurance.

They were in trouble, outnumbered, and utterly alone. One of the boys snickered as they eyed Marie, who appeared to be the easier prey.

Catherine started counting with her eyes: one, two, three, four, five, six boys. They weren't much taller than she or Marie, but they were still boys, and one of them held a thick wooden branch in a way one would a whip or another dangerous weapon. She needed something she could use to defend them against the boys closing in on them.

A sturdy piece of wood with a sharp corner, the kind used to start a fire, was judged an effective weapon. She set the soldier's bag on the ground and ran to pick up the wood. Seeing them up close, she recognized one of the boys from her science class—Jean-Marc, not the nicest person, but neither had he ever been rude to her. Today, his eyes bared unguarded disdain. *But why? What have I ever done to you?*

Jean Marc was now shouting insults at them, and the other boys mindlessly followed suit. Catherine took a few quick steps back and whispered into Marie's ears.

"Run, I'll be right behind you."

She closed her eyes and swung the piece of wood forward as hard and fast as she could. Marie sprung forward and started to run. There was a loud scream, and Catherine opened her eyes as Jean Marc's wounded cheek spurted blood from the deep cut left by her blow.

"She hit me," he said with scornful disbelief. His face reddened and twisted with anger and shame. "You can't hit me!" He clutched the branch in his hand and swung at Catherine's arm.

She let out a sharp cry, not as much from the pain as from the discernment that this was real. The hatred she had seen blazing in Jean Marc's eyes now took form in a physical blow, and she felt it burn her skin. She sped around looking for something else to shield her from the next blow, but there was only the loaf of bread protruding from the grocery bag. She grabbed it and held it firmly in her hands. It was the only thing to protect her now. The boys burst into laughter and one of them shouted: "Stupid Jewish pig!" The cruel words stung a thousand times more than the physical injury.

Marie continued running until she realized she was alone. Catherine was nowhere to be seen. She turned around and felt her body stiffen.

"Are you scared now?"

Jean-Marc sneered at Catherine. This wasn't the time to remember when she helped him with his homework, or when his mother had met her and Maman once at a school performance. How she had praised the young Catherine Aumont for her crowd-winning dancing while he looked on shyly. She had been a rising star and he was an ordinary boy. Standing face to face with him now, he looked taller and more menacing than she ever remembered him. He was only sixteen, but the anger he exhibited made him appear much older and disenchanted with life.

Her lips began to tremble, and she tried to eradicate the thought of Sophie, a little girl beaten to death in a situation much like her own. Not today—she was going home—this was meant to be a joyous day, possibly the happiest in a long time for her and her family.

She prepared herself for the next inescapable blow, but Jean Marc's sneer faded into a frightened expression. He was not looking at her; no, there was someone else. The German soldier stood behind her, his eyes cold and steady as he stared icily at the boys.

"What do you think you're doing?" He didn't expect an answer to his question but demanded to know. He had seen fights far more violent than this.

The boys glanced worriedly at each other, intimidated and frightened by the sudden German presence in their midst. And as soon as the soldier took a brisk step forward, they quickly dispersed and ran away like a defeated pack of dogs with tails between their legs. None of them dared turn back to see what would happen to the girls they had been taunting so confidently moments before.

Catherine kept her eyes low, praying that he wouldn't question her identity. Perhaps he didn't know, but if he found out, would he beat them like Jean-Marc and his friends had intended to? Marie stood at a distance, unsure whether or not to approach them. Besides her own heartbeat and the heavy boots of the soldier advancing slowly towards her, there was no sound. As he got nearer, he paused, his eyes almost smiling but still retaining the coldness they were trained to exhibit.

"What were you planning to do with that?"

Catherine understood that he was talking about the bread she still clutched tightly in her hands. She didn't feel prepared to say anything in response. The strange lump in her throat when she saw him again prevented her from speaking, but his stern eyes showed that he wouldn't accept her silence.

Marie anxiously watched her sister from a distance, and her eyes searched for people she could wave to for help. But who would come to the of a young Jewish girl being interrogated by a German?

He waited for Catherine's answer. He was a patient man and curious as to what this young girl had to say. Her blue eyes and youthful innocence were captivating. She looked directly at him, unlike other children, or even adults, in this town. Her stare was steady, hopeful, and defied the purpose of his being here. He could imagine her interrogating him with those mesmerizing eyes: *What will you do to me? What makes you think that you can control my destiny or whether I live or die?*

"I don't know—hit him in the head, I suppose." She panted as she spoke and felt as though she had been running all this time.

His lips curled into a half-smile but he didn't allow either of them to think he was being friendly. He quickly cleared his throat and tightened his lips again. He stared at Catherine with a look of warning and pointed at the space between her legs.

"Next time they give you trouble; you aim right there. But find a better weapon." With that advice, he turned and left the girls where they stood, obviously dumbfounded by his sudden exit.

When Catherine could no longer hear his boots against the pavement, she dropped to her knees and started to laugh and cry.

Marie ran to her and saw that her sister's arm was bleeding from an attack she hadn't been there to witness. She blamed herself out loud for not staying with Catherine and silently promised herself and Catherine that she would never desert her again.

§

Present—1953, Paris
Catherine

Catherine stood by the door to the theater with a cigarette in her hand. Her dance rehearsal was scheduled in an hour. She wore a long, red velvet dress that caressed her figure like a second skin. The bottom flared like a mermaid's tail. Long dresses accentuated her dancer silhouette, and it attracted many eyes to look her way. Luke loved to watch her when they were happier. When did they first began to fall apart? Or were they ever complete as one? She never blamed the shadow of Marie lurking in the background, waiting to take Luke away from her. He was never hers to begin with. It was Marie who first caught the artist's eye. She was meant to be his everlasting muse, never to be replaced by anyone.

§

Before the war, Catherine had never imagined her sister to be her competition. Marie was always more fragile, and no matter how pretty she was, she preferred to remain in the background. Catherine shone for the both of them, earning them the title of "the beautiful sisters" in Rouen. She was never jealous of Marie and her timid ways. But something had changed in when the war arrived in Normandy. Marie's blossoming softness was halted and then inadvertently hardened. Not many perceived it at first, but Catherine felt the change immediately. Her sister had become stronger and she took on more responsibilities. She consoled Maman when the darkness of the cave became too much to bear, and she listened to Papa speak about the farm and how he was going to leave it to them to care for. He listed the daily tasks that needed to be taken care of. Both she and Marie knew this was intended for Philippe, who was no longer with them. Marie had sat there, her eyes alert and focused, listening to every word without a flinch. Catherine had begun to love her all the more.

§

Wartime—1943-44, Rouen
Catherine

In the beginning, their lives inside the cave were not too dull. It was a whole new beginning, and it brought their family closer together. They had collected the best books, carefully choosing the ones they knew they could read more than once and moved them into their new home. They had to move secretly, only during the night, and when the moon was clouded, so that no light would be seen to expose their shadows.

She and Papa did most of the moving, while Maman and Marie diligently packed their belongings. On the long walks from their home to the cave, Papa would walk behind her, silently and solemnly as if he were marching them to their deaths. When they arrived underground, he would exhale as though he had just walked through a field of mines.

He would give her a look of relief, his wrinkled eyes glimmering with suppressed hope, his lips curled into a subtle smile. They had survived for yet another day. They unpacked fervently and talked as they moved their pots, books, bed sheets and pillows, and the rest of the things they had managed to take. Papa talked mostly about the past, expounding on the good days. His words kept her spirits high and gave her hope. Maybe things will turn around. Maybe she would dance again.

As if it was the most natural thing, Papa one day announced that they were moving into their new home. A solemn silence came over them, and Maman wept silently. Catherine and her sister looked around their house. It was not completely empty, but all the essentials they needed to survive until the end of this war were missing, and no one could tell them when that would be.

They were able to sustain themselves through the first month as Maman used potatoes for nearly every meal. Scraps of ham were rationed carefully, and they all savored the taste of meat on their tongues.

One evening, as Maman prepared dinner, she shrieked in anxiety as she called to them, asking if anyone had seen the potatoes.

"We couldn't have run out already!" Tears rapidly welled up in her eyes. She felt that she had somehow failed her family.

Unaccustomed to seeing Maman in such an agitated state, Catherine silently cursed the war for all the sadness it indiscriminately had prescribed for countless families swept up into a paralyzing injustice.

Marie quietly approached Maman, her hand softly caressing her mother's trembling shoulders. She whispered softly into her ear. "Maman, let me find you some more potatoes." She grabbed her coat and clambered up the ladder, disappearing from their sight.

Before Papa could stop her, Catherine climbed up after Marie. When she came to the surface, Marie was running through the forest, her dark green coat blending in with the pine trees. Forever after, the thought of Marie—her timid, brave sister—revived the image of that coat. She had run after her sister without calling out to her. Marie would hear her footsteps.

And so with one heart they ran through the forest with the moonlight guiding their path and dangerously exposing their vulnerable shadows.

When their beloved cottage came into view, they slowed down and began to tread carefully as they approached the building. It was eerily quiet and they heard their own footsteps on the familiar cement path, betraying their return. They tiptoed towards the entrance and peered into the windows. Everything was just as they left it. Catherine was about to let out a sigh of relief before a small cry escaped from Marie's throat. She was quick to follow her gaze.

Mlle LaCroix and the German soldier walked towards them, hand in hand and carrying grocery bags, talking and smiling like they had not a care in the world. Like walking through rows of deserted, ghostly homes was the most natural thing for them to do. Homes that belonged to people who could no longer lived there and had to hide in unthinkable places. People who fled underground in order to see another day.

Catherine felt insuppressible anger rising inside her. She forgot for the moment who she was and on what dangerous ground she trod. She wanted to run up to him and shout in his face. *Why? Why do you live freely and we are forced to survive?*

He saw them first. His head turned and his eyes caught Catherine's movement as she ducked down. In the manner of a disciplined soldier of war, he approached them cautiously. With his gun cocked and aimed at them, he shouted with unequivocal authority.

"Who's there?"

Catherine discerned a chilling lack of mercy in his voice. She and Marie stared into each other's eyes, mirrors of naked fear, with no room left for courage. The anger Catherine had felt vanished. They were hiding behind a stack of hay, trembling not from the piercing cold, but from fear of being shot to death. And as he approached them, she recognized the familiar sound of German boots. She had forgotten for the past few weeks living underground, safe and tucked away from chaos and terror.

He towered over them like a fearsome statue they didn't dare gaze at directly. He stood only about a meter away, close enough to execute them. But the hand that held the gun was at once lowered, and Catherine sensed his surprise, followed by a look of recognition. Remembering the rare kindness he already had twice extended, she wondered if he would spare them a third time.

Mlle LaCroix called to him. "Friedrich!"

So that was his name.

Her voice sounded shrill, as though worried that something had happened to him. She ran towards them, her face expressing astonishment. She had not expected to see them alive. She smiled faintly while trying to imagine what he was planning to do. They obviously were lovers, but she had no authority over him now, and there was fearful submission in her eyes as she spoke to him in low whispers. He turned and stepped away from them, pulling Mlle LaCroix forcibly by her arm. They stood a few meters away and spoke in hushed tones, his eyes occasionally drifting back to Catherine. There was pleading in Mlle LaCroix's voice, and Catherine wondered if she was negotiating for their lives. He grunted in seeming disagreement and left her behind as he headed back.

He wasn't as tall as Catherine remembered from a year ago. His face had definitely aged. There were fine lines of wrinkles, but his eyes still retained their sharpness and fearlessness in defiance of anything that stood in his way. There was a proudness in his walk, like each stride carried great significance, that somehow he knew that he would leave a defining mark in history.

"What are you doing here?" He spoke with such authority and reprimand that Catherine felt sure she had lost her ability to speak. His confidence was palpable and she wondered if he had been tracking her down all this time. She had heard of German soldiers whose job was solely to hunt down and locate Jewish families like a ferocious dog trained to sniff out pestering rodents. Did he know that they were in hiding? That they had been gone for some time?

"Po-potatoes." Catherine struggled to spit out the word. Marie reached out to her sister and squeezed her arm gently. *I'm here, Catherine. It's alright, we are still together.*

He folded his arms in front of his chest and questioned them again, slowly this time, patronizingly enunciating each word. They had only one more chance to get the answer right.

"What are you doing here?"

"We...we don't have any food. We're practically starving because of the Germans. And . . . this . . . this used to be our home." Catherine regretted the words she blurted out as soon as she had spoken them.

Mlle LaCroix gasped and she covered her red lips with her hands.

Desperate for an ally, Catherine turned to her for help. Mlle LaCroix dressed meticulously for a resident of war-torn Normandy: black woolen gloves and sturdy winter boots that kept her feet warm even as she stood outside in the freezing temperature. Catherine looked down at her own hands, red and cold from the unforgiving wind that tore through her skin every time it blew. Standing inches away, her sister shivered uncontrollably. Having skipped lunch and dinner the day before, she must have been struggling with the same stomach cramps as she—a common occurrence they had learned to cope with since they moved underground. And now her heart ached, a pain different from hunger; it was more a forlorn emptiness, a gaping hole that was slowly devouring her whole.

Friedrich appeared unshaken by what she said, and he watched them, silently and discerningly, like a hunter cunningly planning his next move. She wished she hadn't noticed the gun that hung on his belt. Now she was imagining her own death at gunpoint. Not Marie's. She wouldn't allow that to happen. She raised her eyes and leveled her gaze at him. If faith could move mountains, she would hold on firmly to the belief that they would get through this unscathed. That perhaps, out of an unwarranted act of sympathy, he would let them go.

"Where are you hiding?"

"Nowhere." Her voice sounded small and shaky. How fast she could flee from her interrogator? She dismissed the thought after looking the trembling Marie.

"You just said that you used to live here. I did not hear you wrong. Now, where are you hiding?" His voice was grave and his face held neither emotion nor pity.

She prayed silently, like Papa did every night before he went to bed. He would shut his eyes, allowing a deep crease to form between his brows, sigh deeply, and she would know that he was pleading with God for his family to be spared. And now she was doing the same with a fervent faith she never knew she possessed.

"Where?" A flicker of impatience flashed in his eyes.

She had to give some sort of answer. "I . . . I . . . " She stuttered in fear but couldn't bring herself to betray Maman and Papa. Perhaps she could negotiate for her family. Maman always said she was convincing.

"Friedrich!"

Mlle LaCroix clutched the collar of her coat, an unsuccessful attempt at keeping the wind from seeping in. They all heard her, but only he turned to face her. She said nothing further but let her eyes well up. They were affectingly expressive and Catherine felt sure they were sending him a coded message that only he could untangle. Silence filled the air. He stood still, facing Mlle LaCroix with an unreadable expression. He finally nodded reluctantly and turned back to the girls.

"It's okay, girls. You can tell him." Mlle LaCroix nodded reassuringly.

She spoke in a low voice that made Catherine think back to how she had whispered mischievously while handing Philippe the mille-feuille pastry secretly packed for him. Staring into Mlle LaCroix's eyes, she desperately wanted to trust her. Marie stood beside her and they huddled closely together for warmth. She slipped her hand into Catherine's. Reluctantly, Catherine raised one hand as if detached from her body. She lamented its betrayal and watched it point towards the direction of the Rouen forest.

Friedrich nodded impassively and signaled for the girls to lead the way. Catherine could see fear in Marie's eyes, but she could not say anything to reassure her. Neither of them was prepared to defy the man who held their lives in his hands. Before they left, he turned to Mlle LaCroix, who he called by her first name—Claire, and told her in a nonchalant manner that he would meet her later. This task was just another ordinary errand of the day.

§

Snow began to fall heavily that night, and the trees were now blanketed with a glistening white cover. Catherine felt swallowed by sadness. They may well be marching to their death. Marie could no longer blend into the trees with her green coat. Friedrich made Catherine lead the way, and he followed closely behind Marie, who tread carefully between her sister and the man who may or may not give them another day to live.

They arrived at the entrance of their cave, hidden by thick bushes. The half-hour journey seemed like a lifetime to Catherine. The sisters stood quietly as Friedrich surveyed the area, appearing to be taking mental notes. He would know exactly here to bring his troop the next day to collect their family. Catherine was unable to speak to Marie. He stood between them and Catherine watched Marie's eyes widen with fear and uncertainty. The full moon shone down on them, disclosing their whereabouts, and she had never felt more exposed and scared for her life. His back now facing her, he stayed occupied with his secret plans, his head turning right and left, meticulously analyzing the different paths to their cave. Was there a plan to ambush them tomorrow? Catherine stared at the back of his head, desperately wanting to know whether he had any compassion left for them. As if hearing her plea, he turned and faced them, and with a satisfaction only he could understand, he nodded to himself.

"Very well," he said.

His tone sounded too ambiguous to know whether he was muttering to himself or addressing them. He took a step forward and looked into Catherine eyes, and pointed at her as he would when giving his subordinate an order.

"Tomorrow morning, five o'clock. You wait here."

He began to walk away and Catherine felt unable to move. Moments ago she had felt convinced that her life had ended right then and there. Now she had been given another taste of freedom and life simultaneously so exhilarating and frightening that she had no idea what to do with it.

They waited until they could no longer see the speck that was Friedrich, and they ran towards each other, almost falling as they leapt forward to hug one another. Neither of them cried. There was no use in reporting this horrific encounter to Maman or Papa, who would only become distraught and unbearably fearful. It would remain a secret between them.

When they entered the cave, Maman was understandably furious, though she could not raise her voice in fear of being heard. An advantage to living underground was that Maman was forced to control her temper. At dinner time, they were unusually quiet huddled around the small table, sharing a meagre plate of potatoes seasoned with salt. Papa made sure everyone else had more on their plate than he did, and he muttered about not having much of an appetite that evening.

When they went to bed in their respective corners of the cave, divided by a curtain—the one that used to hang in their dining room—Marie and Catherine settled into their bed silently. Words could not express the fear and worries that muddled their minds. Catherine could hear Marie's suppressed sniffles as she lay beside her. If they both cried, Papa and Maman would suspect that something had happened, and knowing Marie and her incapability of hiding anything from their parents, the truth would be out.

As Catherine rested her head on the pillow, one of the few luxuries they were able to bring from home, she let the most imminent question consume her: is this the end? She imagined a troop of soldiers showing up at their cave, forcing them out one by one. But then she thought of Friedrich and his unpredictable behavior and wished to believe that no harm would come their way in the morning.

Marie, on the other hand, wasn't so sure, and she cried herself to sleep, dreading the morning that would come.

Catherine did not sleep that night. She lay wide awake, impatiently waiting for the dusk to appear. She counted hours, and then minutes, until she knew that it was time for her to climb out of the cave and meet her fate. When she rose to dress, Marie was still stirring in her sleep. Although she did promise Marie that she would wake her, she had already decided not to. She felt special, as if handpicked by Friedrich, chosen for a specific journey. She slipped out of her bed quietly and left Marie behind. As she tiptoed her way to the ladder, it took her a bit longer than usual to exit the cave. She needed to remove the wooden plank slowly enough not to make any noise. When she reached the surface, she was alone. There was no one else in sight.

It was a relief to know that Friedrich had not sent a troop of soldiers to take her and her family them away, but she couldn't help feeling disappointed. Or was this a silent ambush? Were there snipers hidden among the trees, waiting for the perfect moment to pull their triggers? She stood in the snow, wearing Maman's long white coat. From afar, she appeared as one with the wintery landscape, a snow queen in the middle of her kingdom. She sensed him approach before she could hear the fresh morning snow crumble beneath his boots.

He had stood at a distance and watched her for a while before advancing towards her.

§

Wartime—1943, Rouen
Friedrich

He knew the two girls who had disappeared with their family, and not just from previous encounters but from his task as a unit commander to round up Jewish families in the area for relocation. He dutifully sifted through the papers that revealed the Aumont family's disappearance and had his suspicions. In retrospect, maybe he wanted to make it easier for them. He hadn't recognized Marie right away, but he had instantly recalled Catherine's distinctively fierce, blue eyes, and how she valiantly defended herself and her sister against the village bullies. Almost a year has passed since he had seen her; he thought of her from time to time and wondered if they all got away. His curiosity surely had been derived from sympathy.

When he saw her last night, he had felt relief, and it troubled him deeply. This curious sympathy for Catherine stirred within him. Was he glad to find out that she was still alive? He was an excellent commander, well-known in the regiment, and more than anyone understood the importance of his mission. But the sight of Catherine unsettled him. He felt unable to reconcile this newfound empathy for the girl and her family, and it kept him awake through the night.

When he had found them scavenging for food, Claire pleaded for their lives, her eyes wet with tears as she begged him not to reveal their whereabouts to his superiors. He would have spared them even without her insistence, but it soothed him to know that she believed his act of kindness had stemmed solely from her actions. He had little to do with it and would allow them to live only because she had asked him. He repeated this in his mind many times as he lay in bed, his eyes wide open, waiting for dawn to come.

§

He now stood face to face with Catherine, a girl who fascinated him beyond his own understanding. When he saw her again, the weight that burdened his chest was lifted, leaving only a clean breath of air running through his lungs and rejuvenating his heart like a miraculous remedy. Catherine stood still as the snow slowly descended and playfully adorned her hair and cheeks. He admired her courage and defiance, but he also felt troubled by her sharp blue eyes that seemed to see through him. She looked thinner than the first time he saw her at Claire's shop. Her high cheekbones were more pronounced now, and although her eyes were still bright, dark circles had formed beneath them. She must be hungry.

He slid the strap of his bag off his shoulder and tossed it to her. It didn't land close enough for her to catch it but instead fell by her old winter boots, and as it settled against the powdery snow, a few potatoes, sweets, and apples rolled out of the bag. He watched her stand speechless as she stared at the bag full of food and tried to make sense of it all. Still, this act of kindness did not raise the reaction that Friedrich had anticipated. There was a sharpness in her face, as if she looked down on the charity he was bestowing on her. Her display of pride set her apart from the other Jews he had come across. They stood facing each other, and she stared boldly at him, not as a victim of a war that sought to destroy her, but as his equal. His admiration for this young Jewish girl began to grow. The knowledge that she would be fed for at least another two weeks made him turn away in order to hide his smile. As he walked away, he felt the softness of her voice.

"*Merci.*"

Thus, his regular visits began. It wasn't difficult to smuggle extra potatoes and other food items and stuff them into a bag. His battalion rank precluded anyone from daring to question him about the additional food supplies he took from the kitchen. Word had spread, however, that he had taken a French mistress in town so most people shrugged it off. He was careful not to have anyone follow him when he delivered the food to Catherine. Sometimes, when he couldn't get away from his duties, he would have Claire do it, although he didn't like the idea of her wandering at night by herself. He gained more satisfaction whenever he met with Catherine, even if just for a few minutes, to hand over the bag of supplies. He felt bewildered by this young, blossoming girl with the spellbinding eyes. Something within him had changed, but he brushed aside unfamiliar emotions as he would have performed the duties asked of him—with caution and discipline.

CHAPTER FOUR

THE REUNION

Present—1953, Paris
Rita

It took her several hours before she finally admitted to herself that she had lost her only clue. While getting ready to leave her apartment, she casually sifted through her purse looking for Kurt's drawing. Dissecting every corner where it might have been carelessly tucked away, there was nothing left to think other than it was gone. She sat on her bed feeling defeated, trying hard to think back to the moment when she last held the drawing in her hands.

For two days, she had tried to recreate the drawing from memory, but she couldn't quite get it right. She liked to draw, but her skills would never match the genius hand that sketched the portrait of the mysterious woman Kurt was hiding from her. She distinctly remembered the background: dense forest with tall, robust trees, full of leaves, and a small church visible in the background. But without the drawing, it was all useless now. She wouldn't be able to explain it to whoever recognized the location and could point her in the direction towards where "Marie" lived.

Rita found herself dreaming of this place for the past two nights. She was running through the forest, desperately searching for this young woman to no avail. The dream had fragmented into incoherent sequences: She was running down a paved path that led more deeply into the forest. She turned and found herself alone inside an old deserted church—the same as in the drawing—where she stood among empty pews. When she tried to sit down, she was suddenly running in the rain. A familiar scene flashed before her eyes: a man was about to get hit by a car and she pulled him back with all the strength she could muster. They both fell to the ground.

She awoke with her back drenched in sweat. The accident—yes, it was on that day. She had collided with that man on the street a few days ago. The drawing must have fallen out of her hands then and she had been too distraught to notice it. But she was determined to find it again and hastily dressed, grabbed an umbrella, and rushed out of the hotel.

She crisscrossed the same block for an hour to no avail. She felt the leaves crush beneath her heel as her eyes scanned the ground for the lost drawing. Although she wasn't yet tired, she felt thirsty from all the running. The same coffee shop she frequented before losing the picture was nearby. A glass of water would be good and perhaps she would have some luck here, it was a beautiful drawing and therefore not entirely impossible that someone had found it and kept it safe for the rightful owner to reclaim it.

She entered the coffee shop and several heads turned towards her. She couldn't be sure if it was her outfit that was too outdated for Paris, or that her hair was in disarray from the wind. She shrugged it off and sat down and tried to re-arrange her hair in order to look less alien in a city where chic and unforgiving fashion reined.

"Mademoiselle?"

The waiter looked eager to speak to her. "You are so much more beautiful in person."

He spoke in French, and she thought she heard him wrong. She was about to respond when a wide-eyed boy of no more than seven approached her with a stack of papers he appeared to be distributing. The waiter became distracted and promptly chased after the boy

"You can't put up anything on the wall!" he shouted. "I've told you many times already!"

He attempted to grab the boy's collar, but the latter successfully escaped his grasp and contorted his face before he ran away. He bolted towards the exit. Before reaching the door, he tripped on an old man's cane placed by the table, and fell to the ground, throwing the stack of papers into the air.

Rita watched as they drifted downward, one landing by her feet. She casually collected the piece of paper, curious to see what the boy was advertising, and she felt herself staring into her own reflection. The drawing looked like it had been sketched quickly, but the details of her eyes, nose, lips, and even the pattern of the coat she wore a few days ago all had been captured perfectly.

She stumbled as she took a few steps forward to check the other fallen papers, anxious to see if there were more copies of the drawing. Her eyes weren't mistaken, and now she understood why she had garnered so much attention today. She looked up and saw the boy scurrying past the shop window. She cursed under her breath as she clumsily hurried to pick up her belongings and chase after him, each of her steps landing on her portraits that lay scattered all over the ground.

"Hey! Hey you—stop!"

She could speak some French only when not flushed or in a hurry, but by her body language, everyone seemed aware of what she was talking about. A small crowd began to form. Some men thought that the boy was a thief and that she was desperately trying to catch him. They caught up to him and held him captive until she reached them, out of breath and her cheeks reddened from the cold. She tried to explain to the men holding the boy like a criminal that he hadn't done anything wrong.

Following a series of attempt to explain in broken French, a helpful English translator passing by stepped in to clear the misunderstanding.

Rita was sneered at by some when they discovered that the boy was not a thief. Their heroic actions would go unrecognized. Others simply shrugged and smiled apologetically at the boy, and the crowd began to disperse, leaving her to face the frightened boy, who was now in tears.

She smiled and tried to reassure him with a candy that she found in her purse as she apologized profusely in French. When he finally stopped crying, he unwrapped the candy and as soon as he tasted its sweetness, his troubled face broke into an innocent smile.

Seeing him more relaxed, she inquired about the drawing without sounding too stern. "Who gave this to you?"

He looked puzzled and she regretted not having asked the translator to stay.

She pointed to the portrait clutched in her hand, and the way she held it distorted her face until the image no longer resembled her,

"*Qui? C'est qui?*"

The boy was obviously perplexed by her question, but it seemed that he understood her. He snatched the paper from her hands and flattened it carefully it on the ground. He pointed to the paper and then to her.

"*Madame, c'est vous! Vous ne voyez pas?*"

Running out of patience, she exhaled loudly, feeling exhausted from running and furious that someone drew a portrait of her and passed it out like an insensitive joke.

"*Non, non.*" She shook her head, made a quick drawing gesture with her hands then pointed back to the portrait. "*Qui?*"

Luckily, this time, he understood her question immediately. His eyes brightened and he pointed to the left corner at the bottom of the paper, giggling at having led her to the obvious.

"*Madame, voyez ici, le nom et l'addresse.*"

The handwriting looked untidy, suggesting the artist's impatience and contempt for having to spell out the words when drawings are far more worthy of time.

Rita narrowed her eyes to make out the writing. "Luke N. 68 Montepassant, Paris".

§

Wartime—1944, London
Rita

The night sky was clear, and Rita was glad to be sitting outside in her mother's lawn chair. She rolled up her wool sweater and rested her head on it. Stars competed to show which one cast the brightest light. She sighed and her thoughts wandered back to Kurt. *Where is he now, and what is he seeing? Is he watching the same sky?*

§

Wartime—1944, Rouen
Kurt

He woke up with a cracking headache, feeling like he had been violently thrown down in a wrestling match. Kurt flinched at the memory of Freddy Brown, that heavyset lad who always glared at him like a hungry predator before a match. But that was two years ago back in college in London.

And yesterday he wasn't in a wrestling match. Where was he? He opened his eyes but his vision was hazy, and he had to blink several times before he could see the person standing in front of him. He tried to raise his hand and rub his eyes for a clearer view, but he was tied down. *Fuck!* Was he in German hands? The figure didn't appear to be German. German soldiers don't wear blue-and-red-patterned clothing, or a dress. The face that made his heart ache steadily came into view like a dream. *Rita.* Her eyes weren't the ocean-blue he was accustomed to. These were a pale emerald green, and they sparkled as they stared worriedly at him.

"Maman! Il s'est réveillé!"

His body tensed at the sound of the foreign language, and it took him a minute to hear French rather than the German he was trained to hate. He relaxed his shoulders, trying to make out Rita's face and wondered why the colors of her eyes had changed. She didn't speak French, and he was neither back home nor at the base. Where was he? Darkness crept over him again, and he lost consciousness.

He reawakened surrounded by the family who saved his life. He was properly introduced to Claude and Lucille, the parents of Marie and Catherine. They were Jewish and had lived in the underground cave since the beginning of the war. He learned he had been shot by the Germans that he and his teammates had run into, and he had passed out in the snow. Before the Germans could get to him, Marie found him lying outside the entrance to the cave, and he was brought in by Marie, Catherine, and Claude.

"It has been two days," Marie told him. She held his hands tightly in hers, reminding him of the kind nurse at the Paris hospital where he was treated briefly for a stray bullet wound. He tried to disguise his shock, but as he watched her, he was unable to chase Rita from his mind. He felt both comforted and terrified to see her in this stranger and in this place. Rita, whom he loved so deeply—and where he vowed he would never return if he survived this war.

The French Rita stared back at him, her green eyes lit with excitement. He had suffered from life-threatening injuries and no one, including her, expected him to recover.

"It is a miracle," she said softly. Her eyes held him with affection and familiarity. She felt as if she knew him from long ago. He was her miracle, and he seemed convinced that she was his—a guardian angel who had saved him, a request graciously granted by Rita's prayers.

§

Present—1953, Paris
Luke

He unmistakably had seen Marie the day he met Rita, and he still saw her standing in front of him with her blue eyes fixated on him. They faced each other and he restrained himself from lunging forward and wrapping his arms around her slender frame.

Only moments ago he had been thinking about Marie. They had so little time together, but she was his for those fleeting moments. They hadn't enough time to savor each other, to get lost in each other's eyes. And this girl, this reincarnation of Marie, began interrogating him the moment she barged through his door.

He was deeply immersed in his thoughts and didn't hear the first few knocks. He had thought it was Catherine returning to the house to collect her things. There was determination in her eyes when she left him at the hospital, and he knew then that his broken marriage was a lost cause. He opened the door to find the girl he had been drawing for the past several days. Her brown hair was damp from the rain and her hands clutched the drawing he had impulsively done a few nights before when her face wouldn't leave his mind. He had wanted to see her again to know for sure. What better way to find a person than to display hundreds of flyers along the busiest streets in Paris? He wondered how much of Marie he saw in her. The sketch didn't take him long to draw for her face came to him effortlessly. Now, here was the muse herself.

"Is this a joke to you, sir?" She recognized him immediately when he opened the door. It was the man from the streets, the same man who almost got them both into an accident because he had been too inebriated to walk straight.

"I'm sorry, but I'm afraid you must come inside to continue this conversation." He pointed to the rain with one hand while holding the door wide open with the other. She walked through the threshold, and he felt the air she moved through breathed life into his soulless body. The sight of her revived him. They were now in the same space, breathing the same air—he and this beautiful woman unknowingly impersonating Marie.

§

Present—1953, Paris
Rita

Rita was furious and wanted to know why he felt the need to distribute flyers showing her face. Why was he searching for her? When she confronted him at his doorstep, he didn't seem the kind to play malicious jokes on strangers. What was his motive? She pretended to be angrier than she was and strode in silently, allowing herself time to keenly scrutinize her surroundings. The tall ceiling and exquisite marble floor told her that this place was much more costly than its owner made it appear to be. The living room was carelessly decorated with large, simple wooden bookshelves, making the wall look like a literary fortress. The shelves also held clusters of random items as if he were still undecided about his collections. There was an army rifle on one of the shelves, and she recognized it as the type Kurt had. Below it, there was a picture of a ballet dancer—but not any dancer. This was Marie Aumont, the famous ballerina who rose to fame shortly after the war.

She wasn't ready to talk to him yet and she didn't let the shock show on her face. At the center of the living room, where the moonlight shone brightest through the skylight window, she saw a reflection of herself smiling back modestly. The eyes were a clear shade of green and although the tears were not drawn in, she knew they were being held back.

"This!" She heard herself speak. "This is me." She turned and he was standing behind her, only inches away.

"I'm sorry, I didn't mean to scare you." He backed away and walked toward the couch and sat down smiling.

She couldn't tell whether he was looking at her, or at the painting in front of her.

"My eyes are blue." There was a hint of disappointment in her voice, but she made it sound like she was pointing out his mistake.

"Oh." Luke stood up and walked towards her still wearing the same coy smile. He stared into her eyes as if he were inspecting them. "Well, so they are."

She stepped back, feeling uncomfortable and unsure whether she should sit or stand. She attempted to fix her hair, already unruly and frizzy. She must appear foolish to him, although she was here to confront him about his misconduct and not the other way around.

"What is it that you want? You went through all the trouble of distributing these flyers."

The portrait of her was still clutched in her hands, and her voice was steady and unfaltering.

He didn't know what to say. He hadn't actually thought about what he wanted. All he knew was that he needed to see her again and somehow have a chance to prove his eyes wrong—that she wasn't Marie but an imposter who resembled her. Now that she stood in front of him, he was speechless, his mind as blank as an empty canvas. He had met Marie, by chance, out in the woods by Rouen. It was a day he would never forget. Time moved through these eyes, a different shade, but nevertheless reminiscent of Marie's. She looked like her, but by the haughty and self-righteous way she spoke, she reminded him more of Catherine.

"Well," he said confidently, without knowing what would come next. He paused. Momentary silence wouldn't give him away; it would only build up the suspense. He was used to improvising his conversation and seldom had a difficult time finding words or reason to readily answer any sort of interrogation.

He heard his voice falter as Rita gazed at him intently. His mind felt blunted by a besieging force. He looked away from her and his eyes began to search for something yet undefined. From where he stood, he could see his blank canvas, set up months ago, a work he had promised himself to begin. Inspiration seemed to evade him and his natural talent. He needed time to figure out why he couldn't let go of his memories of Marie, why he chose to linger among these images of her, why he tormented himself and never tried to find a way out of the engulfing debris of his past. He could pretend that she was Marie. No one needed to know. He could speak to her in his mind, whisper things he had longed to say, and she would simply sit there. It would be quite therapeutic. He turned to Rita, and although he could barely suppress his newfound joy, his voice was surprisingly calm.

"I want you to be my muse."

§

Wartime—1944, Rouen
Luke

Two days have passed since Kurt has been missing—or shot to death by the Krauts. Luke shook his head at the disheartening possibility. He didn't know him that well but felt like there was a hole in his chest. One of his men was now unaccounted for. He was one man short, and with only four men in his team, he believed he had already failed the mission entrusted to him.

How did he get here in the first place? He had repeated the question throughout the last forty-eight hours, sitting in the dark without even a lit candle for fear his location would be exposed. The Germans were bound to be patrolling the area by now. His father would have been proud. Or maybe he would think him foolish—his youngest son, who had vowed proudly to one day become a famous painter—now a Jed agent leading a team of men braver than himself to sabotage the Germans.

§

It was Christmas day, three years earlier, when his father sat him down at the dining table. They sat stiffly across from each other, separated by numerous plates of leftover turkey, bacon, and a platter of scrambled eggs. Holiday season was the only time he would see his family since he traveled and painted for the rest of the year, living an aimless, vagabond life as his father called it.

"What are you doing, son?" His father's voice sounded dry and flat, but his eyes glimmered with a stubborn hope, unextinguished after so many failed attempts to offer sense to his rebellious son. He believed that Luke, a brilliant student who had a bright academic future ahead of him, wasn't so lost after all.

Luke despised his father for disregarding his passion as if it were nothing more than a hobby for him to pass time. His father sneered at his paintings like they were cheap art that didn't deserve a place in his library. The walls there were adorned with framed paintings by Vermeer, Van Gogh, and other artists his father treasured. There had been no lineage of famous painters in their family, only successful lawyers and well-to-do politicians.

"I'm finishing breakfast, if you don't mind." Luke forced a breezy smile, anticipating the usual reprimand. He enjoyed witnessing his father cringing at his prideful nonchalance.

"Don't take me for an old fool, for God's sake, Luke." His father's voice shook with anger, and Luke knew that his mother was behind the kitchen door, listening intently to their conversation. This was a familiar debate that would remain perpetually unresolved. His father cleared his throat. His hair was graying at the temples but still thick and in constant disarray. He would be sixty-eight this year, but Luke thought him older, and for the first time in three years, he felt a regret for not living up to his father's expectations. A lawyer, a journalist, something with words, his father would suggest pleadingly.

"Anything that would validate your academic gifts."

Luke had scoffed many times before at his suggestions, and their conversations unfailingly escalated to a heated debate every time he went home.

"What are you doing with your life, Luke?" His father let out an exasperated sigh to let him know how disappointed he was. The sympathy Luke had felt for him a moment ago vanished, swiftly replaced with the familiar bitter animosity he felt towards the old man.

"Nothing that would earn your concern, that's for sure." He wiped his mouth and threw the napkin on the table. He was already standing when his mother rushed through the doors, holding a freshly baked apple pie like a peace offering.

"Are you leaving already?" Her eyes were pleading for him to stay, but he knew that indulging her would prove to be pointlessly unpleasant for everyone. His sister's family was staying here as well, and he would be an insufferable grouch throughout the day, scaring his twelve-year old nephew with his manner and snarky remarks. He shook his head as he picked up his bags and headed for the door.

§

That was the last time he saw his father. News of his death came a month later when his sister Edith had called him from home. His mother was too devastated to speak on the phone, and Edith delivered the news in her stead. His father fell from the chair on which he stood while adjusting the Van Gogh painting in his library. The heavy gold-framed painting crashed onto his head. At first, Luke didn't think much of it. The old man was already dead to him. Days later, he found himself deeply unsettled by the creeping sense of regret followed by a sudden pang of sadness. He had missed his chance to explain his decision to his father. If he had persisted, perhaps after several failed attempts to discuss his future, his father would come to understand his passion for painting, even acknowledging the slim possibility of his succeeding as an artist.

When the news of war came several months after his father's death, he put down his paintbrush, packed his unfinished canvases, and enlisted during the first week of the announcement. He would give his father at least that much and give up painting, at least for a little while, and see what life brought him.

§

Soon after he joined the army, he was selected by the Office of Strategic Services to join a top secrecy mission: Operation Jedburgh. He had been chosen mainly due to his fluency in German and French. His linguistic hobby picked up during his college years had become unexpectedly instrumental in dramatically altering his position in the army. He didn't have to take part, and he was well aware of the risks. It was obvious that this sort of secret operation was essentially a one-way ticket to Europe. There was no turning back. If he was going to risk his life in war, he was going to risk everything. He made a promise to himself: if he survived the war and this clandestine operation he had been handpicked for out of hundreds of men in the battalion, he would have earned his right to choose his own path without any guilt.

Along with two-hundred eighty men, he endured the grueling physical and mental training, mastering all the technicalities imaginable in radio communications and espionage skills. By the end of their training, they were able to piece together concise intelligence reports. He never wished for a high army rank and enjoyed being part of a secret operation involved in something cunning and unconventional. He couldn't get enough of the thrill it offered.

This was his first mission as a linguistic army officer. A week before D-Day, he entered Normandy with Kurt and François to gather intelligence for their headquarters to re-assess attack positions. This was the first time he assumed the role of patrol leader in a mission. He felt grateful for the opportunity to prove himself while knowing from the very beginning that he wasn't ready. Even his men knew it. Since returning to their base without Kurt, morale had been low, and he didn't have the heart to organize a second patrol. None of them suggested a search mission for Kurt or would admit to each other that they were scared. They were outnumbered, and while they had been told a few days before that replacements were on their way, they remained alone with a few inexperienced French villagers—maquisards—now looking to him for instructions. He tried to shake off the image of Kurt's body rotting on German territory, and the thought of it made him choke on his cigarette.

"Fuck this."

He threw his cigarette to the ground and didn't bother to crush it. The snow would kill the fire. Maybe the snow would kill his men. They were cold and unequipped for the long winter. He pulled up his collar and buttoned up his coat. Anger fueled his determination and he ventured alone into the forest at five o'clock in the morning on Christmas day. The night before, he had heard the German troop on the other side of the city singing "Silent Night." They sounded a bit slurred and he hoped most of them were still drunk and asleep in their barracks. His one-man mission to find Kurt alive and bring him back would restore morale to his team and gather his men together to fight another day.

§

At first he thought it was a small twig on the ground, but it looked oddly familiar. He tugged at it until he could identify a shoelace tied to an American army boot. Size 9, he thought—Kurt. Who else would it be? No other troops had been deployed in Normandy yet. He was about twenty minutes from the base. Had Kurt been this close to them all along? His eyes darted from left to right, keeping an eye out for an ambush and any sign of Kurt.

A branch cracked behind him. Someone was close by. *Shit, am I being watched?* His hand tightened around his rifle and he turned and aimed at the sound.

A young girl, not more than eighteen, stood front of him. Her light brown curls protruded from the blue scarf she wore loosely around her head. She remained still, and her plain dress looked burdened by the oversized coat draped awkwardly across her shoulders. But she had appeared like a vision emerging out of the air.

Luke withdrew his rifle and stood immobilized by the figure. He didn't want to move in case she ran away or disappeared. Her eyes looked frightened and prepared to flee. He realized how threatening he must seem to her, and he laid his rifle on the ground then raised his arms as if surrendering to this ethereal ice queen of the forest.

"I'm not German." He was unsure whether she understood English, but at least she would hear that he wasn't speaking German. He saw her shoulders relax in acknowledgement that he wasn't a threat.

She walked hesitantly and cautiously towards him.

"American?"

Her voice was as soft as her features. He felt lost in her emerald green eyes but quickly collected himself, wanting to reassure her that he was not a threat.

"Yes." He opened his coat and pointed to his American flag badge sewn onto the inner layer meant to be concealed while out on missions. "See? American."

She sighed with relief and the cloud of her breath etched the air.

Seeing she was no longer nervous, he took a step forward, and as he moved closer to her, the ground beneath him seemed to fall away and he felt a calming warmth radiating from her.

"My name is Luke." His left hand rested on his chest like he was making a pledge to her. *I vow to protect you and to never leave you. Can one fall in love this way?*

Her voice was already fading as a faint shade of pin rose in her cheeks.

"My name . . . is Marie."

§

Present—1953, Paris
Rita

She closed the door quietly behind her. It was a heavy door, meticulously carved from solid wood patterned with a mix of flowers. They were sculpted in all sizes, intertwined with leaves, twisting at every corner. Only moments ago she had stood on the other side of the door, speaking to this man who wanted her to be his muse. She scoffed at the idea at first and thought it inappropriate. She had heard from friends what happened to girls who posed for unknown artists with no known background.

Then he asked her what he could do for her in return. Anything, he said. His eyes locked on her flushed face. She didn't know what to say, and to hide her own embarrassment, she stood with her chin raised indignantly and said nothing.

He began to speak about himself. He would introduce himself properly to reassure her of his artistic reputation. Luke, he said, that was his name. After the war, he returned to France, where he had fought with his men, and stayed on as he gained an audience for his paintings.

"You might have seen this somewhere," he said. He led her to an adjoining room, a small parlor reserved for special guests, and pointed to a painting on the wall without taking his eyes off her.

She drew back in amazement, not expecting to see the perfection that lay so still yet so full of life on a flat canvas. A ballet dancer stood before a mirror dressed in a short, white chiffon dress, looking wistfully at her own reflection as if it were someone else's. Her sad eyes held hope, her shoulders aligned in a dancer's posture. Her long, slender arm rested on the bar and seemed to sustain her entire weight as she stood effortlessly on her toes. Rita felt beguiled by the painting and she moved towards it, her fingers caressing the golden frame that held the ballerina so willfully captive.

She asked if he knew the woman in the painting, and he didn't answer her. But he asked a second time in a confident tone—would she be his muse? She felt herself blush and overcome with emotion. Her own reflection, painted meticulously on an oil canvas—would her eyes shine as brightly? Would her fingers appear as graceful, her silhouette as desirable? Without thinking further, she agreed. As they shook hands, she told him firmly that she would ask for a favor in return after some thought.

He smiled and reassured her that was agreeable. When they would next see each other, she could let him know what he might do in exchange. Standing in as his muse was a most important task, he insisted. He took a step back and walked her to the door.

As he helped her into her coat, they stood inches apart, and she saw him clearly for the first time. He was tall with broad shoulders, and there was an air of a disciplined soldier about him. His artistic side showed in the manner he wore his hair: long, wavy, and disheveled in a rather careless way but nonetheless fashionable. His face was handsome with large, dark brown eyes and chiseled, model-like features. A deep scar on his left cheek bordered his ear. It was not something easily missed.

With one hand gently on her back, he opened the door with the other and bid her goodnight, his eyes pleading with her to stay.

She walked out, almost in a daze. What she had really come here for? She heard him calling behind her.

"I'll see you on Saturday—Rita."

There was a slight hesitation before he said her name. She did not turn back, but she waved to him, acknowledging his reminder. As she walked away, she saw her shadow stretched out of proportion by the full moon, accompanying her on this cold, strange night.

§

Present—1953, Paris
Luke

He didn't go to bed right away, even though he was exhausted. Seeing her again—this girl who summoned so many memories, good as well as unwanted—filled his mind with love and hatred. He felt compelled to pick up his paintbrush so that he might pour this nightmare onto an empty canvas. His passion was detectable only in the first few years of his career as an artist. After the war, his painting style became dramatically more serene and relatable, although no one really knew of the anguish and violence hidden under the layers of paint.

He frequently had asked himself what it was about his memories of Marie that trapped and tortured him so. He'd seen many people survive loss, not just soldiers, but civilians who had witnessed more atrocities than he had, and they seem to be getting on with their lives. Were they putting up a front, pretending they had successfully recovered from these wounds? Or was he a weaker breed, more susceptible to the loss he had suffered, and too frightened to go to bed sober?

He never managed to figure it out, and he began to enslave himself to alcohol, pleasantly surprised at how much it soothed him. At first, he restricted its magic only to evenings before he went to sleep. But then the need for its company began to grow and fill entire days until he was unable to tell what day of the week it was. Being with Catherine changed that. Somehow she managed to retrieve his soul from the underworld in which he lived. They had been happy once, and he believed they had a chance at beating the odds and overcoming a dark past.

On the nights he slept soundly, good dreams came his way. Memories were always from a specific time. He sat up and stayed awake throughout one entire night, recalling his dream and later painting it frame by frame. Too precious to share, he never showed anyone these paintings. Making them public would make them less real. There was one he especially loved. He had dreamed that he could bring Marie with him as he had promised. He led her out of the cave that she proudly called her home. Her bright smile left him aching. She stepped out of the cave and shielded her eyes from the sun. Her head tilted slightly and when her eyes adapted to the light, she faced the sun, welcoming its brilliance. He captured that moment to the very last detail, from the crease near the corner of her eyes when she squinted, to her unruly fingernails, bitten in anxiety and a habit she confessed she hadn't been able to stop since childhood.

Such were the details they shared in the little time they had together. They had seemed insignificant and trivial, but now he regarded them as priceless bits of information never to be traded.

§

Wartime—1944, Rouen
Luke

When Marie first led him into the cave, he stumbled as he adjusted his eyes to the darkness. It was a low, cramped place that was thoughtfully improved to resemble a home. A small wooden dining table in the center space held neatly stacked plates. This must be the living area. Her parents stood timidly by the table., and Lucille, her mother, wore an embarrassed expression, like a hostess ill-prepared to receive her guest. When Marie introduced him to her sister Catherine, he was surprised by the firmness of her handshake. She was a young girl but the fierce determination in her eyes reminded him of a reckless soldier he had reprimanded weeks before they had landed in Normandy. She was beautiful in an extravagant way, and it was difficult not to notice her. He found her charming if a little too young to be so grounded and confident. But it was Marie that held most of his attention with her softly elegant ways and her kindness. She wore her braided hair in a loose bun and as she spoke she pushed back loose strands of hair behind her ears. Her green eyes were at once sincere, timid, and watchful, a combination that he hadn't be able to capture on canvas despite countless tries. He later gave up and blamed it on the fact that he had seen her only a scant number of times—not enough to really know her or absorb all that she was. When he was able to shift his attention away, he began to ask questions, most of which her father, Claude, was able to answer.

§

The family moved shortly after the German invasion, and the cave was known to Claude since he was a young boy. He had chopped trees for firewood in the forest and discovered the cave one day when he fell into the entrance while playing with his cousins. It became a secret hideaway among the children that they never shared it with anyone else, using it as a secret underground fortress and bringing all their valuable toys and trinkets to hide. The cousins took turns tidying the cave and chased away bats that retreated into deeper corners. They grew to have distractions bigger than toys or games like hide-and-seek, and the cave became less and less important to them. Eventually, it was forgotten as they turned into adults with a different world to conquer.

When tensions grew among the Jewish families in the area, Claude began to plot their escape, but with little success as most of the routes were beginning to be monitored and blocked by the increasing numbers of German troops. One day, as Claude walked through the forest to collect firewood for the week, he stumbled upon the entrance of the cave. He and his cousins had marked it in a way that only they could recognize. They had planted an apple tree by the entrance, and since then, it had grown into a majestic thing to behold in the middle of the forest. He rushed home with the news that would change their lives dramatically. They would live, and they would live free.

§

The cave, as primitive as it looked, was thoughtfully partitioned into three areas. Aside from the living area where Luke stood, there was a smaller space, divided by a short bookshelf, and that was the family's washroom. On the opposite side of the washroom, two large mattresses were separated by a curtain that hung from an uneven wooden frame. Luke blinked in disbelief as Kurt, lying on one of the mattresses, looked up at him and smiled faintly. They exchanged a few words before Marie stepped in and insisted that Kurt should rest. She was obviously in charge of his health and rightfully so. As young as she appeared, she was as steady and stern as any doctors he had met on the field. Exhibiting paternal pride, Claude exclaimed that Marie had nursed him back to health and had done everything she possibly could to save him.

When they rescued Kurt, they found shrapnel cuts on his shoulders and arms and an exit wound on his left leg. Lacking surgical experience, Marie consulted her books and improvised her way through the process— and although she never admitted it to them—she felt inadequate and frightened, but her steady hands never gave way to her fear. At her father's insistence, she used the whiskey to disinfect the area and managed to stitch the wound with the first-aid kit tools she practiced with at school.

"When will he be able to walk?" Luke tried to keep his voice low. He anticipated that Kurt might not be able to walk again and didn't want to further upset him.

Marie smiled and reassured him that Kurt would be able to use his legs in two to four weeks. "You can come get him then," she said, glancing towards Kurt almost regretfully since it would mean bidding farewell to her first patient.

§

When Luke was asked to join them for dinner, he politely declined, not wanting to impose. But procuring food must be an ordeal. How inconsiderate he would appear if he left without making sure they had enough food to live on.

"Please, can I bring you anything? Any food?"

Claude and Lucille looked at each other awkwardly and didn't answer him, obviously reluctant to disclose their family secrets. Catherine cleared her throat and stepped between Kurt and her parents, shielding them from his unintentional interrogation.

"No, thank you, we have enough food for the week." Her tone left nothing to debate and she regarded him as she would an intruder.

Luke felt taken aback at her response and confused by her refusal for help. He wanted to question her, but the fierceness in her eyes convinced him otherwise. *Beautiful, yet so thoroughly hardened.* He wondered at her appearance; she was the only one among them who didn't look like she belonged or like she wanted to hide. Their eyes met and he looked away, unsure of whether or not she could read his thoughts.

"But there must be something that you need." He diverted his attention back to the rest of the family, desperately wanting an excuse to return to this place if only for the chance to see Marie again.

"Perhaps something for Kurt—you must be lacking medicine." He nodded at Marie, who rose to her feet as he spoke.

"Yes, yes, of course," she said.

She assumed her duties as a nurse very seriously and attended to Kurt, checking the bandages on his leg.

Kurt let out a soft groan as she removed the first layer of bandage, and she tried to ease the pain him with her touch and whispered something only he could hear.

"Do you need more bandages?"

Luke felt Catherine's watchful eyes on him and wondered if she could see through his purpose.

"Yes, please," Marie said. "A sewing kit, bandages … more bandages— *un, deux, trois, quatre...*"

She began to count her equipment, shutting the rest of them out as she entered a point of concentration reserved strictly for her patient.

He took the list of things she needed and held the paper on which she had scribbled as if it were a sacred scroll. He folded it carefully before placing it in his pocket. Marie guided him towards the exit and Catherine slowly and cautiously removed a wooden plank that shielded the cave from the outside world. They all listened quietly for any movement. The process was excruciatingly measured and almost religious in the way everyone remained still and looked up as though praying for absolution. Luke waited patiently with them, admiring this family for their discipline and determination. It had been with these enduring qualities that they survived the previous six months underground.

Catherine signaled to him that it was safe to leave. He thanked them with a nod and smiled briefly at Marie. She looked as angelic underground as when he first saw her in the snow. He exited the cave feeling light-headed and giddy. He was in love, and she was from another world.

§

Present—1953, Paris
Catherine

The lights were still on, and Catherine imagined that Luke was working fastidiously on a painting, fueled by new recent inspiration. She used to love coming home to him, seeing him so absorbed and lost in his own world. It would fill her with admiration for her husband as she watched him fondly from a distance. But now she dreaded to open the door to see what she expected to find. Most days he was asleep, his paintbrushes nowhere to be seen. Instead of paint sets scattered on the coffee table, she was obliged to clear away empty bottles of whiskey and other liquors that viciously sucked away the inspiration from the man she used to worship.

She opened the door, quietly removing her shoes and tiptoeing into her house, a habit she had developed over time. Luke never said anything, but the smallest noise while working was a serious distraction, something he could ill afford when absorbed in a new project. As she entered the living room, she was surprised to find him up and about, moving around like an excited child with a new discovery. He shifted from left to right, holding a paintbrush in his hand and focused intently on the canvas. It was rare to find him genuinely indulging in his work. She had witnessed his rise to fame and was jealous at how he had accomplished it so effortlessly.

As a dancer, she practiced hours each day, mastering the most detailed techniques apparent to only a select few in the audience. Her career demanded perfectionism, and she gladly surrender to the pleasure of performing flawlessly. Unlike dance, his performance was rarely criticized, and as many would agree, his work exuded a rare purity. One critic wrote that Luke painted through the eye of an innocent child. She knew better than anyone that he was far from pure.

What he had been through, what he has witnessed through the war—a failure in humanity in its ugliest form—how could they not see through his pretense? Whatever he created could be done only after transporting himself to an imaginary world where he had not withstood so much suffering and cruelty. She pitied him when he received praised for his work. The words bore no resemblance to the man. He became fully immersed in his work when he painted through the night, tirelessly laboring for something meaningful and not for his own artistic reputation or to please his crowds of oblivious fans. These rare artistic outbursts occurred only after awakening from his nightmares. He could then unleash his hatred and the pain that he was never able to put into words. He painted it all in forms and shapes that weren't easy for most people to comprehend. But she understood it. His sufferings were familiar to her, and every time he poured them out, she felt more relieved. Her own suppressed memories would be given a moment of freedom.

When he was done and asleep on the couch, leaving the canvas to dry, she took time to embrace the anguish so beautifully translated into art. She had wept when standing in front of an image that reminded her of her family. The colors were primarily gray and black with a swirling pattern repeated in an almost animalistic and sinister way. In the middle of all the chaos, a bright dot emerged, meticulously painted with different shades of yellow, like a light at the end of a tunnel. She stood silently looking at it for a long time. She had felt tears rolling down her cheeks but they seemed like someone else's. Her father, her mother, Philippe, and Marie—they were crying out to her from the painting. Did they ever reach that light? Did they find the peace they prayed so relentlessly for after death?

When Luke woke up and saw her emotional state, he removed the canvas from the wooden stand and threw it into storage. He never brought it out again, but from time to time she entered the storage room to stare at it and grieve for her family in her own way.

Quietly, she walked past the living room and went upstairs. She began to pack her things—it was time to leave for good, and she wanted to make sure that she never had to come back. She left with only a few outfits, and for some reason most of what she took was either red or black, and she got tired of wearing the same colors. Today, she wore a short black dress, and her hair was put up in a simple bun. She walked passed a shop and was stunned by her reflection and how much she looked like she was on her way to a funeral. She laughed a little, first at herself, and then at the situation. It was a sign. Her marriage was dead, and she might as well come to terms with it and move on. And so she went home to collect her belongings and to replace her widow's outfit with something more cheerful. It was new beginning, after all.

Shuffling through her closet, she found a gold dress with a sequined collar. Feeling the silk under her hands as she caressed the material, she nostalgically recalled the story behind the dress. She had bought it for their first anniversary when they were still relatively happy. Luke had asked that she sear something fancy for dinner, and she had spent a ridiculous amount of money in a department store whose customers' daily expenditure was her yearly earning.

He had pulled her chair for her as she sat down to dinner and complimented her on how beautiful she looked. How loving his eyes had looked. They toasted the occasion with a bottle of expensive champagne, but she had secretly thought it was to celebrate the fact that they had gone a full year without mentioning Rouen, Marie, or what happened on that fateful day.

She slipped out of her black widow attire and put on the gold dress. Although it did bring back memories of the good times she shared with Luke, she was more than ready to let them go. She toasted herself in the mirror with an invisible champagne glass. To the happier times. She heard Luke's footsteps in the doorway before she could close the bedroom door.

He cleared his throat when he saw her and he looked beyond her into the past they had shared—a happy one, even ever so briefly.

"You're back." He stood in the hallway with his hands in his pockets, his eyes tracing the outline of her body.

"Yes, but I'll be leaving soon."

She pretended not to care and continued folding her clothes. She hesitated before putting them into her opened suitcase on the bed. What was she afraid of? He already knows that she's leaving him, so why are her hands trembling? She stood up brusquely and pretended to be occupied as she mindlessly shuffled through her clothes in the closet.

"Listen, I have to finish packing. I have a ballet function tonight."

"Did you want me to go with you?"

It was a straightforward, legitimate question. He usually accompanied her to all her dance functions. But today, the question begged a finality she didn't expect to acknowledge just yet. There was an impassivity in his eyes as he waited for her to respond.

"No." She reciprocated his cold stare. Beneath her serene appearance, turmoil stirred within her as she mentally paced between the blurred events of the past few months. What did she do to deserve such contempt from the man she thought she knew?

§

Present—1953, Paris

Luke

When Catherine left, he remained sitting on the bed. He might have run after her, but he let his anger anchor him. A useful thing that was—his anger towards Catherine. He heard the door close downstairs, and he felt safe enough to move around and see for himself if she had taken that piece of hateful evidence with her.

He moved to the shelf with the wooden jewelry box only to find that it wasn't there. She must have taken it. He had wanted to ask her so many times, let his anger explode from his chest and interrogate her like he had so many Nazi soldiers. Except that he wouldn't torture he; no, he would torment her with memories. But he couldn't bring himself to break their unspoken pact. Neither one of them ever spoke of the dark past, the cave, her family. They tiptoed around the subject expertly, almost competing to see who could hold out the longest. It turned out they were equally triumphant.

With all the force he could muster, he pushed the drawer back so violently that it broke and fell to the floor. He jumped back and inadvertently tripped on his own coat thrown carelessly near the bed. Defeated, he lay on the floor. He would ask her the next time they meet. *Why, Catherine? Did you do this? Did you kill them? Do you have Marie's blood on your hands?* If she denied it—he was almost certain she would not—he would demand to know where she got the SS insignia. He would watch tears roll down her cheeks. Only then would he be free of the toxic mixture of love and hatred that consumed him.

CHAPTER FIVE

THE DREAM THAT WAS

Wartime to Post-war—1944-1953
Catherine

It had been five years since she accomplished her dream. When she relocated to Vallée de la Loire, she was supported by Hélène, her mother's cousin, for three years. Hélène did not share her love for art and dancing and deemed it frivolous and too expensive to support. But she became close to Hélène's eldest son, Henri, who was two years older. It didn't occur to her at first, but Hélène kept a watchful eye on them. This would be the first of many female jealousies that she would encounter as she glided her way into adulthood, unprepared, and without the constant parental love and care she had grown up with.

When she didn't have school, she spent her time dancing and daydreaming in an abandoned clothing factory. The walls were so high that if she ignored the broken windows and rows of deserted sewing machines, she could pretend she was performing onstage in an opera house, winning the crowd over with her grace and flawless techniques. She didn't have many friends but didn't feel lonely during the daytime. When her heart ached for Marie and her family, she banished them from her thoughts until dark. Night was the time she reserved for mourning.

She danced most afternoons, and although she did well in school, she sometimes purposely failed her exams just to see if any of her teachers might approach her and try to understand her. None ever did. They seemed intimidated by her sharp mind and confused by her deft academic performance during class in contrast to less-than-favorable exam results.

In the beginning, nearly all the boys in her class admired her, but very few had the courage to speak to her and she didn't bother with those who did. She shut herself off from the boys that surrounded her, and the admiration and curiosity they had for her gradually turned into spite. Someone spread a rumor that she preferred girls, and her chance of finding friends among her already jealous female counterparts completely vanished. But she was happier alone, she told herself repeatedly, she was strong, and she would be stronger still.

She had difficulty sleeping most nights, her mind invaded by the last poignant moments that led to her family's execution. In the dark silence, she imagined the heartbreaking cry that escaped from her mother's mouth as a German soldier dragged her out of the cave. Through tightly shut eyes she saw her father clearly, with his stooped shoulders and sad, worn face. She reached out her hands, stretching them as far as she could so that she could caress him. Alone in her room, she sensed and could almost touch Marie, her sweet sister, her dress pulled at the seams by German soldiers, laughing as they ripped it open. And where was she? She was being pulled back, restrained, and unable to run to her family to shield their pain only for a second.

It had happened so quickly, but in her mind their pain and shame lasted for an eternity. She prayed that she would not think of them every night before she went to bed, but as soon as she crawled under the sheets and shielded her eyes, those moments raced through her mind over and over again. Her rightful punishment for surviving the war.

Henri was kind to her, and of everyone in his family, he was the only one who showed her compassion when she felt unable to leave her room because of the recurring nightmares. Hélène called them episodes, and she questioned her niece with a particular disdain she reserved for petty children and liars. Other members of the family whispered when they thought she couldn't hear them, and sometimes they wondered aloud about how she had managed to escape German hands while everyone else in her family perished. Henri was different. He would bring her breakfast, and as he sat on her bed, he solemnly watched her eat until she had finished everything on her plate. Sometimes they would talk. He knew not to mention her family, so they would speak of trivial things, like how the family cat got chased by the neighbor's dog again; and she would laugh wholeheartedly. She momentarily forgot why she was in this house among strangers and not back in the dark cave that had become her home.

They also spoke of their dreams. As the clever one in his family, Henri immersed himself daily in classic literature, collected old novels, and composed poems; he aspired to become a writer. His mother disapproved of the idea and openly declared she would support his education only if he were to study law like his deceased father. Unfortunately for Hélène, that did not sit well with him, and he regularly plotted his escape with Catherine—a game they both enjoyed playing. He admired her passion for dance and sympathized with her as they were both dreamers without the means to turn their dreams into reality.

One morning, as they sat outside watching the world go by without them, he turned to her and asked in a half-joking manner how she felt about running away with him. She laughed and became quiet when he didn't join in. *How would they do that?* He grinned as he showed her a thick bundle of cash tied with a length of ribbon. He nodded before she had even asked the question.

"I stole it from her," he said with not the slightest hint of regret or shame. "I counted it. We can live on this for at least a few months."

He paused. The next thing he said would turn her life around, and he wanted to be acknowledged for it.

"There is also enough for you to sign up for your first semester of dancing school".

She embraced him tightly. "She's going to have a fit in the morning," she whispered, resting her chin on his shoulder.

He laughed, and as she joined him, he reached for her hand. They sat together and at once knew they were stronger. They would no longer be dreamers.

They had plotted their escape that very afternoon. As the sun was setting, Hélène was busy in the kitchen preparing dinner, and Catherine looked around her nervously, searching for those invisible spies she knew were hiding somewhere. They had already packed and now waited for darkness as their accomplice in an escape that would forever alter their destinies.

Their plan was to meet at midnight; Henri would sneak into her room and they would use the fire escape to climb down. There was no train running then, but they would run to the farthest train station and wait until morning.

She sat up on her bed, trying to stay awake, and with a soldier-like diligence, she counted the seconds on the clock that hung above the door. The excitement of planning their escape had drained her energy, and she began to drift away, nodding, as she entered a familiar and dangerous dream.

When Henri came to her, she was already screaming. He shook her so violently that she slapped him as she came out of her nightmare. They heard footsteps in the hall, and as the doorknob was turned, he sank to the floor and slipped under her bed.

Hélène stood at the door, her face expressionless. She looked at Catherine and sighed.

"What is the matter now, dear?" Her voice was flat and without concern. "Do I have to remind you that it is very late and people are sleeping at this hour?"

Catherine shook her head, worried that Hélène would see Henri. She sat up and dangled her feet, hoping to shield him. Hélène was still half-asleep and she muttered under her breath as she walked sluggishly out of Catherine's room.

That night, Henri and Catherine walked away, hand in hand, without looking back, leaving their past behind and prepared to tackle the world. They took a small apartment in a rowdy neighborhood in Saint-Germain-des-Prés in Paris, but it suited them. For once, they were both free to their lives unsupervised. To protect themselves from unwanted gossips only too eager to latch on to their next victims, Henri told the landlord as well as their neighbors that he and Catherine were brother and sister. No one had any doubts about their naturally platonic relationship. They slept in separate bedrooms and ate their meals together; their bond was strong, and there was an invisible barrier that neither of them dared to cross. They understood that they were family, linked by blood. But there was something more, a forbidden realm of growing sexual tension they did not dare venture into. At seventeen, Catherine was blossoming into an attractive young woman, and everyone around them, including Henri, took notice of her beauty.

Henri worked for a moving company, a business that was booming as Paris became the center of everything, and people swarmed the city as if it were the only livable place in France. It was a fascinating time, and Catherine was glad to be caught up in it. She found a job waitressing in a local brasserie, and with the grace of a dancer served her customers deftly. She caught the attention of many customers, including that of Monsieur Lapardieu, a senior instructor at the Paris Opera Ballet School. He didn't view her first as a dancer but as a conquest he openly lusted after. He was a powerful and wealthy man with little patience, but for a week, he sat at the overcrowded brasserie, staring at Catherine as she moved from table to table.

She wasn't entirely oblivious to Monsieur Lapardieu's lecherous gaze and kept him at bay until she realized who he was. A man of fifty, he was old enough to be her father, but his thirst for beautiful young women was not quenched by the advancement of his years. On the contrary, with his growing authority and powerful grasp on the school, his ability to attract young women with dreams to succeed as a ballet dancer was shamelessly manipulative.

When he invited Catherine to his home to discuss her potential as a student in the school, she told Henri that she had to work late, and that he needn't wait up for her. Her youthful inexperience left her feeling nervous. And despite the effort Monsieur Lepardieu exerted to make this meeting appear like a formal interview, she was not oblivious to the scandalous rumors circulating about him and was apprehensive of his less than honorable intentions towards her.

She had imagined that her first sexual experience would be romantic, but she was aware of her circumstances and this was the only way for her to achieve her onstage dreams. The money that Henri set aside for her allowed her to attend ballet class in a small, untidy building. She was taught by a disillusioned ballet instructor who did not care for perfection when, to her, utter perfection was what made ballet a magical art form.

As she was being led into Monsieur Lapardieu's bedroom, where the meeting supposedly was to take place, she took a deep breath and began to understand how deeply she loved to dance. This was only one of the many sacrifices she would have to make.

His voice was low and arrogant as he ordered her to remove her clothes slowly so that he might examine her. He must make sure that her movements were graceful, and he instructed her how to unbutton her blouse in the manner of an intimate dance performance. He immersed himself in the private recital, sitting in his upholstered velvet chair, staring at her with dominant, hungry eyes.

"It's an inspection," he said, haughtily making his way towards her,

She felt smaller and weaker as he approached her in all her nakedness. His hair was already graying at the temples, and while though he attempted to maintain a youthful look by the fashionable choice of his suits, she saw the skin on his jawline had begun to sag.

Despite his observable signs of ageing, his insatiable desire for beautiful women hadn't been subdued. Later that night, as Monsieur Lapardieu impatiently climbed atop her, panting over her taut body, she let herself go limp and forcibly shut her eyes to envision a brighter future. One year, she promised herself, one year and I will shine on the stage. All the hiding, the time spent underground, shielded from the world in order to survive, at last will have been worth it. The man who undoubtedly held the key to her success moved rhythmically, grunting with pleasure as she winced at the smell of his whisky-stained breath.

He got up rapidly, and she felt an indescribable emptiness inside her, but the grief was soon replaced by the relief that it was over. He returned to the bed with a bottle of fine red wine and two glasses. He drank with her in celebration of his satisfaction. He prompted her to drink, and they finished the bottle. She put down her empty glass and saw the lust return to his eyes. He grasped her again impatiently, and she shuddered, her body helpless and unable to show refusal or the disgust she felt at his touch. Desperately wanting this to end, her fingers latched on to the bed sheet while she endured the violation she willfully consented to. She turned her face sideways lest he noticed her tears, and slowly, she drowsed off into a fleeting dream state interrupted by the reality she found herself ensnared in.

She tried to make out the shape of the bottle that danced before her eyes. Thank God for the wine.

When she woke, she found Monsieur Lepardieu fast asleep beside her. She put her clothes back on and thought of Maman and how much it would pain her to know her daughter had resorted to such an arrangement to chase after her dreams. She imagined Maman reprimanding her. "Foolish girl." But if only she knew.

Still infatuated with dancing, her dreams and ambitions now had an altered direction. She was now determined to show the world what she had been forced to hide all those months underground. Her family put to shame, marched to their deaths—the world would know. She would perform only for them; she would dance with all their passion and energy and with every breath unjustly taken from them.

"Catherine, was it?" Monsieur Lepardieu's raspy voice almost made her jump from the edge of the bed she sat. She felt sharply conscious of her nakedness in front of this man whom she barely knew. She was already regretting the rigid, unromantic intimacy they had just shared. There were no soft kisses laid on her neck as she had imagined, no gentle touch of a lover's hands gliding up her thighs. There was only a hastened, undisguised act of desire that made it seem like a contractual agreement forced upon her due to circumstances, and one that he gladly satisfied.

His eyes still lingered on her bare shoulders and he asked if she would come to his office at the school tomorrow.

"I will make arrangements," he said with a satisfied grin. "And I hope to see you again." He adjusted his shirt collar, knowing that he would have power over her education, her career, and her body.

§

It was a long walk home. Monsieur Lepardieu insisted on sending her back with his chauffeur, but she politely declined, as she did not wish to prolong her evening with any more reminders of him. The streets were quiet, just as she wished. She attempted to find a gleam in the starless sky. She imagined stars as her fallen family watching over her.

When she arrived home, Henri wasn't asleep but sitting upright at the dinner table, and the sullen look on his face told her that he knew. His eyes reprimanded her impetuous actions, as if they had cost them the happiness they were both stumbling towards.

"Where were you?" His kind eyes usually smiled unreservedly whenever he spoke to her. On this night, they looked frighteningly stern as they scanned her discerningly from head to toe.

She felt vulnerable and weak from the evening spent with the man who would now be her sole benefactor. She was unable to gather her courage and confess to him. She did not wish him to know, nor to even understand what she had done.

"I'm tired, Henri," she said wearily without meeting his eyes. She walked past him unbuttoning her heavy wool coat.

With an unexpected brute force, he seized both her arms and forcibly pinned her against the wall. The collision caused the replicas of Picasso paintings to shake on the wall. They had bought them at the flea market on a whim when they had first moved in. "For our new home." He had laughed heartily as he hung them on the bare kitchen wall. It was a silly gesture and she told him they shouldn't make this a permanent place. But he stubbornly held on to the hope that they would one day have a home together, and that he was demonstrating to her what it would be like. She eventually gave in to his efforts of purchasing trinkets from the markets and odd- looking furniture that he repainted to make appear new and in harmony with their "home."

There was a look of betrayal in his eyes that she did not immediately understand. *What did you expect? What role are you asking me to play?* She wanted to shout at him, but the words remained trapped as her lips tightened. She had to give him the satisfaction of playing the role of a lover. It was the only way for him to understand that this could never be. The look in his eyes was unforgiving and cruel. She was convinced he wanted to tear her apart. She felt him breathing heavily, and the smell of cheap whisky clung to his quivering lips. Henri seldom drank.

"*Salope,*" he muttered contemptuously, but clear enough for her to hear. He glared at her disheveled golden locks, her lipstick smeared by a stranger he instinctively despised. Even so—even in her worst state, she was undeniably desirable. He wanted to slap her, and her fierce blue eyes stared back defiantly at him, daring him to. But to what end? What had he wanted for them? And how could it ever be? He softened his grip on her arms and then released her with the intention to never having her near again.

How he had found out, she never knew, but it hurt them both to know that the truth was out. The truth tantalized them every time their eyes inadvertently met in the place they had called home. She had sold her body in exchange for a convenient shortcut to her dreams, the dreams that Henri promised to grant her. He determinedly worked day and night as a mover. And she had heartlessly left him behind. She was ambitious and not patient enough to be the idealist he expected her to be. Nor would she ever be satisfied with the level of happiness he was able to provide for her.

He never forgave her for that night, and he began to dine out on most evenings. They no longer shared the intimate details of their day or their dreams. He purposely distanced himself from her, spending as little time at home as possible until one day he just didn't return. It hurt her to know she had been abandoned by Henri, someone she cared deeply about. Shortly afterward, she moved out of the apartment they had shared for almost a year and moved into one that Monsieur Lepardieu privately arranged for her near his home on Champs D'Élyssées.

It was a lavish space on the fifth floor of an historical building that gave into residential housing demands. She was relieved when told that it was not decorated as she preferred to not have his artistic tastes dictating to her in her own home. She salvaged a few chairs and an old rustic table left out on the street by her wealthier neighbors. The cheap Picasso replicas she had become fond of followed her into her hallways, giving the place an interesting dissonant mood. She enjoyed arranging and rearranging her new apartment, filling it with her collection of records, fresh flowers, and countless tablecloths to match her varied flower arrangements. It was a new freedom that she found herself in. But it also came with a price. Soon after she settled in, Monsieur Lepardieu visited unannounced and expected to be pleased.

The nights were initially unbearable. She would often lay awake in her bed, her heart pounding as she waited for his bloated shadow to appear outside her opened bedroom door. She endured his visits, and sometimes, if she was still drowsy with wine and half-asleep, she pictured a different man embracing her with the assertiveness and gentleness that she craved.

Along with the many long nights spent with Monsieur Lepardieu by her side also came her long-awaited acceptance into the Paris Opera Ballet School, with a generously subsidized tuition fee. As the new student in the advanced-level class, she continued her formal training awkwardly, struggling to keep up for the first few months. But she didn't allow this setback to faze her. There was nothing she could do about her past. She had been trapped underground, and she allowed herself the time needed to catch up and perfect her techniques.

When she first entered the class, she was introduced as a mature student by the instructor. She chose to ignore the snickers among a group of girls who regarded her with contempt. Her blurred past, the absence of a wealthy family, or one that had firm roots in the ballet realm, made her vulnerable to ridicule from not only the girls but the teachers as well. It hurt her to find herself friendless in a world that she loved so dearly, and she made herself appear impervious to callous remarks, and eventually, the bullying came to a halt. She became invisible to the other girls. Her skills were wanting, and she made more missteps than anyone else in the classroom. But she had survived to be here as she would constantly remind herself. She had endured winter underground with her family, and she emerged from the Rouen forest as the sole survivor. She would make it here. With her ardent determination and undefeated ambition, she believed wholeheartedly that it wouldn't take her long.

§

One late evening after Monsieur Lepardieu left her bedroom, she submerged herself in the bathtub, anxious to wash off any trace of his touch and lingering scent from her body. When the task was completed, she lay back and allowed her thoughts to drift to somewhere nostalgic and far away as a reward to herself.

Friedrich appeared in the misty forest maze. She set aside the anger and betrayal she associated him with and wanted to run towards him, yearning for his approval like she used to do. She would show him she was no longer the weak, starved little Jewish girl that he pitied. What a magnificent dance she would perform for him! She rose impetuously from her bath, wrapped a towel around her, and propelled her body outwards in a beautifully executed chaîné, twirling her way into the living room.

As she danced her heart out for Friedrich, she became so immersed in her movements and wrapped in emotion that she was unaware of Monsieur Lepardieu's presence.

He stood watching her from the threshold of the doorway. His bathrobe hung loosely on him, and he rubbed his chin with one hand, a habit when he was deep in thought. He had found his new protégée.

"Do you want to be great?" His playful gaze was replaced by a professional sobriety seldom shown to Catherine.

She was unable to speak. Staring at the towel on the floor, she stood naked before him. She felt suffocated by vulnerability and shame. Had she detected sarcasm in his voice? She didn't know what to make of his question. Or did he genuinely ask because he saw potential in her? In the weeks that had known each other, they barely spoke of anything as most of their contact was physical. She usually complied with his demands and rarely offered opinions of her own.

"Dance for me again."

She timidly nodded, feeling ill-prepared and apprehensive. Now, with a spectator—and a rather enlightened one—she breathed deeply and readied her stance. She raised her arms to the fifth position and leveled her gaze on the man who supposedly could make her "great." She stepped out of the shadows and sprinted forward onto the moonlit floor, feeling as though she was being effortlessly carried by a force greater than herself. Unbound from her surroundings, free of her current predicament, she leapt and twirled like an injured bird who has found new wings.

As she neared the end of her improvised dance sequence, she executed her pirouettes with such clarity that a gleam of pride made her heart flutter and she broke into a triumphant smile. At the end of her performance, neither of them spoke. They each knew that she had won. Her dance was her battle, and her enemy was her fear. She stared back at her benefactor and waited for his inexorable approval, no longer a helpless young woman, but a distinctly ambitious dancer whose indestructible passion and talent were waiting to be unleashed.

§

And so her life took a different turn. Monsieur Lepardieu saw the unique and limitless potential in Catherine, and he began to treat her less like a lover and more like a valued project that would in time yield him additional fame and fortune. Through the next two years, he took her under his wing and created vigorous training. Countless nights were spent inside the practice room he designed for all his "favored" students, and she soon became his prima ballerina in the making.

On nights when he didn't demand her to practice, he poured glass after glass of the finest wines, and they would sit and chat like old acquaintances. Stories of her past would flow freely, not told to any particular listener—certainly not to Monsieur Lepardieu—but she would forget his presence and tearfully recount the days she spent surviving underground, in a darkened cave, surrounded by loved ones.

As good a teacher as he was, he also was an equally shrewd

businessman who knew how to market his dancers. He began to spread the rumor of a young dancer in his ballet company, who, in a brutal war, successfully evaded the Nazis' grasp by hiding underground with her family. She was the only survivor, the miracle that no one had believed possible under the circumstances. He made her his miracle. Press began to feed on this story, and journalists poured over the details, most of the information over-dramatized.

She was at first angered by it all but the unwanted attention shed on her past had begun to work in her favor. However much it pained her, she let the press tell their fabricated stories adorned by scraps of facts received from Monsieur Lepardieu. The sensationalized image of a poor, young, battered Jewish girl, achieving her dreams of becoming a ballerina had the power to transform her into the most adored and celebrated dance figure of the decade.

Just as Monsieur Lepardieu had planned, she rose to fame and became the most sought after dancer in Paris. Not only were her flawless techniques and matchless grace in every performance acknowledged, her eye-catching beauty was blinding to most, and the queue of admirers, both male and female, grew exponentially. Thus, she became a sensation as her fame extended beyond the ballet world.

§

Present—1953, Paris
Catherine

Tonight, after all those years, she would celebrate that success with the most important role in her dance career: the female lead in *Romeo and Juliet*. She stood in the middle of the ballroom in her long white-laced dress and pearl-adorned neck, her chin held high. All eyes were on her, and she sensed the whispering activity seen wherever she turned was about her. Monsieur Lapardieu, who had elevated her from the status of a nameless dancer to ballet royalty, no longer controlled her, but nevertheless remained an important mentor. He watched her with an almost parental pride as he introduced her to wealthy fans. With every hand he shook, his beguiling smile became a little less modest, and the sound of his laughter traveled through the room, boldly and ostentatiously announcing his presence.

Throughout the evening, her thoughts drifted to Luke. While he did not appreciate ballet, she knew that it made him proud to witness her achievement. A small piece of her heart held on to the belief that he loved her, and deeply so. Not in an infatuated, romantic way, but with a love that stemmed from the acceptance of her past. He could then embrace her faults and light the darkness she had been trapped in for too long. That he had rescued her was not an overstatement, and she believed that she did the same for him. Their mutual salvation lasted for the length of their tumultuous relationship. She often woke in the night and the mere scent of his hair and the warmth of his body lying under the same cover would lift the heaviness from her heart. She always felt soothed from the shock that otherwise lingered after her many nightmares.

The love had shifted somewhere along the way. She couldn't determine the exact moment, but she had felt it as unquestionably as his love in the beginning. The first change was in the way he looked at her. Adoration and lust was replaced with skepticism, which soon turned to spite. But like his changeable moods while he was engrossed in a new canvas, the love she felt and the spite she received frequently shifted back and forth like a stubborn pendulum.

A few weeks earlier, puzzling changes were made clear after a drunken outburst.

She had removed her coat after returning late one evening. The night was cold and the smell of alcohol reached her before he even appeared. She walked a few steps along the hallway as saw him scowl at her with bloodshot eyes. A bottle of wine hung from one hand while the other steadied him against the wall. He put the bottle on the floor and tugged at his tie, trying to free himself from irritating bondage. She was familiar with his pattern: celebrating a successful exhibition in the dedicated companionship of alcohol.

Taking a step forward, she attempted to help him. His arm swung forward as if repelled by her touch and he inadvertently pushed her to the ground. He didn't hit her, she convinced herself; he didn't mean it.

When she stood up, his face was inches from hers, and he muttered a question that drastically broadened the distance between her and the man she thought had saved her.

"Was it you? Did you lead them there?"

The question needed no clarification. Her eyes met his and the unbridled hatred that looked back had since haunted her. She feared he was right to suspect her of an unspeakable crime, and in that damning moment, her heart began to harden again. She had yet made another mistake. He had not saved her; no one could. This silly union, this game of a marriage they gambled on had failed. She must reclaim her masked, impenetrable self.

She walked away, and when she closed the bedroom door behind her, she imagined him barging through the door holding a broken bottle with sharp edges to hurt her. She had kept the one object from the war that could thwart her role as victim. She ran to the shelf where the kept her jewelry box and opened the lid. It was still there. She couldn't tell whether it had shifted, but she had placed her pearl necklace on top of the Nazi insignia the last time she opened the box. Now it lay innocently undisturbed above her pearl necklace and earrings.

When he joined her for breakfast the next morning, he seemed to have no recollection of his outburst. She handed him the basket of bread and he smiled affectionately, muttering an apology for coming home drunk. She wished he would finish his interrogation so that she could receive her due punishment for deserting her family.

A gentle nudge on her shoulder awoke her from all-too-constant thoughts of Luke. Monsieur Lepardieu motioned to a plate of desserts being offered to her by a waiter. She smiled apologetically at the young man now flustered as he nervously held the plate. She took a small piece of the mille-feuille cake as a silent tribute to Philippe who loved them. Trying to appear engaged in the conversation, she nodded to the droning voice of the elderly millionaire beside her as he praised her performance at the opera house.

She took the first bite and felt the nostalgic sweetness transporting her back to the past. Marie smiled beside her as they ran towards Mlle

LaCroix's pastry shop. She began to cough uncontrollably, her eyes pleading for someone to help her escape an invisible assailant. A crowd quickly formed around her, and Monsieur Lapardieu hurriedly led her towards a chair. She leaned helplessly on his arm.

"Is everything alright?" His eyes searched her face and his voice was full of concern. For the first time, she thought of him as familiar and recalled the face of her father.

She nodded and smiled apologetically to the strange faces crowded around her. Then she saw them: her father, her mother, Marie, Friedrich, and Mlle LaCroix. They surrounded her, their hands laid gently on her back, on her shoulders, and caressing her arm.

"Is everything alright, dear?" she heard her mother ask. It hurt too much to answer, seeing them as if they had never left.

"Where . . . where is my cake?" Her child-like question drew laughter from the gathering, and a middle-aged lady with an extravagantly feathered hat held out the plate of unfinished mille-feuille with a bony, bejeweled hand. Her chiffon dress brushed the ground as she knelt beside her.

Catherine's hand trembled as she took a second bite, preparing herself for the truth hidden in the pastry layers. The saltiness of her tears mixed with the cake's sweetness and she was roused by a bewildering sense of certainty. This was Philippe's favorite dessert and one that had been too expensive to buy. But every once in a while, Mlle LaCroix secretly packed it up for him when Catherine came to buy bread for the family. She stared down at her plate. Mlle LaCroix's lovely face smiled back at her.

$

Present—1953, Paris
Rita

Rita was not accustomed to sitting still for a long time, and she was actively restraining herself from brushing away the strand of hair that tickled her face. Luke had asked her to wear her hair in a loose bun and adamantly asked her not to change anything after pulling one strand of hair and leaving it loose. It was their third meeting, and she felt she was beginning to know him. While good-natured, his temper was erratic and wild. Something as minor as an electrical hum from the heater could set him off, and she found it quite amusing, like watching a child throwing a random tantrum. An uncle was an artist as well, and she found them to be vaguely similar in temperament. Luke had instructed her not to speak and to sit still, but she was permitted to look wherever she liked. This gave her the freedom of exploring his home with her inquisitive eyes. They wandered from corner to corner, looking for the answer to a question she did not yet have. As he drew, he seemed more involved in the canvas than in her, the muse he had convinced her he desperately needed.

Before they began, he briefed her about his work. "Mostly landscapes," he said nonchalantly.

After asking around at the art galleries she had visited earlier, she knew he had reaped a fortune from his paintings. He hadn't done many portraits since the last collection that had made him famous, the primary work of which was Catherine Aumont, the renowned ballerina. Did he know her? Rita couldn't help but ask, her eyes glittering with curiosity.

"Yes, I knew her quite well," His voice was thick with regret, and she assumed their relationship had been romantic.

The room was filled again with silence, and she began to formulate in her mind the story of how they met. Maybe he had been commissioned to paint a portrait for her. Or he fell in love after one of her performances and pursued her relentlessly. Unsatisfied with her imagination, she sighed and sat listlessly on the green velvet couch looking up at the high ceiling from which was suspended an extravagant chandelier. It was an amazing thing to behold, and Rita smiled faintly as she thought about the perfect wedding that she had planned for Kent and herself.

She felt a gaze so intense the hair on her arms rose. She turned to face Luke, who seemed caught in a trance and unable to escape. His face twitched as if in pain. She called to him several times before he stood up curtly and left the room. She heard him close an upstairs door and found herself alone with her portrait. Recalling her uncle and his artistic tantrums, she didn't feel compelled to run after Luke; instead, she walked over to the canvas, glad for the opportunity to steal a glance at the work.

She wasn't happy with what had been drawn so far. The hair that he so impetuously demanded her to perfect was not drawn in detail. Although the strand was visible, everything else was still a blurry sketch, obviously to be filled in later. As she stood in front of the canvas, her eyes searched for the feature that took most of his time and focus. And then it struck her. The oval shape, the large irises, and even the subtle fine lines around her her eyes were meticulously drawn, line by line, with shadows filled in at all the appropriate places, given them a life of their own. But they were not her eyes. They appeared extremely sad and seemed to be holding back a tragic story. She wondered what things they must have seen to cast such a crestfallen look. When he put his hand on her shoulder, she jumped at his touch, almost knocking the canvas off its frame.

"Please sit down."

He spoke with such calmness and authority that she obediently walked back to her seat. Something had unbound him from himself and he began to speak to her. He asked her about her family, about her life in America. Did she like it here?

She answered his with ease and allowed him to probe into her life. They spoke openly, like old friends, and she felt herself coming back to life with the kind of spark she had possessed before Kurt returned from the war.

"Do you have someone back home?" Luke asked without taking his eyes off the canvas.

She fell silent and he noticed the sudden shift in the mood of their casual conversation.

"Of course you do," he said, embarrassed at his own impetuousness. "Would you like to take a short break?" His hands fumbled as he tried to put down his brush. It dropped to the ground.

"We were happy." She began to speak as if she hadn't heard him. "It was a long time ago, but we were happy. I don't blame the war—I know it was something that the world had to go through. But he came back so changed that I just don't recognize him. I'm not sure what to think…"

Her voice trailed off and she looked down at her hands, her fingers working at an invisible knot she attempted to untie.

"It changes you. War does funny things to people," Luke said as if he was addressing himself. He wanted to tell her his stories and give her answered from his own harrowing experience but felt powerless as he searched for the right words to begin. He couldn't bring himself to speak. He met her inquisitive eyes and gave her an apologetic smile. No more questions today. Perhaps it was best for each of them to face each their demons alone.

§

Wartime—1944, Rouen
Luke

When he walked back to the base, he saw François, and two maquis—Antoine and Benoît—running towards him, their faces colorless as though they had seen a ghost. He didn't know how long he had been gone and he could tell they were scared out of their wits. He began to explain where he had been and that he had found Kurt who was now being cared for by a family in hiding and didn't elaborate on there whereabouts.

"We received orders to move out in two days," François took out a map and showed him the route they were ordered to take to secure a crossroad. "What should we do about Kurt?"

The question confounded him. He hadn't been thinking about Kurt but about the girl that had held his mind enthralled since seeing her that morning.

"He... he can't move just yet, and it's too risky to move him from where he is to the aid station. We don't even have a vehicle." Luke felt something like jealousy when he thought of Kurt lying underground and cared for by Marie and her family. He shook the image from his head and felt a pang of shame.

"I'll go to see him tomorrow and let him know that we can come back for him. We'll move out in two days." He closed the map and walked back to his foxhole thinking about the dim cave as he shut his eyes.

That night, he dreamed of Marie and the vision of her was so real that he could almost reach out and touch her. It was one of the last good dreams he would have in a long time.

The next morning, he woke in high spirits, knowing that he was going back to the cave. He dug around in his bag for chocolate bars he knew he had saved and smiled when he found them still intact in their wrapping. He walked rapidly, and when he saw the apple tree come into sight, he could hardly contain his excitement.

He knelt and began to dig for the wooden plank as instructed by Catherine the day before. When he felt the hard surface with his hands, he knocked gently, and waited for a response. He heard one knock, and he whispered the code word given to him by the family. "Haver." Friend.

Claude opened the door and led him into the cave. When he saw her again, Luke was ecstatic to find she was exactly how he remembered her. Her hair was braided into a bun, a loose strand caressing her cheek as she moved about the room, bringing water to Kurt. Lucille, unsure whether his presence signified good or bad news, looked uneasy as she handed him a cup of water, her eyes lingering at the rifle by his side. Catherine was nowhere to be seen.

"Where is your sister?" He felt grateful for something to ask Marie if only to hear her voice again.

"She went out to collect firewood." Marie tried to hide her anxiety but the tremor in her voice betrayed her. Her parents wore the same distressed look on their faces.

"Is everything okay?" He stood up, spilling the water as he rose.

They heard a knock followed by a soft whisper from aboveground.

Claude moved quickly across the room and pushed up the wooden plank to reveal Catherine dressed in a white winter coat, her nose red from the cold. She climbed down with ease, like a child entering her secret hiding place. Her hands shook from the cold as she handed a basket full of bread to her sister.

She turned towards him, her eyes purposely averting his gaze, but she greeted him with a forced smile. He stared incredulously at the basket filled with bread and fresh pastries. How would a young girl be able to procure all this food in the middle of a forest? She seemed to have read his mind and spoke nonchalantly.

"We have people who help us." She met his eyes with defiance, silently warning him to back away. He was an intruder and his concern was unwelcomed in this place. She glared at him with an animosity that bemused him. And yet, despite her unpleasant manner, he found her gaze intensely alluring. Her eyes were a shade of the deepest blue he had ever seen. A shame, he thought, that a young girl so beautiful was not more kind.

Marie signaled him to follow her. She smiled shyly as she walked between him and Catherine. A clever diversion, he thought, but he gladly obliged without further questions. She led him to Kurt, who was fast asleep. His bandages had been changed and he had more color on his cheeks.

"He is healing fast," Marie said. She adjusted Kurt's blanket to cover his shoulder. She measured his temperature as she tenderly felt his forehead. Her eyes revealed her relief. Her patient was recovering and she had fulfilled her duty as his caretaker. The zeal in her eyes could only be interpreted as elation, and he was moved by her pure joy and the rare innocence that shone so conspicuously through her young soul.

"Do you have any news for us?" Catherine's voice was steady and slightly accusatory. He wasn't a guest and she wanted him to know that. She held her arms rigidly across her chest as she waited for his response.

Her unwelcoming gesture made him want to distance himself from her even more. "Right," he replied.

He explained that his team would be moving out the next day and that they needed to leave Kurt behind to let him get better. They would try to return within two weeks when he should be able to walk again. Would they mind looking after him for the time being? He addressed the question to Marie, his eyes holding her bashful gaze. She blushed, sensing that his attention was becoming apparent. She nodded before turning away to attend to Kurt.

"What about us?" Anger rose in Catherine's voice, and Lucille frowned at her daughter but her face showed a hint of hope as her eyes drifted to Luke.

He felt unable to answer immediately, but he had already determined to bring Marie along. Would she leave with him?

§

Present—1953, Paris
Catherine

When Catherine found the strength to stand on her own again, she walked around languidly, asking each waiter in the room if they knew who was catering the party. She felt in desperate need of this information. Several heads turned and followed her as she scurried past in search of the person who might hold the key to her past. She was determined to learn whether her memory was playing tricks, or if this splendid cake was, in fact, crafted by Mlle LaCroix. There was no reason or traceable evidence, but she instinctively knew that Mlle LaCroix and Friedrich had survived the war and were now in hiding, just as she and her family had lived underground to escape death and persecution.

Her thoughts had remained with Friedrich. Was he living with a deep sense of regret and shame, or was he making the most of newfound freedom where people knew nothing of his past and the atrocious crimes he had committed? She had never forgiven him for what happened that day but neither could she bring herself to hate him. As she grew older and looked back on past events, she came to the realization that their relationship was complex and beyond understanding. She felt certain there was love, although undeclared; and she continued to believe she would never be able to reconcile her feelings. She was trapped in an obscure past blurred by the eyes of her young, irrational self. Was it love she had seen in his eyes? Or was it hate disguised in pity and forced sympathy?

She finally found the girl who had organized the catering and was told that the truck that brought the pastries was pulling out the driveway. She raced towards the door as her thoughts tumbled wildly in her head. Perhaps it was Mlle LaCroix. Or Friedrich himself. If she could only speak to him, if he could explain what had really happened on that day. But would it change anything? She unconsciously slowed her pace, and as she descended the marble steps, she saw the truck pulling away from the driveway. From where she stood she could see only a faint shadow at the driver's seat and was unable to tell whether he had Friedrich's tall nose and arrogant eyes, or if he would turn back and look at her longingly with something like affection, on the mornings they used to meet outside of the cave.

She struggled to stand and managed to grab on to the railings by the stairs. She leaned there lifelessly, hungry for the stale bread she used to share with her family, something she vowed to never eat again if she survived the war.

§

Present—1953, Paris
Friedrich

When the reception organizer called the shop, it was he who had answered. He knew about the event consciously, that Catherine would be inevitably present, and kept the information from Claire, and his guilty conscience chased him relentlessly throughout the day as he loaded the order onto his truck and drove to Paris.

He slipped out before the crowds entered the room, hoping their paths would cross and all the while dreading the possibility of seeing her again—the great Catherine Aumont. He watched the lingering shadow from his rearview mirror and hoped it might be her. But even if it had been, their meeting would be disastrous. He had nothing to offer her. She was no longer a helpless, starving girl who needed the food he brought to her. He had felt like a mighty savior—now he was far from that.

He had ordered executions of fathers, mothers, brothers, and sisters, all whom reminded him of the underground family he secretly protected, attempting to justify his actions with every reason he believed the war was being fought for. Before becoming entangled in his act of kindness, he didn't dare question the validity of the killings of Jews. He wholeheartedly believed in this mission, and he was able to follow through on execution orders without faltering.

When he first met Catherine and Marie, he couldn't tell they were Jewish since they didn't wear the Star of David on their shoulders, and Catherine so lacked the brokenness he was accustomed to seeing. Before he could put a stop to it, he found himself more and more astonished by this headstrong girl who possessed a rare strength and determination found only in the bravest of soldiers. He didn't always tell Claire when he would go to see Catherine, and he wasn't sure why. After several visits with Catherine, Claire's eyes would become clouded when he told her about his day. Deep concern then sharp relief crossed her face when she opened the door to let him in. She was worried for him and frightened for them both if one day his deeds were discovered.

No one could deny Catherine's blossoming beauty and he was no exception as he fell prey to her ocean-blue eyes. But there was something else. There meetings developed a familiarity that grew each time he saw her. He began to look forward to seeing her appearing out of nowhere like a mythical creature. In the short time they had outside the cave, they would sometimes speak about trivial things and other times let the silence take reign of the moment.

He always decided the next time they would meet and instruct her when to come up to collect the food basket. One morning he had walked to their meeting point two meters from the apple tree under which her family lived. His troops had invaded a nearby town and sound of explosions and raids could be heard even underground. She appeared shaken from the commotion heard from the cave, and he saw the fear in her innocent blue eyes. She remained silent as he handed her the basket, her eyes sullen and downcast. He had begun to walk away and heard her say, "I'm glad that you're alright." He didn't turn back but paused briefly to acknowledge her concern for him.

He was known to his men as a stern, unforgiving commander. The image helped him discipline his soldiers and earned him a legendary reputation in his regiment as a cold-hearted, merciless tyrant. But when he met with Catherine in the snow-laden forest, his eyes would soften as he beheld her tiny frame approaching him. When her face came into view, his practiced disciplinarian gaze would take over, and he would speak to her with an indifference he knew they were both familiar and comfortable with.

He stopped at the traffic light and watched the snow fall rhythmically on his windscreen, almost like a song, and it soothed him. Adjustment to the unhurried pace of life after the war had been hard, but he had managed with the sweet, understanding Claire by his side. She was the only one able to cut through the hardened exterior that he put up for others. Yet he was unsure that she really knew him at all. She must have thought him to be kind or else she would never have accepted him so easily. But the darkness that hung over him was heavy and enmeshing, and even he could not lift it after all these years.

A young man on a bicycle came to a halt beside his truck and he thought he saw a face he daily attempted to obliterate from his memory. Nikolaus, a young, dedicated private from his regiment. Nothing about his appearance was particularly striking, nor was he very articulate, which did little to help him make himself known to his superiors in order to rise in rank. But despite his plain looks and reticence, Friedrich had taken special note of him. He was extremely loyal, following orders without question, and he had an unparalleled admiration for Friedrich that was only too obvious. It eventually turned against him as he was deemed far too eager for his own good. It soon became clear that he wasn't going to be a fine soldier in the battlefield, and if he did get sent out, in all likelihood, he would not last long.

Friedrich had devised a plan to keep Nikolaus around—and alive— for whatever time he was to serve in the army. He ordered him to do most of his errands, typically trivial things like bringing the post; he soon had a new protégé under his wings and observed him closely. Nikolaus always completed his tasks early, and he hardly blinked when spoken to, focusing his energy on every word, as if the menial daily tasks given to him were as urgent as direct orders from the *Führer himself.*

Even as Friedrich kept him close as an unofficial protégé, he never let his guard down and kept a placid demeanor around Nikolaus. He spoke little of himself and limited discussions to military-related matters.

One afternoon, as he began to scavenge for food to bring to Catherine, he had difficulty finding bread in their supplies room. He called Nikolaus and asked him to find bread in the next platoon station while he attended to a call from the base in Berlin. Nikolaus returned two hours later with a bag full of bread he eagerly handed to Friedrich. His face betrayed his keenness for an explanation or at least an order to deliver this extra supply of bread. But Friedrich exhibited a stolid indifference as he waited for the young private to take his leave. He had never thought of Nikolaus as any kind of threat and now felt a sudden twinge of fear. His confidence was shaken as he pretended to be unperturbed by it all. Nikolas mumbled apprehensively about an errand he had to attend to and hurried out of his commander's office, leaving the bag of bread and his doubts behind. Friedrich impatiently waited until sunset when most men retired to their posts. He left his base, feeling lighter with each step, as though shedding the weight of worries he had to carry throughout the day.

The walk through the forest was always an intimately tranquil time. He savored the silence like it was an unattainable reward encountered by mere chance, and he let himself freely indulge in the serene, enthralling sound that the branches made when the wind blew through them, like a violinist playing the strings on his instrument. He sometimes closed his eyes as he walked towards the cave, intuitively following the path. At times he felt a measure of happiness, but he could never be sure because it was always so brief—like a passing stranger accidentally brushing against his shoulder. He considered himself a fulfilled man, but true happiness seemed to be out of his reach. Claire made him feel at home and her presence began to take on meaning in his life. He turned to her for comfort and companionship.

His epiphany occurred one evening as she stood cooking with her back to him. Stooping slightly over the stove as she stirred the stew, she hummed a French tune he had never heard before, and it was then he knew that he was not destined to be alone. But despite their closeness and lustful attraction, his adoration for Claire was more a fleeting experience. She never gave voice to her suspicions, but he felt she knew that she wasn't enough for him.

As soon as he spotted the tall, magnificent apple tree from a distance, he awakened from his thoughts of Claire and his eyes began to search for Catherine. In the moments he waited for her to appear—anxious moments that excited him beyond his understanding— he felt like he had returned to one of his fondest childhood moments, impatiently waiting in line to purchase chocolate at the shop around the corner from his home. When he saw her that afternoon, she was not wearing the white coat she usually did—he assumed she had wanted to blend in with the snow, and he admired the tactic. Instead, she had on a soft blue coat that perfectly matched her eyes, and he marveled at the color that shone from her angelic face.

As if right on cue, the snow began to fall, flakes dancing in the air as the wind blew gently towards Catherine, a snow queen standing tall in the paradise specifically designed for her and her alone. He stood still, enjoying the resplendent apparition, and he must have smiled without realizing it because her lips curved into a faint smile in reciprocation.

He started to move towards her until the sound of a branch cracking made him come to a halt. He grabbed his pistol from his side and spun around to face the intruder. His face turned as pale as the snow that draped the forest. Nikolaus stood still, with his hands in the air, but his eyes, filled with doubt and deep regret, nervously darted from Friedrich to Catherine. He had followed his commander into the forest and had unknowingly stepped into a forbidden territory that revealed a secret too shocking to comprehend.

He watched Nikolaus, his errand boy—not even a soldier—who no doubt had followed him with the intention of ensuring that his commander was safe. He looked utterly helpless, staring back at Friedrich's pistol, which was still pointed at him. A pang of shame fell over Friedrich like a bucket of ice water thrown at him, and he was jolted from the dream he had woven in his imagination. That Catherine could actually make him happy—he began to laugh, and his shoulders trembled. He pushed back tears that had no place here. Silently, his steady gaze on his protégé, he pointed to their base, and as he watched Nikolaus' face relaxed, he knew that he had understood the order.

He and Catherine watched until Nikolaus disappeared in the distance. With one hand in his pocket, and the other holding the basket containing a week's food supply, he waited for her to say something.

"Who is he?" Her voice showed no concern but her eyes widened with fear. Was he going to come back? Would he disclose her family's location?

He wondered what it would take for him to remove the overshadowing doubts, and instead, to light up with the happiness he wished he could offer her.

"I will take care of it." He regretted the impulsive promise as soon as he had spoken the words. He hadn't thought of what to do with Nikolaus, but his heart had caught the words more quickly than his mind.

He walked back to the base, his heart heavy and unsettled. More now than ever before did he feel the guilt that sprang from his misconduct. He felt out of place as he passed his fellow soldiers in uniform. Their salutes drew a sour taste in his mouth as a nearby platoon marched past him, their proud, straight shoulders in disciplined alignment. When he arrived at the station, he didn't look for Nikolaus immediately, expecting that he would come to him. He waited until the men started to scatter back to their posts. Nikolaus had yet to appear.

He was unable to sleep as he sat upright at his desk, battling his conscience and pondering what should be done with Nikolaus.

The next morning, as Friedrich drummed his fingers on his desk, waiting for Nikolaus to bring him a cup of coffee, his mind began to panic. Had he already gone to someone and told what he had seen—a German commander helping a Jewish family in hiding? Footsteps continued to pass outside his door bearing no sign of Nikolaus. He stood up, determined to sort this out himself.

Outside, the infantry regiment had gathered for a briefing. The sun was strong, and he had forgotten his hat. He felt even more diminished, more out of place in this world where discipline trumped other merits. He scanned the area and spotted Nikolaus, whom he had kept safe from the violence and atrocities of the war, speaking to First Lieutenant Hans Witt, a petty man who conducted missions only if they earned him a medal or other recognition that would move him up in rank. Nikolaus appeared nervous; his lips quivering as he struggled to explain something of vital importance to the officer who stood in front him nodding indifferently.

Friedrich contemplated his own fate. Would this be the end? And how would Claire survive without his protection? Would his men raid her house after they found out she was an accomplice in helping a Jewish family? Would she be tortured to death, as he had witnessed others many times before? Nikolaus courteously ended his conversation with the sergeant. He turned around and met with Friedrich's harsh gaze. Timidly, Nikolaus saluted him and disappeared briskly in the crowd.

The next morning, Friedrich didn't expect him to show up. But with a brighter-than-usual complexion, he appeared holding a cup of coffee and smiled cheerfully as he handed it to Friedrich. The day had begun with no trace of sun in the sky, and Friedrich found Nikolaus' buoyancy irksome and misplaced. The young private seemed relaxed, much more so than the day before.

Friedrich's mind flashed with thoughts of Catherine's thin frame standing in the snow then with the view of Claire's back as she dutifully prepared his dinner. What would happen to them if he were denounced as a traitor to his country—the country whose ideal he fought so hard to uphold?

Feeling a premonition of what was to happen, Nikolaus backed away, leaving Friedrich denied the chance to make things right. Without thought to the consequences, Friedrich drew his pistol and killed Nikolaus with one shot. He could still see the horror in his eyes, like a loyal dog shot by its master. Other soldiers rushed in after hearing the gunshot, but no one questioned what he had done. They prompted him to tell them what crime had been committed, crowding excitedly around his body like anxious spectators at a ferocious battle, thirsty for more blood.

"I gave him orders to join the patrol tomorrow, but he refused," he heard himself say calmly. He felt surprised at his ability to remain composed.

Laughter erupted, and Friedrich felt a pain rip through him as if he had been shot.

"Well, he's always been a coward," a private added, while others joined in agreement in nods and low whispers. No one had respected Nikolaus when he was alive, and their reaction to his death reinforced his unpopularity among his peers.

The clouds lifted unexpectedly and the sun shone, its warmth creeping into Friedrich's office. He was aware of how suffocating the room felt. He muttered an apology to his men and walked out as he unbuttoned his collar, allowing him to take deep breaths. He hurried past the officers' barracks and heard someone call out his name. It sounded like Nikolaus but he dismissed the thought of him and turned to face First Lieutenant Hans Witt instead.

"Sir, I heard about Private Nikolaus Werner." There was a genuine remorse in Witt's voice. "A shame." He gazed fixedly at Friedrich's pistol resting on his belt. "Yesterday he came to me, asking for permission to join our front-line combat unit. I told him that he had to work on his rifle aim, but the boy insisted."

Friedrich felt his cheeks burning, and he tightened his lips as he waited impatiently for Witt to finish. They both knew that it was his word against a well-respected and widely admired captain of the SS.

"Shame," Witt shook his head sadly. A sly grin appeared on his face. "But a great disciplinary action, Captain." He nodded respectfully, but his eyes glittered with sarcasm and malevolence. "We all have soldiers to discipline from time to time, don't we, Sir?"

Friedrich no longer cared to linger and listen to Witt, and he walked on without answering. Witt obviously knew nothing about what Nikolaus had seen in the forest; otherwise he would have denounced him right then and there. It was his churlish behavior and the way he made light of Nikolaus's seemingly insignificant life that disgusted Friedrich. He vowed to kill him on the battlefield at first chance. It was the least he could do for Nikolaus.

He spent the next several days grieving Nikolaus' death and made up his mind that the next time he met with Catherine would be his last. He began to gather extra supplies, enough to last the family for at least another four weeks. He didn't pack the food in the usual way but took one of his leather bags that had the insignia of the Waffen SS sewed on the side, and filled it with bread, cheese, canned pickles, and apples scavenged from the kitchen. He asked Claire to bake a few of her famous pastries, and he knew his request surprised her as he rarely asked her to bake anything.

The evening before he met with Catherine, he brought several bags of flour and sugar to Claire's apartment. He stood by silently as she began to weave her magic in the kitchen. Her lush, dark hair was secured in a bun, something she rarely did since he preferred her with her hair down and she readily complied with his wishes. He watched her longingly, her voluptuous body moving back and forth as she kneaded the dough with her hands. He felt a rush of love for this woman as he leaned on the wooden bookshelf holding dozens of recipes and cookbooks that she had collected since she was young. He lit his cigarette and wondered if she knew as a little girl that she would be a pastry chef. He had first walked into her shop in the spring of 1942, without the slightest idea that he would change both their lives forever.

She knew well the effect she had on men and had smiled at him flirtatiously. He nodded back knowing that he was going to make her his. He visited her shop on an almost daily basis, and when she jokingly asked how many soldiers he had to feed, he blushed and hadn't didn't return for a week. When he saw her again, he boldly asked her to dine with him with no intention of returning her home before the next morning. And when they first made love in his car, he made sure that she understood that she would not share her body with anyone else from that night onwards.

The daily excitement soon turned into a routine. Friedrich visited her apartment every day after dark. He would find her baking in her kitchen, her face caked with flour like a mischievous child. She smiled broadly at her German lover as he walked through her door unannounced. He didn't tire of seeing her, as she expected him to. Her insecurities were apparent but her face would relax into a smile when she saw him the following night. She was admired by countless men of all ages, and he enjoyed watching her from the other side of the shop window, knowing that the charismatic patissier and her voluptuous body that others lusted openly after belonged exclusively to him. Word soon spread among his men that he had taken a French lover, and when they found out who she was, no one in his regiment frequented her shop out of respect for him.

Their passion was loud in the night, but when they awoke in each other's arms in the morning, they had little to talk about and gazed into each other's eyes, giving voice to their love in a silently intimate form of language.

The day they discovered the two girls standing behind their home, something changed in him, and it didn't go unnoticed. Although it was Claire who initially pleaded with him to help the girls, she later realized that he hadn't needed much convincing after all. He sometimes lay awake at night, speaking to her about the Jewish families he had executed, his eyes wide open as he recounted their deaths—how they were brought to their knees and shot from behind, sometimes indiscriminately if they attempted to run away. She had asked him to stop and he complied, but his troubled eyes continue to tell the many stories that haunted him during the night. She associated his strange commitment to Catherine and her family with the guilt he felt, and she willingly surrendered a part of him to Catherine in order to have her lover sleep soundly at night.

§

He trod the familiar path slowly, pausing at every tree in gratitude for its silent, indispensable company. There would be no returning to this forest. Catherine stood at her usual spot waiting for him, and he wanted to retreat if only to delay their last meeting. But he walked on, and with the heavy bag slung across his shoulder, he felt his heart sink deeper with each step he took towards her.

"That's a big bag," Catherine said. Her bright eyes crinkled as she smiled.

He patted the bag and laughed aloud, a sound that made her jump. She had never heard him laugh before and glanced at him curiously. He seemed different today. Her childish wonderment made him nervous. Did she know something was amiss? He dropped the bag on the ground and looked around them. Nothing had changed since they last met. The forest remained an unsullied ground, the tall pine trees soaring from the ground like a fortress sworn to protect them from outside threats. The wind caressed his face and whispered encouragement in his ears. Time to bid farewell. The dreaded words rose in his throat.

"I won't be coming back," the steadiness of his voice reminded him of his deliberate lie about Nikolaus' death. "I—we will be redeployed to another city."

His eyes held hers as he lied and watched her face become clouded with disappointment. Where would their help come from? Who would bring them food? He attempted to shoot down these thoughts like the birds he hunted as a child with his father. The first time he shot a bird he had cried and his tears kept on falling as he thought about the life he had taken. His father reprimanded him harshly and slapped him across the cheek. Only later did he understand it was done only to make him stronger. He must remember who he was, and who they are. He was a hunter, and the birds were means to an end. They were just birds.

"Oh, I see." Catherine read his troubled face and suspected that it might have something to do with the young soldier whom Friedrich had ordered back to camp.

"This," he said, pointing to the bag slumped on the feathery snow. "This should last you for a few weeks, and I—I . . . " He heard himself stammering. Sweat began to form under his hat and he felt like he was being devoured by his own guilt and her visible disappointment.

"Thank you." Her voice sounded older than her years and carried a tone of self-assurance that he seldom found even in the men he served with. She looked at him with gratitude and her lips trembled. "Thank you."

She shifted her balance on the snow; the weight of her boots seemed to be pulling her down as she struggled to stay on her feet. She mustn't appear weak in front of Friedrich. Within the chasm of a time filled with the violence and cruelty of the Nazi regime, a bridge had been clandestinely formed by their bond.

There was a growing ease and affinity between them. She relished the thought of seeing him, and although her family's life depended on his kindness, she believed that she had somehow become accustomed to seeing him and grown to care for the man whose inexplicable behavior had allowed her and her family to live. Beneath his rigid exterior, he must have pitied her. Why else would he supply them with food and keep their hiding place secret? To her relief, he never showed pity eyes. She knew where she stood in this war; the life she and her family led underground was reminder enough. She kept a steadfast poise until she reached the bag and bent down to collect it.

As she struggled to swing it over her shoulders, Friedrich kept solemnly still. He couldn't bring himself to help her; if he so much as touched her, the compassion he felt would be exposed. He stood rigidly and watched as she staggered away weighed down by his last gift. She turned to him and there was renewed hope in her eyes—that look of determination he loved about her.

"We're leaving soon, too. Someone is rescuing us." She spoke with a hopeful innocence, unmindful that she was conversing with the enemy in a horrific war. To her, the forest was surrounded by an invisible barrier, marking neutral territory—a refuge for those who wavered in their allegiance.

He nodded like a father sending his child to a distant and unknown land. The thought of her being free and able to shine elsewhere made him smile. His gladness helped him forget for a moment who he was and what she represented in an unfinished war. As he walked out of the forest, he gave way to an optimistic glimpse into an unlikely future for himself and the girl he loved.

§

He continued to drive on and his thoughts drifted back to the present. Catherine Aumont. He was no stranger to that name—it has been five years now. When she became a household name—the most promising ballerina of the century—he had felt compelled to closely examine a large poster on a building wall. He had to see it for himself. She was pictured in a white chiffon ballerina dress that wrapped around her body like a second skin. She posed with the resplendent grace visible even during the war, but now accentuated and perfected. Her long arms were raised in a flawless circle over her head like an oversized halo. She smiled at the camera and her fierce blue eyes showed the same determination despite all the improbabilities and obstacles that had threatened her. He stood staring at her on that poster and felt proud, as if he had raised her himself, like the child he never had.

In the three previous years, Claire had suffered four miscarriages. They both understood and accepted that it must be retribution; an unspoken penance to be paid for the countless lives destroyed when the war had moved was in his favor.

The tires screeched as they reached the driveway of his home—an old brick cottage that had belonged to Claire's great-grandmother. When the war was almost at an end, he knew that his side stood no chance against the waves of American, Canadian, and European allied forces that invaded Normandy. He and Claire fled to Chantilly, and they settled down in secrecy until surrounding neighbors no longer held suspicions about the couple that had charmed their way into the area as Claire set up a much loved *pâtisserie* in their home.

§

CHAPTER SIX

———

THE RESCUE

Present—1953, Paris
Luke

Lenny was in his early forties, a short, flamboyant bisexual who valued art above any man or woman in his life. He had met Luke in New York five years before at an exhibition put on by Luke and an amateur painter friend, and he knew that he had found a rare gem. He flirtatiously asked whether he would be interested in showing his work in Paris. Luke grabbed the opportunity with anticipation and fear. He still struggled with a dark past, most of which stemmed from his time in France. But he was drawn to the idea of going back. It was like an addiction too difficult to fight off. He met with Lenny several times a week to discuss his work, and fought incessantly on how to refine it and make it more appealing to the French audience. He felt there was a lot of nonsense in Lenny's artistic advice but eventually took it in. He began to draw what was considered beautiful by others—a group of haughty socialites whom Lenny deemed exclusively worthy to exhibit for in France. Within a few months, Luke had packed his bags for Paris, wrapping his paintings with great care in fear of the potential damage they could suffer on the plane. During the flight, Lenny had talked incessantly about the intoxicating beauty of Paris. Luke didn't share his enthusiasm but had looked forward to returning as he looked out the window and saw "La Ville Lumière" again for himself.

§

With a cigarette in one hand and a glass of champagne in the other, Lenny sat across from Luke, who was momentarily distracted by the waiter. He raised his brow and observed the artist he claimed to have single-handedly transformed into the most avant-garde painter in the country. Luke hadn't aged much except for the few strands of gray in his hair. His face was still ruggedly handsome, and the expression of ironic humor mixed with boyish melancholy worn like a fashionable accessory made him approachable and irresistible to French women. But today he appeared sullen and tired, his eyes duller than when he had first returned to Paris. They now carried a gloomier, defeated look.

"What's wrong, darling?" Lenny pursed his lips and managed to disguise his worries behind a comical act. He knew about Catherine and had seen this coming a long time ago. But he didn't like to be the deliverer of bad news, so he kept his predictions to himself.

"Why do you ask?" Luke took a sip of his whisky, a usual choice for him during lunch. His steak remained untouched; he was never as hungry as he was thirsty.

"No reason. I mean, it's not like Catherine just left you or anything."

Lenny paused and waited for Luke to react. When he caught on and met Lenny's playful eyes, their explosive laughter sounded like this had been the funniest thing they'd heard all day. When the laughter subsided, Lenny playfully blew the cigarette smoke in Luke's direction. His sullen face looked even more attractive, unevenly blurred by the smoke.

"You didn't love her." It was a bold statement, but Lenny hardly surprised Luke anymore. He stared at Luke with a coy smile, waiting for another reaction.

"I didn't?" Luke swirled his glass and watched the ice knock against the sides.

"No, I don't think so," Larry said. "Maybe you loved someone else and have been with the wrong woman all this time—like most people I know." He laughed, thrusting his head back and slapping his hand on the table as if making more noise would make his joke more convincing.

Luke smiled and attempted to search for some truth in the words. He never told Lenny about Marie—he didn't share the story with others— at least not when he was sober. He may have mentioned her name to strangers when sitting drunk and by himself in bars. Alcohol drew out a side of him that he usually kept to himself. He rarely spoke of what he had seen during the war. As charismatic as he seemed publicly, he kept his life private and maintained a comforting distance.

But after a few drinks, Luke often voluntarily broke down his wall of isolation, craving human closeness. He wanted others to hear about his sufferings, he wanted to describe to them the pain he kept like a thorn on his chest that he refused to remove, too frightened of what it would be like to live without the thought of her. He wanted someone to find a cure for the unknown sickness he had been cursed with since the day Marie died. Catherine never completely understood his polar opposite personalities that appeared when he drank. She took it personally, as if Luke blamed her for surviving instead of Marie. *Why was it she that came to him that day and not her sister, the one he loved?* But was it love? It had been so brief, and they were both so young and ready to rush into love during a time when staying alive was a luxury no one dared to take for granted.

After lunch, he and Lenny parted ways. He was to meet Rita later in the day and continue her portrait but now he decided to go for a walk at Bois de Boulogne. He liked to indulge in these lazy afternoon walks, especially at this time of the year. The trees had begun to show colors again, and new leaves sprouted from the bare branches. A group of laughing children ran past him as they chased each other around the park. Spring had always been Luke's favorite season especially while growing up. The flowers in his mother's garden always bloomed into something so extraordinary and different from just one season before. He stood in awe, transfixed by nature's colors and variety. But he had since lost his childlike wonderment of life and allowed himself to sink into the harsher realities of adulthood. He sat idly on a bench, shut his eyes, and tried to remember when he last felt such nostalgic, childlike happiness.

§

Wartime—1944, Rouen
Luke

It was a Thursday afternoon. He remembered that day down to the last detail and mentally replayed it for weeks after it happened.

Before he left with his men for Milton Hall, he was able to return to the cave once more and ask if Marie needed any medical supplies to treat Kurt. She was relieved to see him as they were running out of bandages, and it was difficult to sterilize anything underground. Kurt was recovering fast, and Luke had a few words with him, although he still winced whenever he moved his legs. Claude had been struggling with recurring headaches and back pains and was in desperate need of medication. The worries of the entire family hung in the air. The faces of Marie and Catherine were tense, and Lucille tried to appear composed.

"He needs acetophenetidin," Marie said. he watched her father lying on his mattress with a cold compass over his forehead. This was the best care she could give him, but it was not nearly enough.

"Yes, well, I think we might have some back at the base. I'll have to check the medic's bag. He . . . well, he's no longer with us, but I could definitely check for you, if . . . if you . . ." Luke stammered and felt excited that there was something he personally do for her.

"Can I come with you?" Her question startled everyone. It had been too long since she was aboveground. Everyone could see that she had tirelessly tended to Kurt and rarely had a moment's rest. Even in her dreams, she sometimes wondered out loud whether her patient would walk again. She must have desperately wanted to feel fresh air. He watched her intently and wondered if she reciprocated his affections. Was it because he and his men would be leaving tomorrow? When he announced their departure, her gaze lingered on him. He pretended not to see and it dawned on him later that sometimes love could be declared in the quietest moments.

Since they met a week ago, not many words had been exchanged between them, but she must have sensed that he didn't always come to check on Kurt but had another mission in mind.

"Yes, yes of course, if you'd like, we can go together, and I'll bring back you here safely." Luke was careful to let everyone know he would get her home safely, and he didn't want to miss this opportunity to spend time alone with her.

Wartime—1944, Rouen
Catherine

Catherine would tell that her sister wasn't used to the attention, as boys and men oftentimes are distracted by her, who enjoyed being admired, while Marie preferred to fade into the background. She believed that her shy sister was patiently waiting for someone she would one day leave her family for. They had moved underground, away from the enemy's reach, and far enough from anyone to take notice of them. But Luke noticed Marie. And she was beginning to sense that her younger sister didn't mind his intense gaze when he visited them. When Marie asked to go with Luke back to the base to fetch medicine, it became apparent that this young American soldier was who Marie was waiting for.

Catherine stood beside her sister, and while she said nothing, she waited for her parents to deny Marie her foolish request to leave the cave. They did frequently wander outside to collect firewood and to meet Friedrich for their food supply, but rarely would they be permitted to walk very far. When she finally realized that her parents had acquiesced to Marie's request, it was already too late for her to protest. She watched Luke lead her sister out of the cave, and for the first time in her life, she felt abandoned and slighted by Marie.

§

Wartime—1944, Rouen
Luke

Quietly, they walked towards the base, and Luke cursed in his head for not having anything to say to her—the girl he had been drawing at the base at night before he slept and in his dreams. He watched her silently, wanting to remember the details of her delicate features, the pale freckles on her soft cheeks, her flaxen hair shimmering in the sun, the way her eyes squinted into a fine, the line when she smiled. She looked nervous, and he was uncertain whether it was because of him or because she was walking on unfamiliar ground out in the open. She didn't speak, but there was an unassuming confidence that lay beneath her appearance. She seemed to be at ease with him and found such comfort in the silent walk that this became his fondest memory of her.

Finally, she broke the silence.

"Would you mind if we walked a little bit slower?" She looked straight ahead and her smile broadened with each step. It was a magical sight to see her face brighten and her dark brown curls sparkle under the fading sunlight, minutes shy of dusk. They already were walking at a leisurely pace, but he didn't mind slowing down.

"Of course we can." He tried not to appear too eager to comply but was happy to do so and slowed his pace dramatically. With Marie by his side and the breathtaking view of the Rouen forest, he could almost forget his place and purpose in the war, imagining their walk as a Sunday stroll where he could breathe the same crisp winter air as the girl he was courting.

Neither of them spoke for several minutes. He opened his mouth several times to utter something then quickly dismissed it. Whatever he was about to say was too unimportant or unworthy of this precious moment he shared with Marie. His base came into view and the palms of his hands began to sweat. He must say something or forever lose his chance.

"I . . . I think that you . . . well, I mean . . ." Her eyes were on him now, ever so curiously, probably finding fault in his crooked nose, or maybe his unshaven face.

He was interrupted by Jacques, a young maquisard in his team, who came running towards him from the base. Seeing Marie, he smiled slyly at Luke, who didn't reciprocate his warm welcome.

"Sir, what—uh, I mean, who did you—"

"Where's the medic's bag?" Luke interrupted him before he could continue to probe into Marie's identity. He couldn't trust his men to keep secret her sensitive hiding place. Jacques ran back to the barracks in search of the medic's bag.

They were far from the cave, and he wondered how safe Marie felt when not in hiding underground; of being alive, yet at the same time invisible to the world on the surface. The wind was blowing east, and its force made the trees sway, sending clusters of snowflakes fluttering downward, some falling on Marie like stardust. The snow sparkled in her hair, and couldn't help but think about how he might capture this moment on canvas. He would start with her hair, filling in the details of each strand that fell so perfectly on her face, over her light gray scarf, or carried by the wind. Her eyes looked pensive, as if she might be dreaming of another place, and he wondered what she was thinking and wished he had the rest of his life to find out.

She had begun to shiver from the cold and he removed his jacket and draped it over her trembling shoulders. The sudden gesture surprised her but she didn't shy away from his touch, thanking him with a smile.

"When you come back in two weeks for Kurt, what will happen to us?" Her question startled him, and while he had felt intimidated by Catherine, he believed he could tell Marie anything.

"We would take your family to safety." His next words slipped out without any warning. "But I would like to take you with me. I mean, when the war is over."

He had said it aloud and with determination, like there was no further discussion on the matter. She was leaving with him, and that was that. They stood side by side and he couldn't see her expression but thought he saw a faint smile appear. He felt hopeful and bolder than he had ever been with a girl. He turned and pulled her gently into his arms, tightening the collar of his jacket around her neck so that the cold wouldn't touch her skin.

Her face softened to reflect a trace of happiness. She laughed and he fell more deeply in love as her smile widened unabashedly. He took this to mean yes, but he couldn't be sure and kissed her gently on her still-trembling lips. He had never felt as warm throughout the past weeks spent in the Rouen forest.

Jacques hurried back with the medical bag and handed it to Marie. As she inspected the contents, Luke began to dream of their future; he couldn't wait for the world to know that she belonged to him. As they walked back to the cave, they spoke with a newfound ease, still shy, but now there was an understanding between them. They were falling in love in the most unlikely place and under the most doubtful circumstances.

Before they reached the cave, he asked her to stop for a while beside a small thicket. Time was running out and he was impatient to demonstrate his love for her. This time, he didn't restrain himself, kissing her with a passion so wild she began to resist him. Feeling her body tensing, he lightly caressed her cheeks, reassuring her. She let her guard down and began to kiss him back. He could taste the sweetness in every kiss and felt there was nothing else that would satisfy his hunger or thirst from this day onward.

"I'll come back for you, and your family," he said. He held her small hands in his, wanting to keep them warm for as long as possible.

She said nothing in return but smiled in a way he would always remember—a rare smile that encompassed the deepest sense of joy and hope and allowed him to dream recklessly of their future.

§

When they moved out to join with the rest of the OSS officers in Milton Hall preparing for the Normandy assault, Luke carried the hope he found with Marie. The thought of her waiting for him to return gave him more encouragement than he had initially prayed for. But he had underestimated the horror and fear that war brought to the battlefield.

He had seen things before—men getting shot as they jumped from planes, their parachutes wide open, ready to land them safely on the ground. Kurt, lying wounded and half-conscious on the bed. But he hadn't seen war. He was a linguistic OSS officer, and he wasn't prepared to see this much blood, or men older than himself crying for their mothers, and he was shocked to find that his hands trembled uncontrollably after each shot he fired. He was never a good shot to begin with, but he began to doubt his place in the operation and whether he would actually survive the war. Marie was never far from his mind, and with each day that passed, the night seemed longer. He repeatedly awoke from sleep, fearfully checking to see if his limbs were still intact and wondering if he was not dead already.

The two weeks he had promised Marie turned into four, and each sabotage mission they had to carry out as officers of the OSS became more and more grueling. He wondered if she and her family had enough to eat. He prayed that whoever was supplying food for them would continue to do so. Or had the Germans already discovered their cave? He struggled to stay alert, vacillating between dreams of the Rouen forest and the hideous reality of war, sometimes questioning if she had ever existed at all or whether it all had been a figment of his imagination.

Two months had passed, and he found himself alive, his legs and arms still intact, and he stubbornly held on to the hope that he would find her before the Germans did. Time after time he reported to Milton Hall that they still had one wounded officer in hiding with a Jewish family in Rouen, but he never heard back. He clung to the single thread of possibility he believed could lead him into a future he spent his nights dreaming about. He must have appeared foolish to all his superiors, pushing for an early assault on Rouen, but this was war—and everyone had their own agenda.

§

He was called to the office of Lieutenant-Colonel George Richard Musgrave's, commanding officer of the Jedburgh Operation. It was a simple room with a few chairs scattered as if incidentally and without expectation of anyone of importance occupying them. Boxes of rifle ammunition were piled high, passing for a serviceable bookshelf.

The Lieutenant-Colonel sat in the far left corner of the room, his face unreadable. He sat, preoccupied, behind his desk, paying no attention to the young sergeant.

His voice sounded stern when he spoke. "Sergeant Newman, you asked several times about Rouen."

He didn't take his eyes off the paper on which he wrote—more secret sabotage missions planned for the next few weeks. A single drop of sweat fell onto his desk. He frowned disapprovingly and tried to dab it dry with his finger.

Luke tightened his hand into a fist as he thought about where he would be sent to next. Did he hear him right? Did he say Rouen?

"Yes, Sir, I did."

"I heard Private Friedman was wounded in Rouen and is still in captivity."

His eyes scanned the pages that covered his desk, which remained in disarray.

"Not in captivity, Sir, he's wounded and in hiding."

The Lieutenant Colonel stared at Luke, exhibiting unquestionable concern for Kurt, a soldier he had never heard of until today. He scrutinized the young man who stood before him. They had, in fact, met several times before. He had personally congratulated Luke on his success in leading the mission on the Beseancon-Belfort route in the Doubs Valley, where they managed to stop several German convoys.

"A job well done, Sergeant," he had said to Luke and patted his shoulder. But that was weeks ago, and he doubted he remembered who he was.

"You said he is in hiding? And wounded?"

Lieutenant-Colonel Musgrave stood up, his tall figure towering over his desk, He ran his fingers through his hair, and his eyes flashed with surprise. "Since May, when you first came back from Rouen?"

"Yes, Sir, that is correct, Sir."

Luke had hoped for weeks that this moment would come, and now that it was here, he felt surprise at his calm behavior before his commanding officer. Perhaps this was one of those effects the war has on a soldier: to behave according to your rank, to follow orders without questions, to risk your life in the certainty that your death would contribute to a higher cause.

"Well, damn it, why didn't anyone go for him sooner?"

His impatient response surprised them both. The Lieutenant Colonel quickly recomposed himself and cleared his throat.

"The Canadian troops are going in—in a few days. We're sending in Team HUGH ahead of them. I'll let them know that you will be joining them."

Luke felt a wave of relief and his knees almost buckled. He blinked a few times before saluting the man who may have granted him the future he was fervently praying for.

§

Present—1953, Paris
Rita

The house seemed emptier, and she thought it felt different today. She looked around the room, no longer shy about being drawn by Luke, always so immersed in his work. They spoke only at the beginning and end of their session. And each time, Rita learned something different about him. Oftentimes, the traits she thought she had figured out seemed to contradict each other.

On some days he appeared genuinely interested in her life in America, asking her questions about her hometown, or why she enjoyed riding horses. On others, he remained quiet, unable to say anything that hinted at kindness or concern for her other than his instructions on how to position her face or body towards the canvas. Today, he looked focused and immersed in his work. If she were to ask him questions, or inquire about anything in his past, he would answer dutifully, in a robotic kind of way to signify that he wanted to carry out his work without interruptions. She found him to be interestingly approachable in this mode, and she enjoyed speaking to him while restricting her questions to intervals of fifteen minutes.

"Do you think you changed much after the war?"

She regretted her question and bit her lips, watching Luke's face for signs of anger—a reaction when they spoke about the war. He never told her exactly what he did, and she didn't care to probe. He didn't speak much about his duties as a radio communicator either. But she was intrigued about how the war changed a person. How did it wield the power to transform someone so profoundly? Sometimes she thought she could see Kurt in Luke. They bore a similar sadness when asked about the war.

Luke paused with his paintbrush in his hand, letting it hang beneath his chin. He appeared deep in thought, but she couldn't tell whether he was searching for an answer to her question or if he was far away again.

"Yes. And no." He answered thoughtfully and slowly then resumed marking the canvas with his artistic, seemingly random strokes.

"I—I don't understand. I mean, how did you change, and how did you not change?"

She felt silly trying to spell out her question again to accommodate his answer. She had to be specific if she wanted a coherent response. The desire to understand Kurt's transformation was too strong for her to mind her manners.

"Can you move your chin slightly upward?" Luke signaled for her to do as he ordered, like a puppeteer handling his stubborn, unheeding puppet. "Good, good. Stay there, please."

She gave him his fifteen minutes of silence before persisting with her questions. After two weeks as his muse, she began to know how to draw a response from him without sounding brash—a trait that he despised. He enjoyed giving orders but hated receiving them. She assumed with certainty that they now had formed a rare kind of chemistry common to the artist and his muse.

"I changed." Luke broke the silence first. His mind remained bound to the canvas, and his eyes stayed fixed on something that he was meticulously perfecting with a thin paintbrush. "I changed because I am no longer the same person. And I didn't change because ever since the war..." His voice trailed off and his express was clouded.

His hand didn't wander across the canvas, and she understood that he his pause was not caused by indecisiveness on where to paint the next stroke, but how to continue his answer.

"Ever since the war, I've been trying to get back to who I was."

The empty house echoed his words. Then it struck Rita. It wasn't that the house was emptier; it was simply no longer a mess. He had cleaned it.

§

Present—1953, Paris
Catherine

She reached into her jewelry box to find her earrings and brushed against something familiar. She knew what it was the moment she touched it. She took it out and held it in her hand. It weighed close to nothing, but to Catherine, it held all the burdens in her heart. There was a time when she took it out every night for a quick glance. She wondered if he had really done it. Her fingers glided the surface of the eagle, caressing its open wings. She flinched as she remembered what it stood for. She read the lettering embroidered beneath the eagle: Waffen SS. And then again. And again. She shut her eyes and saw him again. Friedrich. She still remembered the way he looked at her when they met, and when she thought would be the last time she would see him. He had stood with a look of longing as he carried the last bag of food that she and her family would receive from him, a German SS officer. The strangest act of kindness from a man she could never have imagined benefitting from in the eye of the most violent storm to date in history.

And she had believed him.

She believed him to be different, and that because he kept their hiding place secret, he would never let harm come her way. She had confided her family's escape plan and could hear herself utter the fateful words. "We're leaving soon, too. Someone is rescuing us." She must have appeared like such a fool to him. Granted, she was still a child then, and she couldn't have known that the man who fed her and allowed her family to live underground for so many months, who had become an irreplaceable figure in her childhood, would later become her family's executioner. She had seen it with her own eyes.

§

Wartime—1944, Rouen
Catherine

It must have been at least two months before Luke returned to rescue them as he had promised. She had doubted him from the beginning, despite what Marie told her. She had never seen her infatuated with anyone before, and she didn't think that her sister would ever find someone—at least not before she did. She was sworn to secrecy, Marie made her promise that she wouldn't tell Maman and Papa.

"When Luke comes back, he said he would take me with him."

Her eyes showed dreams of a future that was seemingly impossible. Catherine watched her sister curiously when she spoke of this American soldier she barely knew. What could he possibly have done so that the most rational person in the world she knew would choose such an uncertain, unrealistic road? She tried to reason with Marie and discourage her from dreaming about a bleak future.

At night, when Maman and Papa were deep in sleep, they talked under the blanket, their bodies pressed together against the hard soil that was their bed for many months. For the first time since they lived underground, Marie had become angry with her for being so deliberately unsupportive of her decision. She fell asleep first, leaving Catherine lying awake and unable to close her eyes as she pictured her life without Marie by her side. She couldn't believe how selfish Marie was being, having so little remorse for leaving everyone else behind. It struck her that Marie was not the noble, loyal sibling she always thought she was. It bothered her how much Marie resembled her. She imagined that she would have made the same selfish decision if she had met someone who valiantly risked his life for her.

The next morning, the family gathered round the table to share a meagre breakfast. They were on their last batch of potatoes and sugar. Luke had promised her family that he would return in two weeks, but only Maman seemed to know it would take much longer than that. She had carefully rationed their every meal so that the food supplies would last for at least another month. But now the supplies were running low, and a plate of potatoes for breakfast had turned into a small piece of potato coated unevenly with sugar. Kurt, who had since recovered from his injuries, sat with them, refusing to eat any more of their food. At Papa's insistence, he took one bite of potato and declined the rest.

He had worn a look of guilt for six weeks now as if regretting having survived. He must have felt that he was a burden to the family. Many times, he gently pushed away the generous portion of food that Maman put on his plate. But Papa wouldn't hear of it. It became obvious to Catherine that her father had taken a strong liking to Kurt, largely due to his uncanny resemblance to Philippe. It wasn't just that they looked alike, but there was something familiar that even Catherine had begun to recognize. It was subtle, but she could see a faint shadow of Philippe when Kurt sat on the ground, deep in thought, with his hand supporting his chin, the muscle visibly tense as he clenched his jaw. Philippe used to do that when Maman reprimanded him for stealing sugar from the jar.

Kurt would smile at Maman when she brought him a blanket and pillow at night before he slept. It was a look of gratitude, but to the rest of the family, it was a missing piece from what used to be happiness when Philippe was still alive.

Three weeks after Luke's departure, the hope of being rescued that the family, including Kurt, held on to, began to dim. Now, they all sat quietly in the darkened cave and surrendered to the reality no one was ready to admit but had all accepted: they had been deserted. No one was coming back for them. It hit Marie the hardest; she rarely spoke, and when she did, it would be Kurt she inquired after.

Catherine felt unfairly slighted by her sister, and she was furious at Luke for deserting her family and for taking Marie's affection away from her. Maman prayed more fervently than ever, sometimes so loud that Catherine had to muffle her ears with her hands. She couldn't bear how desperate she sounded. God was nowhere to be found in the cave. They had been deserted not only by Luke and his men, but even God had left them behind. *Why would anyone else come for them?*

§

It was Papa who heard it first. They all thought it was a squirrel. Kurt had recently caught one outside the cave. The meat was not as tender as that of a rabbit, but they still enjoyed sharing a meal that was not always potato and sugar. They heard the sound again, and Papa's look confirmed it was not squirrel but dreaded footsteps. They came closer and death felt preordained.

Marie wrapped her arms around Maman's shoulders as she began to sob. Catherine heard her sister whisper, "It's okay, it's okay Nothing is going to happen to us." She so wanted to believe Marie as she held her breath and stared at the surface. If this was to be the end, she wanted to look into the eyes of their executioner and search for a truth she stubbornly held on to: guilt—a deep sense of regret for extinguishing another life.

Kurt took a step forward, his gun clutched tightly in his hand—the only weapon the family had to protect them. When she saw the gun, Catherine wondered if she should ask Kurt to shoot her family first. It would to be a less painful death than the ones she had heard about: Germans rampaging through villages allegedly hiding maquisards; women and children screaming as they were burned alive locked inside a church; grown men crying for the lives of their families.

They had not witnessed these executions, but hearing about them was unnerving and demoralizing.

The shuffle of footsteps convinced Catherine that there was more than one person. Three or four people were now above them—their executioners. She approached Kurt and her sudden movement startled them all. Before she could utter the unthinkable request, a familiar voice called out from above.

"*Haver.*"

No one dared move. Papa blinked a few times before he was able to respond to the code word he had taught Luke several months before.

Maman let out a soft cry before she fell to her knees, and Catherine felt the cave shake. God's hands were delivering them out of this darkness.

"Yes, yes. *Haver. Haver—Haver!*" Papa rushed to the opening and scrambled to find the wooden plank that separated them from the world above them.

Catherine turned towards Marie, who appeared calm, her face serene and unflustered as she waited for their rescuer to make himself known.

Luke jumped down, nodding to Papa before he saluted Kurt. His eyes were filled with love when he saw Marie. She had waited for him and he came as he had promised.

Catherine felt a pang of sadness tugging at her chest, but she didn't allow it to show and met Luke's eyes with a level gaze.

Two other soldiers waited outside the cave and there was urgency in their shouts. "Do you see Corporal Friedman? Is he there, sir?"

"Yes, he's right here," Luke answered impatiently. He signaled for Kurt to exit the cave.

In those few seconds, Kurt was forced to say his goodbyes and express his gratitude to the family who had sheltered him. He was unable to say everything he wanted to say. Only Marie reacted fast enough, and gave him a quick hug before he left.

"Sir, we have to go now. There is movement at two o'clock, sir!"

Maman's hopes of being rescued had been trampled. They were being deserted again.

"Listen, I'm coming back for you."

Catherine couldn't tell if Luke was speaking to them, or only to Marie. There was no time for her to ask; he was already rushing towards the exit. But he nodded to Papa before he climbed the ladder to the surface. She had to believe him. The wooden plank was hurriedly covered, and as the muffled sound of the soldiers faded away, the cave was once again dark and quiet. It felt like it had been a dream, and they had awakened to find themselves alone again, huddled together underground, but this time without Philippe or Kurt.

When night fell, Catherine unfolded their wool blanket, and as she draped it over Marie, she saw that she was fully awake. Her sister, always so docile and unassuming, had hardened in a manner that Catherine almost respected and feared. She found herself envious of Marie's determination to love. As she turned away to hide her anger and disappointment, she wondered what she could do to convince her to stay.

The next morning, Maman and Papa sat on the ground. Maman had packed a few family pictures and pieces of jewelry that she would sell for their survival. Papa held her hand and waited solemnly for Luke.

It seemed appropriate to say goodbye to the cave now, Catherine thought, as her eyes scanned the place they had called their home for the past year. A small wooden box that became a bookshelf for Papa's old newspapers, a few selected favorite teacups that was brought underground out of her many set of expensive collections were placed on the edge of a protruding corner of the cave. There were things that they couldn't take with them, things that would be left behind, as traces and undeniable evidence of their lives underground. She remembered looking around their old house the same way before they prepared to move underground. *Would their future be a bit brighter this time?* She closed her eyes and as she imagined her life outside of this place, she could see it—she would dance. She would be freed from this cave to perform on the stage for the world to see.

"Papa!" A sudden thud shook her from her daydream. Marie knelt beside Papa, who lay on the ground, struggling to breathe. He had already suffered a heart attack a year before the war, and his health had been deteriorating since they moved underground. Maman ran to the medicine box to find the pills for his heart condition.

"Where are they? Where are they?" Her hands trembled as they went through the box and her voice sounded desperate and high.

Marie pressed on Papa's chest with both hands. What did it mean— was he dying? The color was fading from Papa's face. Life was slipping away from him.

Unable to move, Catherine stood still beneath the exit of the cave, her eyes on the wooden plank that was their only way out. There was no one there to help them. Was this it? They were going to all die, suffocating in the cave they thought would be their best chance of survival. Was she going to disappear underground, like the dead—buried and long forgotten by the living? She wasn't dead yet— her heart was still pounding.

She didn't know how it happened, but now she was running outside, past the apple tree, kicking fallen fruits as she ran. Her legs sprinted above the ground; she felt the grass, soft and wet beneath her—and then—only then did she realize that she was running barefoot. There were no walls to enclose her, and she was free of the smell of soil. The darkness that had bounded her for so long was no longer a concern. She was not dying; she was running free for her life. After what seemed like an eternity of running, she was out of breath and began to slow down. She breathed in the fresh air and as impossible as it seemed, she felt it passed through her lungs, miraculously rejuvenating her whole body. She was alive. Her ears were getting used to the sounds she had missed for so long: birds, wind blowing from the east, grass crunching beneath her feet— she was free from the cave.

She had become the deserter she accused Marie of being.

§

CHAPTER SEVEN

──────

THE FOREST

Wartime—1944, Rouen
Catherine

She was lost in the woods and disoriented. Almost an hour had passed since she ran from the cave. Disoriented and frightened, she felt as though she was walking in circles. She couldn't be sure if she was on her way back, or moving further away from the cave. The skies were clear and it reminded her of a day she spent playing outside with Marie and Philippe, without a worry in her mind. As she kept moving, pushing away the branches in her way, she thought she saw something move from a distance. Then she saw them: dozens of soldiers in the uniform she associated only with kindness and not the malevolence it had become known for. The distinctive gray-green almost blended with the trees. They moved swiftly on the other side of the forest, leaving her shocked to see them taking a familiar path. The cave. Her home. Her family. They couldn't hear her from where she stood, but she stifled the cry that escaped from her lips.

The last words she had spoken to Friedrich resonated clearly in her head. "We're leaving soon, too. Someone is rescuing us."

Betrayal took the form of a knife that cut deeply and mercilessly into her chest. It must have been Friedrich. She had foolishly, unguardedly told him of their plan to escape. *No, this couldn't be.* She shook her head violently.

Who will be there to protect her family when they find the cave? Marie had said that Luke's base was hidden somewhere nearby. She glanced around, looking for signs of an American uniform, or Kurt, or Luke. A bandage on the ground caught her attention. It looked like the kind that Marie had wrapped around Kurt's wound. She hurried towards it and picked it up, turning it back to front, trying to verify that it could belong to Kurt. The ground was dry and she was overjoyed to find footprints that led to a path covered by wild thickets. It didn't matter that some of them had thorns that pierced her dress and scraped her bare calves, She ran, desperately wishing she would find something akin to hope at the end of the path.

§

Present—1953, London
Kurt

He woke from what seemed like the longest dream and adjusted his eyes to the blinding brightness of the sun shining through the window. This was not his room, nor had he been asleep.

"A coma," they told him. "You've been out for a few weeks now."

When he had asked about Rita, his family and her parents were surrounding his bed. He felt an odd animosity from his mother-in-law, as though he had done something unforgivable to her daughter. His first thought was that she had died, that he had lost her in the accident, and he wanted to weep. His mother read his expression and stopped his track of thought.

"No, dear, she's all right." Her usually sharply contemptuous expression had lifted today. Her eyes looked apologetically warm and sympathetic.

"So where is she? Where is Rita?"

No one answered him; awkward glances were exchanged, and his uncle Harold cleared his throat, while others shifted uncomfortably. Everyone seemed to know the answer but no one wanted to be the one to give it.

Then it hit him—as obvious as it was all this time. He had failed Rita, in almost every way possible. His visitors began to disperse after words of affection and pats on his still-aching shoulders. He found himself alone with his parents and Rita's mother, who had lingered behind.

"Rita—is currently away," she said.

Her mother's graceful quality was matched in Rita's behavior. There was something that stood out about her, however simple the tasks carried out. Whether dusting cupboards, arranging flowers on the kitchen table, or speaking to him about trivial things that didn't concern or interest him, she would accomplish each of them as though carrying out a most important task. He loved the curious blend of arrogance and grace that had captivated him. That is, until he came back from the war a stranger to her. Had had pretended for so long that he was oblivious to her pain.

"Where?" he asked. Had she leave him for good?

"Paris."

The city was not a familiar one to him, but the mention of a place, of a country devastated by war only a few years before, brought a kind of revulsion that hadn't existed when he was first deployed as an OSS officer. The long suppressed hatred that he had strived to turn into indifference had broken loose. With his face buried in his hands, he began to sob uncontrollably.

§

Wartime—1944, Rouen
Kurt

When he awoke to find himself in a darkened cave, and not above ground lying in the snow as he remembered, his heart came to a near halt.

Was he in an underground German base?

As his eyes adjusted to the dimness, a face that he recognized from memory appeared—Rita. He called to her, and she looked perplexed and frightened. The fear in her eyes made him shout louder. *How can you not know me?* She answered him in a strange voice distinctively different from Rita's. He listened as she spoke to the others in French. He began to look around him and saw that there were two more people trapped underground with them. A middle-aged couple stood behind her. The woman looked at him apprehensively, but the man had kind eyes and watched him with curiousity.

"My name is Marie. You were injured, and you see—we brought you down here...". Her voice was soft and she tried to reassure him as much as she could, calming him with her gentle touch. When he could breathe normally again, he was introduced to Claude and Lucille who, by now, had lived here for almost a year.

He couldn't believe his ears. A year underground—with all that had been happening on the surface. A world filled with unrelenting violence, fields of lost limbs, lost hope, and lost loved ones.

"There's also Catherine," Marie said in English, her words pronounced clearly and slowly as if she were afraid to make a mistake.

"Who's Catherine?" Kurt heard himself slur as he spoke. It must be the medicine. *Wait. How in the world had she been treating him underground?*

"My sister, she will be back soon."

She seemed reluctant to elaborate and he was too tired to ask any more questions. He felt a familiar dizziness, the same sensation that put him to sleep after the stray bullet. He wanted to ask her—what her name was again—if she knew how much she reminded him of home—no, of someone back home. Someone he would give anything to see again. He stretched out his hand like a child pleading for a mother's care, and he felt her touch.

"It's okay. It's okay. *Il faut que tu dors.*"

§

The next time he opened his eyes, she was nowhere to be found.

149

Instead, another girl with the deepest blue eyes stood observing him. This must be Catherine. Her direct gaze was curious but also seemed to withhold something from him. She regarded him as though he were a spy, or an unknown enemy. She didn't trust him.

"Please, have some water," a deep voice behind Catherine urged. Claude held the cup as gingerly as if it contained holy water. His eyes smiled, but his lips were pursed and his expression rigid.

"*Merci*." He took a sip of water and as he drank, the entire family watched him with admiration, as though he were already a hero of war. But he hasn't achieved anything of significance yet.

He wanted to return to Rita as a distinguished officer. Where was she now, and what was she doing? Perhaps running off to the post office again, sending him letters as she promised she would. He had received them religiously for a year; she never skipped a day. He had missed her while at Milton Hall, but he was distracted by meetings and training, and the adrenaline of being part of a secret mission made him insusceptible to homesickness. Even he was surprised at how unaffected he felt thousands of miles from Rita. He would write to her every so often, unaware of how his periodical silences would sway her moods, and they gradually were sent less frequently than he had promised her. How devastated she must feel with no news from him. If he were already declared dead, how would she react? The wound on his leg was still healing, and although Marie treated his leg with as much as care and medical skill as she could muster, he still felt a great amount of pain. But the thought of Rita waiting for him hurt even more.

"Please, can I?" Marie stood by him holding bandages in her hands. He later learned that they had been cut from bed sheets.

He acquiesced and allowed her to untie the bandage on his leg that was stained with dry blood, and he wondered how such an inexperienced young girl managed to suture and look after his wound. When he winced as she tightened the bandage around his calve, she smiled apologetically and asked if the pain was manageable before she attempted a second time.

§

Over the next two days, Marie sat by his bed monitoring his breathing, dutifully checking his bandages and pleading with him to rest. When it was time to eat, Marie would spoon-feed him, an act of kindness that embarrassed him while others looked on curiously. More than a few times, he overheard Claude refer to him as "Philippe," then realizing his mistake, his eyes saddened and he quickly corrected himself.

One afternoon, as Marie was changing his bandages, he broke the reinforced silence. "Who is Philippe?"

Catherine sat nearby peeling potatoes with Lucille. She looked on with a placid expression, appearing to anticipate Marie's response. He found her quite intimidating. If not more beautiful than Marie, she possessed an unshakable confidence rare for her age as well as an intriguing fortitude.

"Philippe was our brother, he—he is no longer with us. He died before we came down here."

Marie's hands trembled slightly as she secured the bandage with a small pin. She glanced towards her sister as if requesting permission. Catherine met her gaze with an indifferent look. She continued to speak, and her eyes, unable to hide the horror they had witnessed, lost their gleam as she recounted their brother's death.

He was seven at the time.

§

Pre-War—1942, Rouen
Catherine

She and Marie were in the kitchen, making jam with Maman, their hands stained red from the strawberry juice. The sweetness lingered in the air. As Maman carried a pot of the cooled strawberry puree from the stove to the kitchen table, Philippe tiptoed into the kitchen to sneak a few strawberries into his pockets. His hands reached into the basket, and she caught him by the sleeve and pulled him back, inadvertently forcing him to collide with Maman. He clumsily slipped in the spilled jam that now covered him like red paint. With a mischievous grin, he began to lick his fingers and his arms, savoring the sweetness that stuck to his skin like glue.

Maman's, light-brown dress was stained with bright red blotches, and she watched Philippe at first in shock, then to Catherine and Marie's surprise, she began to laugh. Thinking back, it was such a funny sight: Philippe and Maman covered in strawberry jam from head to toe, and soon after both she and Marie laughing uncontrollably at the mess. Papa was confused by all the commotion and at the same time relieved it was only strawberry jam on the kitchen floor and not what he had first imagined.

That same afternoon, while Catherine and Marie were busy studying, Philippe begged for one of them to join him in a game of hide-and-seek—a game for which both had grown too old and important for.

Catherine chose to ignore him, while Marie promised that she would draw with him afterwards. Philippe loved to draw, especially portraits of his family who were always readily available to pose for him after dinner. By the time they realized that he had gone, the clouds were overcast and the skies had begun to dim. When no one could find Philippe, Maman sent Catherine and Marie to look for their brother.

"Another game of hide-and-seek, no doubt," Maman laughed as she shrugged her shoulders and walked back to the house to set the table.

§

The sisters walked all the way to town when they couldn't find Philippe nearby their house. They passed an alleyway and heard shouts and a violent scream that sent them running towards Mlle LaCroix's shop. This was not the first time they heard something similar in their neighborhood. Attacks on other Jewish families were seemingly random, and no one had made any connection between them. Perhaps they were arbitrary, and not linked together by a common hatred that seeped into what they all thought a safe and peaceful town. When the attacks escalated, Maman and Papa became wary of leaving the house and began to worry about their children who remained oblivious to the cruelty they would soon witness.

They ran into the shop, their faces red and flustered, gasping as they tried to catch their breaths. Mlle LaCroix hurried over to the girls and hugged them before she went out to see what all the commotion was about.

Catherine heard her shriek. Were the Germans attacking the non-Jewish French too? Had Mlle LaCroix been harmed? They held their breath before gathering enough courage to move. Catherine walked to the door, wanting to look outside. She stared in horror as she watched Mlle LaCroix carrying Philippe's limp body into the shop. Like that morning, his clothes were stained red, but he wasn't smiling, and he no longer smelled of strawberries.

Mlle LaCroix looked just as shocked as the sisters. Philippe's angelic face with its innocent smile that could brighten Maman's day now was covered in blotches of purple and dirt that spread unevenly across his swollen face. Fresh blood dripped from his nose.

"Philippe! Philippe!" Marie cried.

Their brother's eyes squinted in pain and Catherine's heart broke knowing his injuries were far too deep for any of them to see. He reached out his hands to them and his grip tightened around Catherine's arm. His lips quivered as he attempted to speak, but his breathing accelerated to the point where he began to choke and gasp at the same time.

As Mlle LaCroix frantically moved about the shop to fetch water and towels for Philippe, she sent Catherine to look for Dr. Mencken who didn't live too far from her shop. He had taken care of Marie when she was sick with pneumonia the year before; he wouldn't refuse to treat their families. As soon as Catherine stepped out of the shop, she became distraught and forgot the way to Dr. Mencken's home.

Frustrated with herself and with Philippe for getting into trouble, she began to cry as she stood in the middle of the road. People rushed past her, subconsciously avoiding her, aware of who she was and what she represented. She caught a glimpse of a familiar figure across the street from the shop: The German soldier who had saved her and Marie from the menacing boys. He stood among the other soldiers, speaking to someone beside him. They were gathered round a military vehicle, and appeared to be discussing something of vital importance. He spoke with authority, giving out orders to the rest of the group. As if he could sense her, he turned around and saw her standing there. His expression was so guarded that it was difficult to read whether he was friend or foe today. His eyes shifted to Mlle LaCroix's shop.

From that one look, Catherine felt convinced he knew what had happened to Philippe. She believed that he was sorry for them. But then he turned away and continued speaking to another soldier. She then remembered that Dr. Mencken's green-roofed house was two blocks away from the book shop. And she ran. She ran for Philippe's life.

Dr. Mecken arrived at the shop too late. Philippe's heart had stopped a few minutes after Catherine left. Marie and Mlle LaCroix could only clean him up for when Maman and Papa would come for him. Catherine held on to the counter, her hands shaking as she watched Mlle LaCroix use a white towel to wipe away the blood from Philippe's face, hands, and knees. Marie stood by helplessly, her face wet with tears as she held a bowl of water mixed with Philippe's blood as Mlle LaCroix repeatedly used it to wash the towel.

"Catherine, Marie." Mlle LaCroix's voice trembled but she regained her composure. At that moment she possessed an emboldened kindness and love that Catherine seldom detected in anyone outside her family.

"Go. Go and find your parents. I will stay here with Philippe."

When Maman heard the news, she was unable to stand, and Papa went alone. He couldn't believe the truth until he saw his youngest child lying on the floor, covered with Mlle LaCroix's coat. His blood-stained shirt and trouser were folded neatly on the floor next to him. A sound came out of Papa that neither of them had heard before. It was a loud, low groan that didn't quite resemble a cry. Philippe's eyes were closed and he appeared so peaceful that Papa accepted his death only when he knelt beside his seven-year old child. He picked him up and cradled him in his arms, rocking him back and forth, lulling him to sleep.

§

The week that followed was a difficult one. No one spoke of what happened, but they all knew it was the same group of boys who teased and bullied Jewish children until things got out of hand. No one stopped them. Later, when other families came to offer condolences, someone told Maman that there had been a group of German soldiers who stood by and watched as the boys beat Philippe with baseball bats, laughing as he screamed for help. There wasn't much left to say, and after Maman sent the neighbors away, she muttered a curse on those who had killed Philippe and on the German soldiers who did nothing. The words frightened Catherine. Maman was not one who wished malice on others.

§

Wartime—1944, Rouen
Kurt

Claude was reading by candlelight near the foot of Kurt's bed, turning the pages solemnly, as if reading a eulogy of someone he once knew.

Kurt felt uncomfortable and wanted to say something, He had reminded the family of something tragic, but no matter what he might say, no words would never bring Philippe back, nor bring justice to those who had beaten a child to death.

"You should rest," Claude said as he stood up from his chair. He walked past Kurt and patted him on the shoulder. "You will get better, and then you can go home."

Home. Kurt thought about where that was for him. Back in London. Rita. And he lifted his head and looked about this dark, hollow cave. He searched the faces of his rescuers and vowed silently that he would repay them. He would get better, leave this place—and come back for them.

§

Present—1953, London
Kurt

He struggled to sit up in the hospital bed, clenching his teeth as he gripped the bedframe and pulled himself up. His arms had lost their strength; it has been a while since his last training. He had run track and wrestled in college, and during the rigorous training for Operation Jedburgh, he ran faster than anyone in the mission. The last time that skill had served a purpose during the war was on the day that would change him in unimaginable ways.

The family that had kept him safe during those two months, the same people who had shared their meagre supply of food, the young girl who had nursed him back to life—they were all killed on the same day. As much as he wished to banish the fragment of time from his memory, he could not. It had become engrained with a sharp accuracy. Like a stubborn shadow, it followed him into his dreams and resurfaced whenever he heard the familiar sound of gunfire, or a name that triggered the scene to rerun in his mind. Today, it was the absence of Rita that led him back in time.

It had been difficult for him when he first returned from the war— to bring himself to look at the face that reminded him of timid, sweet Marie, who had taken care of him when he found the pain unbearable. And it pained him to see her. Rita— Marie—Rita. Their faces would oftentimes overlap, and he struggled to tell them apart. When he awoke from his naps, drenched in sweat, and found Rita sitting beside him, he would jump up from the couch as if she were an uninvited guest, or a ghost who frequented his reality all too often. Exasperated by his erratic behavior, Rita wanted to know about what happened so that she could be of help to him. But how could he possibly explain that his fear and his nightmares took the form of her very own flesh? That he felt tormenting guilt when she stared at him longingly. That she was a constant reminder of a family he had failed to protect. He consciously kept Rita at bay so that she wouldn't discern anything from his past. Perhaps he wanted the distance from Rita as penance for his crime, for deserting the family in the cave when he left so abruptly with Luke. For not asking questions. For not insisting on doing the right thing at the right moment.

He pulled the covers from the bed, exposing his legs. The deep gash had healed, although not perfectly. Marie was not a surgeon, and her sutures were amateur when compared to what he later would receive from more experienced hands. She must have been shaken at first when she saw his wound. How could he fathom the admirable spirit of the quiet, fifteen year-old year that had sewn a broken man back together with the means available to her? After the war, when he had trouble sleeping, he found himself gliding his fingers across the protruding, crooked scar. Why hadn't he jumped at the opportunity to save her life, as she so courageously saved his? He thought of her as he traced the outline of the scar. He thought of Claude and Lucille and of Catherine.

Catherine. He winced at the memory of her. The last time he saw her was in the Rouen forest. She showed up at their base at the outskirt of the forest, gasping for breath while attempting to speak. She must have been running. Her face and neck were damp with sweat, her golden hair disheveled, and her large, petrified eyes told of a horror that he would only later find out for himself.

He saw Luke rushed towards her, and though he tried to calm her so that she would speak coherently, his voice was harsh and loud, as though he was interrogating a runaway criminal.

"What happened? Why are you here? Where's everyone else?"

An unintelligible sound came out of her trembling lips.

Luke's hands gripped her shoulders, and he shook her almost violently until she sputtered the words.

"The Germans, the Germans.... I saw them going to the cave. I think—I'm certain, that—that someone found out where we are hiding."

Grabbing the rifle left carelessly on the ground, Luke shouted orders and signaled for others to follow. His team leader's voice sounded calm and authoritative as he led a group of thirty men and headed into the forest. Kurt ran towards the cave alongside Luke and could hear Catherine sobbing. How many shots had been fired? Two? Three? They all came from that direction. And with each shot, their pace quickened. The other men's faces showed little concern other than the tension that furrowed their brows. Another shot. The distance to the cave seemed like a time warp that mischievously held them hostage.

When the apple tree came into view, so did the lifeless bodies of Claude and Lucille lying on the ground as if on display for all to see. Marie lay beside them, her dress stained with blood. A German officer stood over her, still holding the weapon he had just fired. Luke shouted something incomprehensible.

A sense of powerlessness came over Kurt and he dropped his rifle in surrender to the horror unfolding before his eyes.

Catherine, who had been trailing behind them, pushed her way

157

through the soldiers; seeing her family, she fell to her knees and let out an agonizing cry. The sound gave away their location and they were forced to move quickly.

The German troops were startled, and as they were outnumbered, they began to disperse and retreat. Kurt trod slowly and aimlessly. Remembering Catherine, he turned back and watched her sob.

Luke ran to where Marie lay, calling for help in the belief there was still a chance of reviving her. He shouted repeatedly for the medic who rushed towards them more in response to Luke's desperation than in hope for the victim.

From a distance, Kurt watched him weep, his arms wrapped tightly around her unresponsive body. Her dress was torn in several places, and Kurt tried not to think about what the German soldiers had done.

Still inexperienced with deaths, he tried to console Catherine, still kneeling in the same place, a small distance from her family. She had stopped sobbing but refused to move. She stared blankly at Luke as he continued trying to resuscitate Marie while the medic looked on helplessly.

He helped Catherine slowly to her feet. She felt light and he held her arms as tightly as he could in fear that she would be blown away by the wind. He walked back to the base with her, pushing back thorns from the thickets with his forearm. The camp was almost deserted, with most of the men still in the forest, while others were scattered around, on the lookout for German soldiers who may be hiding nearby. He sat with her on half-emptied ammunition boxes—his unexpected reunion with the sole survivor of the family he promised to protect.

"Would you like some water?" He twisted open the cap of his canteen open and handed it to her.

Her eyes flickered, so he knew she understood him. But she made no attempt to take the canteen. Her face was smeared with mud and dried tears. She still looked beautiful beneath the dirt, but her eyes exhibited a terrible sadness.

The portrait of war, he thought bitterly.

"Do you—do you need…" He heard his voice fade. He had no idea how he would supply her with what she needed or wanted. Her family—

no one can give them back to her. Silenced by his own gaucherie, he chose to remain silent beside her. She sniffled from time to time, and he listened intently in case she asked for anything.

When Luke returned, he looked disoriented and refused to speak to anyone. He stared at Catherine coldly, silently blaming her for abandoning her family. No one spoke until Kurt and Luke were given orders to leave. The Canadian troops would stay for their mission that was yet to come.

§

Catherine was to be taken to a hospital later that day, and Kurt wondered if he should accompany her and make sure that she was safe. He felt an obligation towards the only survivor of the family who had taken him in, and he felt bereaved as well. He requested that Luke allow him to accompany Catherine to the hospital, and Luke only nodded desultorily, his eyes sullen and dry. He sat on the ground holding his rifle and resting his chin on the barrel. He didn't speak for the rest of the night.

The drive to the hospital was only a few miles away from the base, and Kurt carefully draped a blanket over Catherine's shoulders. Although it wasn't cold, she trembled as they drove away from the forest. Neither of them spoke during the drive, but as he helped her when they arrived at the hospital entrance, she turned to him and thanked him in French. Her voice was small and her eyes defeated. He watched her walk up the stairs, her feet dragging wearily. Her calves were scraped and had traces of dry blood. The lump in his throat grew as she disappeared behind the door. Would this headstrong girl withstand the loneliness that awaited her?

If they both survived the war, he would come and see her again. Memories filled his head: how she practiced her ballet routine in the cave when she thought everyone else was sleeping; how he fell asleep watching her as she sometimes danced throughout the night. He would wake up at daybreak, seeing her untie her ballet shoes. Perhaps he would watch her dance on stage one day, allowing himself the small glimmer of hope he reserved for the girl who survived against all the odds.

§

Present—1953, Chantilly
Friedrich

Unable to fall asleep, he stared listlessly at the ceiling and waited for flashes of the past to appear like scenes from a nostalgic film he has seen before. Not a day passed that he didn't think about Catherine and her family. More often than not, he lay awake at night recounting the details of what happened that day. By then, the snow had almost melted from view, except for what lingered near the tree bark seeking refuge from the sun and the warmth that spring would bring.

§

Wartime—1944, Rouen
Friedrich

It had been almost four weeks since he last saw Catherine. He was surprised at how quickly he had been able to adapt, and how relieved he felt at the thought of serving in the army without constant self-doubt. Soon after they had bidden farewell, he led a patrol in Le Chambon-sur-Lignon, a small village near Rouen, and he felt revived and more focused than ever. When his men found a Jewish family hiding in a church, he felt as though fate was challenging him, testing him to see where his loyalty lay. At first, he was reluctant to look at their faces, fearing that he might see her, but there was no trace of Catherine. As he ordered his men to execute the family, including the children whose terror-filled eyes begged for compassion, he felt the weight on his chest lighten as each shot was fired. He believed that Nikolaus's death now ceased to haunt him. It was an act of retribution, of justice that had to be rendered. He could finally live with a clear conscience and begin to focus his energy on counterattacks in Normandy.

§

One afternoon, the routine patrol in the city that First Lieutenant Witt was ordered to lead took a sudden shift of focus when someone had reported suspicious activities in the Rouen forest. Friedrich was not informed where the patrol took place, and only found out when he passed by the radio base and heard the commotion. Someone had called in about finding Jews hiding underground.

In the past, his men had sought out Jews in the strangest and most innovative hiding places, but this was unheard of. He suppressed a rising anger that felt like a fiery sensation soaring from his chest and halting in his throat. The sound crackled from the radio and he tried to appear indifferent to the news. The room seemed smaller to him and everyone surrounding him was now the enemy. His breathing accelerated. Someone was trespassing on his territory—the sacred ground he thought could remain a secret between him and Catherine.

He left alone, rushing to catch up with Witt's troop. The thought of someone stepping over the grounds where he and Catherine stood just weeks ago drove him mad. He ran without a plan in mind through the fields, shutting out all sounds, hearing only Catherine's soft footsteps. A familiar sense of urgency alerted him that danger was approaching. This was a war of conflicts within himself that he needed to resolve. There was no sense in running to rescue what he would assuredly lose and what was doomed to happen. But if he didn't arrive in time, he would rot his life away wondering what could have been. Could he save her? Life was where Catherine was, and her death was unthinkable.

As he approached the apple tree, silhouettes of soldiers surrounded it menacingly, like the strange oracle he had seen before in a dream about the Rouen forest. He felt distraught at the sight of invaders trampling over his sacred ground. Witt and his men pushed Claude and Lucille to the ground, their hands over their heads. He moved forward to get a closer glimpse of what he had predicted would happen one day. Still a distance away, he could not see their faces clearly, but from the way their bodies fell to the ground, they had already surrendered to their fate. Catherine's father was coughing violently and struggled to breathe. His wife, helpless and without the authority she maintained underground, knelt beside her husband and sobbed.

No one else emerged from the cave as he searched for traces of Catherine and Marie. He advanced between the trees and felt his uniform dampened by branches still wet from the rain that fell earlier in the day.

The seasons had shifted artfully. Whatever the snow had meticulously covered, it now laid bare.

A scream ripped through the air as one of the men aimed his gun at Claude. Was it Catherine? Friedrich ran at full speed. He needed to shield her from the horror that was about to unfold. But it wasn't Catherine—it was Marie who fled from the cave and threw herself in front of her parents, her arms boldly outstretched as she pleaded for their lives. His legs came to a sudden halt. He had seen this all too often: parents pleading for their children, children pleading for their parents. Witt stepped in and forcibly pulled Marie away. She shouted hysterically in French and Friedrich wondered whether she was hurling insults at her family's executioners, or telling her parents how much she loved them. He believed it was the latter, that those words were the last that Claude and Lucille heard as shots were fired into their chests.

Their bodies slumped to the ground, and with no snow to cushion their fall, the sound of their weight was as deafening as the gunshots that ended their lives. Marie's sobs saturated the air. The men dragged her away and began to tear off her dress. Friedrich could do nothing but watch the horror play out in front of him. He ran as if meeting the enemy head on, with a temerity that could only be seen in the cruelest of battlefields. Without a second thought, he pulled out his side pistol and fired two shots. The men tugging at Marie's dress stopped, instantly setting her body free as she laid in a pool of her own blood. She had been shot through the chest, twice, by his perfect aim. He walked to where the men stood placidly and he examined her body with a practiced indifference.

"We don't fraternize with the enemy." His voice was dull as he pointed to Marie's lifeless body. He callously scrutinized her bloodstained dress as if she were a stranger; no different from the other Jewish bodies they had previously discarded.

He knelt beside her as if to further examine her as would a field medic, but instead of spitting on her body like frequently done, he covered her bare thighs with a piece of her torn dress. No one spoke; the men appeared stunned by his actions. Witt began to make his way to him, his eyes proud and exhibiting a kind of malice that Friedrich detested in soldiers. Before Witt could say a word to him, a high-pitched scream tore through the silence. Catherine's trembling mouth was covered by a young maquisard who held her since she was too weak to stand. So she was not in the cave. Friedrich felt relieved and overjoyed but unable to explain what he had done—what had to be done. He was almost panting as he searched her eyes for understanding, for a trust he knew they had formed in this forest; she must know the truth. But how must he seem to her with all his conspirators and the condemning evidence surrounding them. Friedrich would not forget the way she looked at him—with horror and disbelief that haunted him throughout each day and into his dreams. In her disquieting eyes he saw himself drown in the violent waves of guilt.

A group of maquisards began to form around them. Witt, standing close to him, saw that they were outnumbered, and he shouted orders to his scattering men. Most of them began to retreat, but some stood their ground bravely and shot towards where Catherine stood.

For a split second, Friedrich was confused as to which side to run to. His sole confidant had become his enemy and he decided not to linger, knowing that his innocence could never be proven, and if he lost her, he still had a war to fight. And Claire—he still had Claire.

§

And he still had her now. He climbed into bed and watched her sleep soundly, her eyes closed, but he could see them move as if she were dreaming. He brushed her hair away from her eyes. It had been a few years, and she must be tired of hiding. Their *pâtisserie* was known for its rich taste, a sweetness that could not be perfected elsewhere. But Claire was unable to greet her customers and hear their praises for her work. They must lie low in order not to draw unwanted attention. Their identities remained unclear among their neighbors, but most people ignored the past and heartily accepted the beautiful couple, who made sweets for a living.

CHAPTER EIGHT

LA BALLERINE PERDUE

Present—1953, Paris
Luke

It still didn't look right. It was incomplete, and for the life of him, Luke couldn't tell what was missing. He paced back and forth in front of his unfinished canvas. The work was near completion; even the colors were filled in and he had given light to the eyes, the most difficult task. The eyes are the window to the soul—he knew that to be true.

He stared into the familiar face and she obligingly returned his gaze. Halfway through drawing Rita, he had realized he was beginning to confuse the two. Was he drawing Marie, with Rita sitting in as a muse? Or was he attempting to draw Rita with the memories he had of Marie? He threw his paintbrush on the floor and allowed himself to sink into the couch. It wasn't going according to his plan. This was supposed to be his big comeback. Granted, he hadn't lost his foothold in the artists' circle. His last work was still among the most praised—at least among the critics he knew whose verdict mattered. But he had let himself go during the past few months; he voluntarily retreated into the background, away from the fame he so lavishly embraced and at the same time despised for the past few years. Somewhere deep down, he never forgave himself for betraying Marie.

His act was materialized in the painting he drew on the night he met Catherine again after six years. He completed the work while his mind was muddled by inebriation, falling in and out of dreamlike state. Lenny discovered it the next morning and took upon himself to unravel Luke's irreconcilable guilt to the world. When Lenny submitted it for the Prix de Rome in 1950, he spontaneously gave it a title that managed to further fuel the popularity of this impromptu work—"*La Ballerine Perdu.*" It was praised by the circle of elite French critics as the most painstakingly accurate interpretation of beauty and youth.

§

Post-war—1950, Paris
Luke

Catherine Aumont was not yet then a household name, but she was on her way to becoming a renowned ballerina. Her beautiful and flawless techniques were too apparent for anyone to ignore. He would meet her by chance again at her debut as the principal dancer for the Paris Opera ballet.

§

After the war, Lenny spoke about Paris and its incandescent magic, about how it could potentially transform Luke into the city's most sought after artist. He couldn't help but feel caught up in a dream. He leased his apartment and bid farewell to his mother, who remained skeptical of his plans but nevertheless dutifully supportive. He packed his bags and left to join Lenny in Paris, "the City of Lights", which promised all the impossible dreams he sought to replace his recurring nightmares of the war. He couldn't quite admit it to himself, but he willingly returned to the country that caused him so much pain with the faint hope of confronting it. He wanted to shake his fists at the same sky that had looked down on him without mercy, at God who was both present and absent from the darkest moment of his life.

During his first week, he was busy preparing his first exhibition, unpacking all his proudest works, even finding time to add a few more paintings to his collection. One afternoon, as he was working on final touch-ups, he received a call from Lenny whose voice was excitedly high.

He had tickets to the ballet at the Theatre des Champs-Elysees. They had been a generous gift from one of the rich art patrons he had befriended in the exclusive social gatherings he managed to invite himself to by the most mysterious means. At first, Luke politely declined. He had a legitimate excuse—he was busy preparing for the exhibition. When Lenny insisted, Luke promised that he would try, and if he finished his work in time, he would join him during the intermission, but he still would need a few more hours before he could leave the house.

As fate would have it, Luke found himself finishing the preparations early, leaving him with no choice but to join his friend and sit through a performance that in no way interested him. He was aware of his inappropriate casual attire for such a splendid event, and he reluctantly entered the Théâtre des Champs-Elysées, a grandiose hall that had hosted musical legends he had never neither heard of nor cared about. Among the crowds of people gathered at intermission to exchange praise for the first half of the performance, he found Lenny engaged in a heated conversation with a man whose nostrils were so flared with disdain that he thought it prudent to step between the two men.

"Oh Luke, there you are," Lenny said. "I'm so glad that you could make it tonight. This is Monsieur Lepardieu, and we were just talking about—"

Before Lenny could finish his introduction, Monsieur Lepardieu interrupted him mid-sentence, his extravagantly manicured mustache twitching as he enunciated every word.

"Well, your insolent friend here seems to think that my very best pupil has no place in my ballet. An absolute outrage! *Incroyable!*" He turned and left, red-faced and puffed with anger.

Lenny stared back at Luke incredulously and awkwardly adjusted his black framed glasses while surveying the retreating man whose profession he had inadvertently insulted.

"But he—was it really—oh, fuck. Well, there goes my connection to the ballet realm." Lenny took a sip of his champagne before looking back at Luke. They both laughed heartily.

§

When the intermission ended and the crowd was ushered back into the theatre, Luke casually glanced at the programme he was given when he entered. And as he saw the name of the principal dancer, he saw his own pathetic silhouette, holding his rifle, unable to stop all the killings he witnessed. It was a familiar sight, triggered by a most familiar name. He read the name again and again. *Catherine Aumont.* It couldn't be the same Catherine he had met in the underground cave. Marie. Rouen. The source of all his nightmares.

"Let's go, I got the best seats in the house, can you believe it?" Lenny giggled as he tugged at Luke's sleeve and pulled him into the theatre.

When the music started, Luke was unable to take his eyes off the stage, ardently searching for that familiar face. But his vision blurred, and he couldn't see any faces distinctly. He felt the dampness in his hands and discovered he had been crying.

"Oh, here she comes," Lenny whispered as he nudged Luke with his elbow and eagerly watched the prima ballerina's entrance.

Luke saw her now as clearly as the day he first met her.

The music came to a sudden rest and the strings paused in mid-air as Catherine emerged from offstage and fluttered towards the center of the stage. The orchestra crept back in; the music serving as a shadow accompanying her every step. She looked much taller now, her frame less fragile than when he last saw her. She moved gracefully as though carried by the wind, transforming herself into a bird. She leapt effortlessly into the air with her invisible wings and her chiffon dress swayed rhythmically. Her features were dramatically accentuated by the stage make up but easily recognizable. Here was that young girl of sixteen, with eyes so blue and inquisitive that he had always felt vulnerable under her defiant gaze. From that moment, he never lost sight of her throughout the performance. He consciously followed her every move and every beguiling smile meant not for him but for the audience, and he felt a disconcerting jealousy towards the equally captivated crowd.

The performance came to an end, and she returned to the stage to receive a standing ovation. Monsieur Lepardieu stood beside her, his arm wrapped around her waist as if she were a valuable possession that he owned. Luke wanted to run up to the stage and steal her away to a place where no one would recognize her. They would flee together to somewhere not yet tainted with memories of the past. He could start over and she could come with him. This otherworldly creature he had just seen on the stage—would she take him as he was?

Not long before, he had asked himself the same irrational question without considering the consequences that were bound to follow. He felt a familiar pang of sadness as he watched her face dissolve into the delicate features of Marie. How had Catherine survived all these years in a war-ravaged country? How had this young girl, after losing everything and so brutishly persecuted, managed to dodge all manner of obstacles and now stand onstage showered with praise and admiration? He sat back in his seat, speculating on her past, tracing her steps as an orphaned Jewish girl to her rank as a widely admired ballerina—all based on his imaginings and assumptions.

The crowds shuffled to the exit; Lenny had already left his seat and now trailed behind Monsieur Lepardieu. Luke smiled in admiration of his friend's fervent, unabashed need to please others; his mind always preoccupied with paving the way into another exclusive Paris artistic circle.

He lingered in his seat long after the crowd exited the auditorium into the lobby and rested his arms on the upholstered velvet surface of the seat. He stared blankly at the empty stage. Was she really there? He blinked a few times before he looked down at the programme, repeatedly reading her name. *Catherine. Catherine Aumont.* Yes, this was the same Catherine he had met in a time he had tried to abolish from his memory. He stood up and headed towards the exit, keeping his head low as he scurried through the crowd still raving about the performance. Was he ready to see her again?

"Luke!" Lenny's high pitched voice sliced through the noise, and several heads turned.

He looked up and found himself staring into Catherine's eyes, as sharp and blue as he remembered them. She stood only a few feet behind Lenny, and while her lips moved as she spoke to the group huddled around her, he felt the force of her gaze into his new and unfamiliar fears and all the accumulated pain he could never rid himself of. She disguised her surprise well. He watched her divert her attention back to her avid fans, her eyes occasionally darting back to him to make sure he hadn't disappeared.

"Luke, there are some people I'd like you to meet."

Lenny didn't waste any occasion to introduce him to potential art patrons, and the gleam in his eyes was most obvious whenever he sensed that "big money" was nearby.

An elderly English couple visiting Paris with the sole purpose of seeing the ballet, stood on either side of Lenny. Both were meticulously dressed in a fashion that reflected their extravagantly expensive tastes.

Luke stood by trying not to cringe as Lenny began to boast about his friend's painting artistry. His gilded compliments were presented with a broad smile. Despite his insincerity, his plan seemed to be working well. The couple listened to him intently, nodding as he spoke about Luke's exhibition the following week. Their enthusiasm grew as Lenny described Luke's latest work in rhapsodic detail. He referred with pride to "a rare masterpiece."

"And did you enjoy the performance?" the woman asked Luke.

Her long, wrinkled neck was adorned with diamonds, and her eyes stayed fixed on his inexpensive tie. He felt as though she was judging his worth and deliberating whether his artistic work would coincide with her status.

He didn't answer her immediately, feeling uncertain about what he should say. Catherine's head tilted slightly, also anticipating his response.

"I think . . . well, I'm not sure if I would be the best judge of performances such as this…"

The broad smile on Lenny's face turned into a frown and he quickly changed the course of his response.

"…but what I do know is that the main dancer did a magnificent job. Magnificent indeed."

This satisfied his potential patroness and she smiled approvingly, nodding as he enunciated "magnificent." They continued chatting aimlessly, much of the discourse revolving around the best restaurant in town and which ones offered the best selection of wines. It ended with a surprising invitation to dinner after Luke's exhibition, which they would undoubtedly attend. Lenny wished them a good evening, and as he waved to them, he nudged Luke with his elbow, giggling excitedly.

"This evening wasn't such as waste of your time after all, was it?"

Before Luke could answer, he felt a hand softly tap his shoulder.

"You said I was magnificent. Have you ever seen me dance before?"

Catherine stood next to him, addressing him with a nostalgic familiarity, yet at the same time, without acknowledging that they had ever met. She stood confidently before him, emanating a deeply rooted sense of self-worth. She knew that she would take the world by storm after the evening's distinguished performance. The sheen of her pale blue sequined dress reflected her translucent blue eyes—or was it the other way around?

"Well—no, in fact, I have not."

Did she recognize him? Of course she did—he couldn't assume otherwise.

Lenny glanced dubiously at him, trying to decide whether it would be prudent to leave him alone with the star dancer. This was a connection he couldn't afford to lose.

"He is a fan of your dancing, truly, he is."

Lenny adjusted his glasses, staring at the ballerina standing before them, her eyes fixed solely on Luke. Seeing she was unresponsive, he retreated to find other potential patrons to charm as well as to salvage his dignity, as he couldn't bear being ignored in a conversation.

"Well, there's Monsieur Lepardieu. I must congratulate him on this wonderful show."

Lenny took his leave and Catherine nodded politely. She shifted her attention back to Luke and maintained an intriguingly distant courtesy as she continued to speak.

"Did you really enjoy the show?"

Her smile was affable, but there was something missing. Luke searched for the recognition that should be there in her eyes but stubbornly remained hidden.

"Yes, yes I did." He felt puzzled by her manner. She was playing a game of pretense. Was she really not going to acknowledge who he was?

"Well, then, you enjoy your evening now."

And with that, she left him for another group consisting mainly of other dancers from the ballet, their faces still flushed with sweat from the flawless performance. As soon as she joined them, the voices became more animated, and laughter could be heard all the way to the other end of the hall. They were celebrating their success, and Catherine was their star.

He was unable to move from where he stood, dumbfounded by the encounter with the girl who now transformed into an alluring young woman who playfully refused to acknowledge him. Her attitude was disquieting and he considered the idea of confronting her.

Lenny found him staring aimlessly at the crowd and insisted he join him for drinks with a few other "big money" patrons he had befriended.

"Think of this time as an investment, darling," he whispered as he forcibly dragged Luke towards the exit.

Still entranced by Catherine's reappearance, Luke's eyes searched for her in the crowd. He believed he spotted her before he went through the revolving door, but the twirling action of the glass distracted him, and he lost track of her. His last glimpse was of her standing by Monsieur Lepardieu, her lips smiling, but her eyes indifferent and tired. She appeared discernibly restless and unable to break free from the crowd that claimed her attention. The thought of her being trapped brought back a troubling sadness, and as he left the opera house with Lenny and the inebriated crowd, he wondered if he should have rescued her. Yet despite his overpowering yearning to turn and run back to her, he couldn't bring himself to do it. He had already failed once before.

§

Post-war—1950, Paris
Catherine

Moments before her first performance as the main dancer, Catherine recited aloud the instructions her Rouen ballet teacher had whispered in her ears. No trembling. No missteps. And no failure. She had to keep herself focused and pretend she would be dancing on an empty stage, with no audience to judge or reprimand her when the show was over.

Monsieur Lepardieu had lobbied hard for her role as lead dancer. There were many other viable options in the class, some younger and significantly more experienced than she was. When the final cast was revealed on the board outside the ballet school's main hall, she could hear the class comments. But when she read her name scribbled in an almost illegible handwriting beside the lead role, she felt a gleam of pride and didn't care that she may have won by climbing into bed with her teacher.

To be fair, he hadn't called her into his bedroom for the past few months, and she suspected he had his hungry eyes set on a younger freshman, or that he simply wanted her to focus on her dance as he had stressed many times before.

"What a rare and beautiful talent you have," he had told her. "I am going to make you great and unforgettable. Mark my words, Catherine."

And she did. She practiced tirelessly every night in the empty classroom until the school closed, and in her airy, spacious apartment—fit for a dancer—that Monsieur Lepardieu generously paid for.

When she finally won the role she knew in her heart that no one else deserved, she believed she had paid for it with her own blood and sweat. And this was not just counting the nights she spent with Monsieur Lepardieu. She had laboriously and tirelessly put in much more effort than anyone else in her class; even Monsieur Lepardieu saw that. Her devotion to dance developed into an unstoppable obsession, beginning when she became aware of the way other girls looked at her. The rumor had spread that Monsieur Lepardieu favored her over those who slept with him and was confirmed when he was seen entering her apartment and allegedly not leaving until dawn.

She didn't care much for her notorious status as the teacher's whore, but she found it particularly strenuous to deal with the outside assumption that she won the role merely because she had been intimate with her teacher. She felt irritated by the lack of recognition she deserved for her skills and technique as a dancer and was determined to prove them wrong.

And so began her grueling hours of practice. There were nights she didn't stop even when blood was visible on the tip of her pointe shoes. She sometimes practiced from evening until dawn, and when she stood by the classroom ceiling-high windows, feeling the sunlight caressing her cheeks, she felt overwhelmed with gratitude for the second chance at life and would thank Maman, Papa, Marie, and Philippe for their support. When she felt weary, her determination worn to the ground and replaced by a bitterness that gnawed at her insides, she lay sprawled out on the floor, devoid of motivation—and she would feel them. Maman whispered encouragement in her ears, Papa's kind eyes winked at her, Philippe's innocent, bright smile cheered her, and she always felt Marie's unwavering support for everything she did. And that was how she stood up again, knowing they were on her side, and remembering who she was dancing for. I will shine for you, she promised herself and her family. The light temporarily dimmed by your unjust deaths will be lit again.

§

When that first performance was scheduled, she could hear her unruly heartbeat, but nevertheless felt thrilled to be on center stage. This was her moment, and she would prove them all wrong. She sat in her dressing room powdering her face and adjusting her costume. She breathed slowly as she stared at her reflection in the gold-framed mirror.

She had Papa's eyes, a rare color of deep blue—almost violet—and she was once told that she was beautiful because of them.

"Your eyes seem to have a life of their own, like they can tell a remarkable story. Could I take a picture of them?"

Jacques, her first boyfriend in Paris had told her. He was a freelance photographer and later left when he discovered her unscrupulous relationship with her teacher. She recalled his praises as she observed herself.

Her skin glowed with the sweat resulting from her excitement. She wore a mix of gold and violet eye shadow that accentuated the hints of violet in her blue eyes. They looked occasionally fierce, mostly due to her driving ambition to succeed. But on this night, they were softened, knowing that despite the countless hours she put into her tireless practice, she could stumble at any point and become the laughingstock that everyone in her class expected. But she would not be dancing for them. No, this is an exclusive, intimate performance reserved years ago for her family. The rest of the audience existed by chance. She would not be influenced by their judgments. She left her dressing room and closed the door behind her. She was ready.

Though not flawless, she knew she had excelled far beyond what Monsieur Lepardieu and the rest of her class had expected. She did not stumble, and every part of her dance was seamlessly executed with such effortless grace that even she was shocked after each segment. Did she just master that pirouette, that grand jeté, and the final battement? Although the stage lighting was too bright for her to see into the audience, she felt sure she was able to recognize a familiar shadow. Was it Papa? Maman? Philippe, or Marie?

When the performance ended, she went backstage without realizing that the full house was giving her a standing ovation. She dabbed her sweat furiously with a towel as the stage director rushed behind the curtains, frantically gesturing her to go back out. She walked onstage in a daze and the audience's pleasure and admiration took the form of uncontainable applause. Stunned, she could only smile and appear calm. There would be no crying today. This was a good day.

As she changed out of her ballet costume and into her evening gown, she could hear the whispers behind her. Many girls, once jealous and bitter about her being chosen for the role, were now hesitant about approaching her with congratulations on her spectacular performance. She cared little about what they thought now, and she wanted to waltz out of the door with newfound pride that had crystallized the moment she had won the audience. But as she removed her pointe shoes, her feet sore and tired, she had no interest in making more enemies. She didn't want to live her life segregated from the rest. Seclusion was something from the past, and this was the future.

She approached one of the girls and began chatting with her, smiling as others joined in—all eager to win her approval. When she entered the hall of Théâtre des Champs Élysées, she felt a rush of renewed energy and ambition soar through her body. Heads turned as she passed by, whispers of her beauty and flawless dance techniques could be heard from the crowds wherever she walked. She approached Monsieur Lepardieu who embraced her in a fatherly manner, and she had a deep sense of repose intermingled with the knowledge that her dignity had been restored. She was no longer regarded as another dancer—one that he could flirt with carelessly—no, she was now *the* dancer. And although she was still his to flaunt at more events such this, she would be respected now.

"How do you do?" She smiled through dozens of introduction within twenty minutes of her entrance. The exhaustion kept at bay for so long had overpowered her; so much so that she came close to falling asleep while listening to the droning voice of an elderly man who expressed his admiration at length.

A high, strident voice jarred her from her subconscious doze so abruptly that she lost her balance and had to grab onto the dull speaker beside her. She stepped back and apologized while Monsieur Lapardieu laughed merrily, excusing his star dancer for her uncommon clumsiness.

"You wouldn't expect that to happen on stage, of course!"

She joined the rippling laughter as her gaze followed the voice who had shouted the name both nostalgic and daunting to her ears. It evoked memories she had struggled with for years before she could sleep soundly at night. *Luke.* The very same Luke, almost just as she remembered him, appearing in a sea of unfamiliar faces. It seemed like only moments ago that they stood together in the Rouen forest, screaming on top of their lungs, wishing for the nightmare to end—the recurring nightmare he has undoubtedly struggled with just as much as she had. He hadn't changed much. He still had an air of a trained soldier, but his shoulders were more relaxed and his hair unkempt. She tried to remember him in uniform, but all that came to mind was an indefinable military figure.

She felt exposed and unprotected and wondered what he must have thought when he saw her dancing. She was now free, and after tonight, successful, and although it wasn't really her, the personality she had become for the role was carefree, full of innocence and goodness. But in his eyes, she must have appeared guilty and shameful for dancing with joyful exuberance after what had happened to her family—what she had inflicted upon those she loved and later abandoned. She felt as though she wore a written confession around her neck as penance for her sin. But he couldn't have known. Her mind wavered so violently she wondered whether if she should run away. Like that day when she ran from the cave, from her family—from what now meant everything to her.

She must have appeared calm and indifferent since no one inquired if she was all right. The conversation continued and she kept smiling and nodding at her admirers. The voices surrounding her took on a pacifying sound. She looked back at Luke, who sometimes met her gaze, and at other times listened so closely to the person speaking that she wondered if he recognized her at all.

When the knot in her heart tightened and became too painful to ignore, she made up her mind to approach him and ask where he had been all these years. He owed nothing to her, nor did she ever try to seek him out. But as she moved towards him, the returning familiarity made her more despondent and peculiarly hopeful. As she got closer, she overheard his praise for her performance, which she understood as a generic response. She doubted if he had ever been to a ballet performance. She smiled and wondered what Marie would say to her now, and she wished that she could tell her sister what she was seeing now. Luke, who was just as tall and handsome as she remembered. She was standing behind him now, and it surprised her that she was able to distinguish his scent. Or was it his presence that evoked the memory of the scent of forest pine trees and the distinctive musty smell of the tree barks? But instead of the tall trees, a large crowd of people surrounded her, all speaking excitedly to each other. The women's elaborate dresses glittered under the lighting, screaming out for attention. Something deeply nostalgic was triggered within her. She longed for the peace and quiet of the cave. Funny how the heart changes. How desperately she wanted to leave and return to that darkened place she had loathed as a child.

She watched Luke, his back facing her, and wondered if he would recognize her, acknowledge where she came from and who she had become. As confident as ever, her identity nonetheless had felt confused since the day she emerged from the cave alone. She thought she was freed when she left its confinement, but she had become tangled in the traps of reality without anyone to turn to and confide in about the day that forever changed her. There was no one to understand the reason for the penance she sought. This was her chance. She reached out to Luke and tapped him on the shoulder.

"You said I was magnificent. Have you ever seen me dance before?"

CHAPTER NINE

"THE PORTRAIT"

Present—Paris, 1953
Rita

When the phone rang, she thought the unimaginable had happened. Her heart pulsated violently against her chest, and as she picked up the phone, she realized how empty and meaningless her life would be without Kurt. When her mother told her the news, her legs buckled and she had to support her weight with her arms on the kitchen counter.

"He woke up, Rita." Her mother's voice was calm and absent of emotion.

Rita remained silent and could hear her mother breathing on the other side of the Atlantic.

"Will you come back?" Concern filled her voice and she was a mother again, wanting to comfort her youngest daughter.

"I—I'll need a couple of more days," Rita said. She rubbed her temples with her hand. She was already tired from sitting for Luke through the whole day, staying as still as he demanded for the painting. He hadn't been in a talkative mood, and the silence suffocated her. Now she felt even more exhausted.

"I'll be back soon. Tell him—tell him that I'm coming back."

When she hung up, she sat up on her bed for hours before she had the desire to fall asleep. It was only half past six, but she had no energy left to do anything else. Her fingers traced the flowery pattern of her bed sheet and the motion calmed her. Perhaps this was why Luke was so immersed in his drawings—the act of drawing paved the way to some kind of therapeutic healing. She smiled faintly at the thought of Luke as he recovered from his invisible wounds. And Kurt—what of his injuries? She felt relieved that he was awake. But she contemplated with a heavy heart their future together. Was there any future, any hope of happiness left to salvage?

She rested her head on the pillow and thought of Kurt in his hospital bed. Was he thinking about her too? Or had his thoughts wandered to someone else—someone she was trying to find to no avail. She had lost that piece of drawing.

As she began to drift off to sleep, her thoughts about Luke and Kurt and their similarities and differences led to a moment of profound realization. She jumped from her bed fueled with a new purpose. There was no time to waste. She dressed and searched for her coat. When she closed the door behind her, she felt renewed and invigorated. She may be able to solve the mystery after all.

Present—1953, Paris
Luke

Resting his head on one end of the couch, Luke took a much-needed break. It was a beautiful painting—one of his finest works. The outline of the body was ill-defined—almost rushed. He purposely had painted it that way so that the beautiful face with the celestial features and crystalline green eyes would enthrall admirers, inviting them to do nothing but revere her beauty. He didn't have to open his eyes to see it but could effortlessly recall every detail of his canvas to mind. The subject was someone who daily had haunted his mind through the past years.

He didn't rise immediately when he heard the knocking; his dreams kept him willfully impervious to outside noises. The second time, it awoke him from his daze and he walked sluggishly to the door, irritated at the thought of an uninvited visitor.

"Rita," he said, surprised to see her.

"I . . . I know what I want." She was still out of breath and obviously had run all the way to his home.

"What do you mean?" Still half-asleep, he looked at Rita and wondered why her eyes were not green like he had painted her.

"I want you to draw me a place. From memory—well, my memory. Can you do that?"

"I thought I was the artist and got to decide what I want to draw." Her request sounded curiously funny and he subconsciously allowed himself a vague smile.

"This was part of our deal."

She was not smiling and looked as serious as he has ever seen her. He cleared his throat and tilted his head up to observe her from a different angle. Of course—she hadn't agreed to sit in as his muse just for the fun of it; he had promised her anything she wanted. He laughed as he deemed this request to be a poor choice of "anything." She wasn't vain, but he did expect that she would request a monetary reward. He nodded and tried to restrain himself from smiling again lest she misunderstand it as belittling.

"Yes, yes, of course. Well, do you want to come back another day, or—".

Without answering, she walked past him and searched his living room with a peculiar familiarity that mystified him. She may know his home better than he did. With a blank canvas under her arm, and a stand clutched in her other hand, she walked to the center of the room and determinedly set up the new canvas as if she were the painter. She moved swiftly, placing the canvas carefully on the stand and positioning his chair in the way he preferred it when working. When she was done, she stood with her arms crossed, impatiently waiting for him to approach his new work station.

"Please. Won't you sit down?"

He approached her warily, intimidated by the emboldened Rita. He seated himself, feeling uneasy while staring into the blank canvas. He wasn't accustomed to working on two projects simultaneously. But he nodded in deference to her request and prepared his paintbrushes.

"So, what is it that you want me to draw?" He felt like laughing. How the table has turned: his muse commissioning a drawing from him. But he feigned enthusiasm and was intrigued by her whim.

"A place."

Her brows furrowed as she paced around the room, and he knew she was anxious. As his muse for the past five weeks, he could read her emotions. Before she grew impatient from sitting too long, her eyes would stop glancing around the room. Her curiosity about him showed in her searches for anything she could attribute to the formation of his character.

"I've never seen it," she said. "It was in a drawing that I found—the one I lost when I first met you." She recounted the details of that day, her voice more self-assured now that he was listening more closely.

As she spoke, the things that had happened gradually came into his mind like a dream that was only now unravelling after a moment of déjà vu. He had fought with Catherine the night before after arriving home drunk. As usual, he must have uttered things that upset her. It usually pained him afterwards—never during when he would say thoughtlessly callous things. Remorse always came a day too late. As Rita spoke of the drawing, he realized this wasn't a trifling request for a beautiful work, but that her future and happiness were attached to the realization of this drawing. He didn't hear much detail as to how she came into possession of it, but he understood that it served as a clue to something—a puzzle she needed to solve on her own.

"Could you draw it for me if I described it as accurately as I can?"

He glanced back at his unfinished work then back to the blank canvas that held no promise of reward for either his career or his own enjoyment. He looked at her, his stand-in muse whom he had approached only to use as shadow of someone he once loved. An awareness that he cared for her dawned on him. The feeling wasn't strong, nor was the moment dramatic or life-changing, but it warmed him from within, and he felt a willingness to help her without anyone prompting him to do so. He hadn't felt compassion for anyone in a long time. Catherine may have been the last person he truly cared for, and within the seconds of contemplating his life and the lack of people in it, loneliness hovered over him like a stubborn shadow.

"Yes. Yes, I'll try."

§

Post-war—1950, Paris
Luke

As much as the incidental meeting at the Théâtre des Champs-Élysées affected him, he hadn't given it much thought during the weeks that followed. When he returned to his apartment from the drinking party Lenny had dragged him to, his mind was too numb to reflect on what had just happened. He stumbled through the door, tripping on his shoes after awkwardly removing them. His head spun violently and he was unable to sleep. So he painted—his most effective remedy for recurring insomnia.

He settled into his favorite thinking position and waited for the inspiration to come. His mind wandered back to the ballet and Catherine. Now he was running back to the Rouen forest but couldn't find her. Her face filled his reverie so completely that he couldn't make out Marie's features. Desperate for another glimpse into his past, he got up and rummaged through the boxes of his military belongings until he remembered giving the drawing to Kurt.

§

It was the night before their mission to rescue the Aumont family. Luke would take Kurt and twenty Canadian soldiers to escort the family out of the cave and into safe perimeters. Alone in his foxhole, Luke took out his small drawing pad—a routine to distract him when he couldn't fall asleep—and he drew. Pages and pages of Marie, as though his mind was suffocating from endless images of her, and the only way for him to breathe was to actualize her on paper. Her face, the way she smiled, and her healing hands. He added poorly imagined details and promised himself he would authenticate them when he saw her again. Unable to remember if she had a mole on her lower neck, he nonetheless meticulously drew it in. He had always found her neck to be a sensual feature and he faltered momentarily. He drew by the light of the moon, transfixed by the figure that took shape under his roughly sharpened pencil, willfully entering into his own world.

Someone jumped into his foxhole and he drew his rifle.

"Jesus, Friedman! Announce yourself before you scare the shit out of me! I almost shot you in the goddamn head!"

"Hey, quiet over there!" a voice hissed from a few foxholes away.

Luke shot a dirty glance towards the private he almost killed and signaled him to sit down.

"Sorry, Sir," Kurt said sheepishly as he found a sitting position in the already cramped area. He glanced at Luke's drawing pad. "Is that Marie, Sir?"

"Yeah, yeah, it is," Luke felt irritated that his feelings for her had been discovered. He began to put the pad away, stuffing it into his pocket.

"Sir, if you don't mind—could you draw me one of those?"

"What?" Luke snapped before he realized what Kurt was asking him.

"I mean, that portrait of Marie, could I have one?"

Luke glared at the insolent private. Who was he to ask for such a thing, and what happened between him and Marie when he was in her care? He had spent so much time with her in that cave.

"No, Sir. I—I mean, uh, she—my fiancée back home, you see, she looks an awful lot like her. I—I lost her picture the day I got shot, sir."

Luke hadn't imagined that Kurt might have a family and a girl back home and regretted his overly protective reaction. Didn't they all have something to return to? This was a young man who had a future waiting for him. Why does it even matter if Kurt was infatuated with Marie? She would be his after tomorrow. He laughed softly and gave Kurt a reassuring pat on the shoulder.

"Yeah, of course, I can do that."

Kurt didn't speak during the whole time he drew for him. Maybe he was scared of another outburst, but now that he thought back, recalled the way Kurt sat, his eyes intently watching as if he were a magician bringing his fiancée to life on paper.

It was a simple picture drawn in a rushed few minutes. He quickly outlined the Rouen forest as he remembered it. The pine trees were skeletal versions with bare branches. He imagined a church up on a hill, although he was sure that no such building was there. But it would have been nice, he thought, and drew it in. But when it came to Marie, and her face, he subconsciously slowed down, generously letting time slip by, as if it were a common luxury. He drew fastidiously as he outlined her face then filled in details with the extreme care. When he drew her smile, he felt her soft lips should curve upward. His moved his pen swiftly and with certainty until it lingered above the paper, hesitating above her hands. With each stroke, she became more real, and some fifteen minutes of drawing, he was done.

He handed the portrait to Kurt, who took the paper in his hands as if it were a sacred artifact. Then he folded with painstaking care and inserted it into his front pocket.

"Thank you, Sir." Kurt saluted him quickly before he jumped out of the foxhole and disappeared into the darkness.

§

Luke wondered where he was now. He had wanted to know the fate of all the men he served with and heard news of him when he returned home. He later realized that while most of the other men had taken up posts in the high ranks of the army, only he and Kurt remained uninterested and had left the army for good. The last he heard, Kurt was working as an engineer for an aviation company. A good job for a fine lad, he thought and left it at that.

Now, as he sat on the floor by his closet, the boxes of memories unfolded one by one, luring him back into the past, he wondered if he would have felt happier had he never met Marie. And now Catherine. Catherine. He repeated her name again, this time out loud.

"Catherine".

He began to draw fervently if only as a way to survive amidst all the uncertainty and finished the painting without allowing himself a moment of pause.

He filled in the last shade of blue, which he layered atop the dark purple used for Catherine's eyes, remembering them clearly. A sense of betrayal overcame him, and he wept. It began as a soft sob that grew as if suppressed for a long time. His pulse resonated throughout his body. It was done—the evidence of his betrayal.

The next morning when he woke up, his headache was gone, and he found himself under covers, remembering nothing of going to bed. The morning light seeped through his half-opened curtains. He got up grudgingly; the anger he felt the night before hadn't subsided. Walking hesitantly to where he had left the canvas, he was shocked to find it missing. Did it even happen? Or did he fall asleep when he came home and the painting was only a fragment of a dream? He sat sprawled on his couch, trying to determine if he could have dreamed everything. The damning evidence lay beneath him: dozens of sheets of papers, drafts of the painting, were scattered on the floor. But where was the final work? Perhaps he never got to it.

§

A few weeks passed, and he received a letter from the board of Prix De Rome, congratulating him on making the finalists' list for the year's competition. He couldn't recall submitting any work to Prix De Rome. He'd call Lenny, who was notoriously known for doing things on a whim.

"Prix De Rome?" Lenny's voice sounded groggy and irritated.

"Yes, do you remember submitting any of my work? I just got a letter."

Before he could finish, Lenny's high-pitched scream startled Luke and he dropped the phone, reluctant to pick it up again. He could still hear him.

"Oh, my God! You received a letter?"

Luke felt annoyed by the fact that Lenny had yet again submitted his work without discussing it with him first. He left the phone on the ground while he contemplated whether or not he should find another associate.

"Oh, Luke! I knew it was a winner when I first saw it! And you say you never do portraits! Liar! Are you there? Why are you so quiet—Luke? Luke!"

"Yes, yes, I'm here."

If he continued to ignore him and then encounter him later at the gallery, Lenny would undoubtedly shout louder at him. He picked up the phone up and tried to remember why he had ever agreed to let Lenny be a part of his life.

"What are you talking about— which painting?"

"The one from a few weeks ago." Lenny sounded confused. "You don't even remember drawing her?"

"Who? I don't know what you're talking about. A portrait of whom?" He felt increasingly angry, wanting to hurl the telephone at the wall and watch it fall in pieces. He wasn't sure whether the anger was directed at Lenny or himself.

"Catherine Aumont!" Lenny said. "I assumed that you drew it out of infatuation. I mean, you did seem a bit shaken after you met her at the ballet. So here's what we'll do . . . "

He could hear only that name resonating like an endless echo as Lenny's voice trailed off. Catherine Aumont. So it wasn't just a dream. That painting—it was going to be displayed in public for all to see. The burning sensation and sharp pain in his heart was back—much like what he felt the night he had completed her portrait. He hung up the phone while Lenny was still speaking and unaware of the crime he had unraveled and exposed. Distraught, Luke picked up the letter and in one motion crumbled it threw it against the wall. As it dropped, he felt the same desperation that had engulfed him when he saw Marie for the last time.

He did not leave his apartment for three days. Thinking that he had fallen ill, Lenny visited him several times, knocking on the door until his hand tired. He shouted from outside, reminding him irascibly that his exhibition would open in five days. After nothing but silence, he began to relent and spoke with less reprimand in his voice, pleading to be let in.

Luke answered tersely to confirm he was still alive and to prevent Lenny from alerting the police. Exasperated but not defeated, Lenny was determined to continue his vigil. He had endured many "artistic outbursts" from several other clients and remained unfazed by Luke's withdrawal, viewing it as a customary storm that would pass.

Luke sat listlessly, as if waiting for absolution, praying for a sign from God that this was the end. He was ready. He could no longer live with this guilt. If only he had pushed harder. The day he took Kurt from the cave was the day he had promised Marie and her family that he would return for them. Their look of disappointment and abandonment still haunted him. Their turn would never come again. He cursed himself for not disobeying orders and acting on his own impulse. He could have taken her with him. He made a choice that day when he turned and left, when he followed the orders to wait until the next day to rescue them.

§

It was the fourth day of his self-inflicted exile when Lenny knocked on his door so violently that several of his neighbors came out to see what the commotion was about. A small crowd gathered and looked on curiously as Lenny, dressed in a fashionable red suit and wearing sunglasses that covered half his face, as if he knew he would be embarrassing himself. He stubbornly stood outside, puffed with anger, and although a small man, the force of his voice was by no means parallel to his size.

"I don't care if you never want to come out of your apartment in this lifetime—but by God—you *will* come to your own exhibition tomorrow! Damn it, Luke, you won third place for the Prix De Rome. Is it really that big of a blow?"

Luke hadn't opened the second envelope addressed to him from the Prix De Rome. He thought he didn't care, but his heart sank a little when he heard he hadn't won the top prize.

"And I even invited Catherine Aumont. Remember her? The subject of your painting? Huh?" Lenny's voice escalated to an unrecognizable screech. "Now how do you suppose that would look?"

The familiar name sent a shock through Luke's body. He rose from the floor where he had sat for the past hour and opened the door.

Lenny, about to leave, was unable to hide his surprise when Luke appeared. "My God, Luke, you look terrible!"

Luke swallowed hard. "Catherine—Catherine Aumont is coming?"

"Well, I would think so. Your painting made her an even bigger star than she already is after her performance of Swan Lake—which, of course, you missed." Lenny was already in a buoyant mood.

"I see," Luke said.

Lenny pushed the door wide open and swept into Luke's apartment full of energy and purpose. "Now, let's get you cleaned up first. We can worry about the mess in here later."

While Luke felt an emotional hollowness only he was aware of, he was being groomed by Lenny and a few of his friends in fashion. Luke shone like a new penny; they had even cut his hair shorter, in hopes to make him appear more presentable. He was forbidden to interject any of his personal opinions into how they dressed him, but he wasn't going to remain silent when Lenny dictated which of his works would be featured during the exhibition.

§

That same afternoon, they had a long, heated discussion which soon escalated to a fight about whether or not "La Ballerine Perdue" would be selected among what Luke deemed much finer works than the latter. Luke found the title to not only be distasteful and misleading—he did not draw Catherine to portray her as someone who was lost, but rather, as someone who was grieving for what was taken from her. Despite his insistence at changing the title of his own work, Luke realized that while his painting did not win the top prize, it had indisputably won over many hearts among the well-respected art critics, and it became increasingly difficult for him to stand his ground when Monsieur Lepardieu called and congratulated him on the fine job at naming this astounding painting which featured his most prominent dancer.

§

The day of the exhibition, he kept the same outfit that Lenny had put together for him the day before. As much as he disliked it, he was too exhausted to argue with him, and changed only the tie at the last minute—a small attempt at rebellion against Lenny's many instructions.

Though confident of his connections in Paris, Lenny hadn't expected this exhibition to draw so much attention, and when crowds swarmed past the doors, he was moved to tears. It soon became clear to both artist and agent that people were coming to see "La Ballerine Perdue," discovered to be the now-famous Catherine Aumont. Others who hadn't heard of her initially would remember her name and beauty after the exhibition.

Throughout the evening, while chatting with interested buyers and art critics, Luke kept his eyes alert for a sign of Catherine in the crowd, but she seemed to be absent. When the evening was nearing an end, he began to walk around the hall, stopping to examine each of his paintings. Despite the many praises he received tonight, he still felt deeply unsatisfied and critical of the collection.

When he approached "La Ballerine Perdue," he passed by a few lingering guests who spoke in hushed tones as if they were standing in front of a sacred statue. Luke slowed his footsteps and listened. From where he stood, he watched a young woman in a long, black overcoat with a matching scarf over her head standing alone by the painting. She possessed a grace and sophistication that triggered an instant recognition: Catherine.

Dumfounded, he watched her from a distance. She seemed enchanted by the painting, her expression full of longing, as if she were mourning something lost long before. When she turned back and faced him, she had been crying. The tears on her cheeks left a subtle dampness that flickered under the lights, and he wondered if he should look away.

He couldn't recall whether she had approached him first or if it had been the other way around. She greeted him courteously and coldly, but there was warmth in her eyes. She regarded him with familiarity but acknowledged nothing from their past.

"That is a beautiful painting, if I may say so." She laughed softly as she pointed at herself trapped in a canvas on the wall.

"Yes, well, I'm glad you like it." Luke felt only embarrassment, and he could think of nothing else to say.

"Do you—want to get something to eat?"

Her face looked radiant, and he couldn't tell whether it was from the lighting or from something within her. Was she glad to see him again? He wanted to believe she was. He looked into the face not of the young girl he once knew but that of a beautiful woman whose eyes looked so inviting that he couldn't resist. They left the exhibition with in search of a restaurant fitting for two lone, reunited souls.

That night they spoke of many things, mainly trivial, such as which restaurants he frequented since moving to Paris, and about the movies or plays they had seen. They evaded the past, that looming hole ever so present but never confronted throughout their conversation. They simply pretended that it didn't exist.

He felt besotted. His eyes held her smiles, and the same grace he had seen onstage was delightfully present even in the most casual steps she took beside him. He felt rejuvenated, and although he recognized the danger of being near her, as memories could come crashing in at any moment, he was ready to risk it—his sanity for momentary bliss.

The inexplicable happiness he once had felt with Marie returned— this time with a greater intensity, as if making up for time lost. The passion he had long reserved for Marie now seemed insuppressible. He resolutely lusted after Catherine's flawless dancer figure. After a late evening dinner at a brasserie near the gallery, they said goodnight. He had longed for this—not just any companionship, but someone who understood his past and who wouldn't question the source of his nightmares. But he also was fearful of what this could lead to. Would they one day have to acknowledge the life chapter they had shared? Would this part of their past return to haunt them? Emboldened by the rich wine they had paired with their dinner, he remained willing to take that risk. As he walked back to his apartment, the street lights of Paris seemed to be nodding in agreement with his impulsive take on love. Take that risk, they whispered to him.

He went home and fell asleep determined to replace all his nightmares with the unspoiled, untouched dream of Catherine.

§

Post-war—1950, Paris
Catherine

She hadn't expected to meet him again after that night at the opera house, although she imagined a dozen different ways they would encounter, if ever linked again by chance.

When Monsieur Lepardieu insisted that she accompany him to the painting exhibition where her portrait would be featured, she declined with the reason of a recurring migraine. Too many people now wanted to depict her as a pitiful, young ballerina who miraculously rose to stardom, and she was tired with the sensationalized version of herself. Her success was not a result of anyone's charity other than Monsieur Lepardieu's benevolence, which she had paid for.

As for "La Ballerine Perdue," she scoffed at the title and despised the artist for choosing to depict her as weak. She had no idea the artist was until she walked past one of the exhibition posters plastered on the wall outside her practice room. It was a portrait of herself, with a faint but visible profile of Luke beside the brief description of the artist's background.

When she met him at the gallery, she felt drawn to the bittersweet nostalgia he stirred up simply by looking at her. He was the strongest link to her past and one she couldn't deny herself access to. Their eyes playfully acknowledged their overlapping pasts, though neither was ready to be unmasked. It was a dangerous game of mutual attraction.

"I think we should see each other again." His tone was lighthearted.

This was neither a question nor a request that should be turned down. They were leaving the brasserie, both slightly drunk from the wine and the exciting beginning of an infatuation. They both felt deliriously elated and mischievous as they tiptoed into a forbidden playground.

Catherine acquiesced with a smile, and she let the answer linger in the air. The crowd had begun to disperse, and they were among the few lively souls who chose to remain out in the street, exploring the possibilities offered by the moonless evening. Occasionally, her thoughts wandered into the past and she thought of Marie, then questioned whether this man beside her still loved her sister as much as she did. But Marie's shadows came and went, like the soft wind that blew over them, never lingering long enough to whip itself into a windstorm.

She allowed herself to be drawn into a dangerous attraction to a man first claimed by her sister.

§

That night, Catherine dreamed of Marie dressed all in white, her favorite color. They were jumping on their beds, simultaneously flinging pillows at each other. The details of her former cottage home flooded her mind: the intricate carvings on their wooden bedposts, the carpet with its exotic, richly complex patterns that Maman bought from a Turkish vendor down the street, Papa's cigars, at once pungent and soothing. When they had grown tired of jumping, they lay on the white linen sheets with their arms intertwined. Marie was laughing even though both knew that she hadn't survived the war. As her laughter subsided, she turned to face her, and even in a happy dream it pained Catherine to know she would never see her sister's angelic face again. There was no sadness in Marie's eyes, but a steady, unfaltering peace that overrode all emotions.

"What will you do?" Marie asked as her quizzical emerald eyes searched Catherine's face for an answer.

She woke clutching her nightgown tightly in her fists. Rarely was she superstitious about dreams, but Marie's question lingered in her ears. What will she do?

Throughout the next few days, she continuously received calls from Luke and would either make up silly excuses of not being able to meet or simply refuse to see him. There was no reason for her to deepen a relationship that would strain over time given their history together— except for the fact that she desperately wanted to see him again.

The next evening, as she sat at her dressing table preparing to go onstage, a handwritten note was delivered to her.

Be my muse.

The back of the business card showed Luke's name and address, but there was no other message beyond the subtle invitation. Catherine thought him foolish, and she bit her lips as she searched her reflection in the mirror for someone who could make the decision in her stead. But no one came to her rescue, and she stared vacantly at her made-up self until the stage director called her name.

After the performance, riding in Monsieur Lepardieu's chauffeurred car, she watched the streetlights of Paris from behind the backseat window. The golden glow of the lights was distorted by the rain, yet she found it comforting, like an abstract watercolor with little structure and mesmerizing in its own way. She was half-heartedly listening to what Monsieur Lepardieu said about her performance. He rambled on about careless, distracted movements and the missteps that no one in the audience other than he and a few other expert eyes would have noticed.

When his ranting came to an end, Catherine felt her mentor's rough hand gliding up her thigh beneath the silken material of her dress. She watched him passively, as though far removed from where she sat, like it was someone else's body being touched. Though he rarely chased after her as he had before, she knew that she now possessed the power to demand that he stop, but she allowed his hands to linger under her dress. He moved closer to her and fondled her breasts. She closed her eyes and tried to imagine what it would be like if a different man were lusting after her. The abstract figure now took on the real-life form of Luke. She sighed as his image crept into mind, and Monsieur Lepardieu, taking this as a sigh of pleasure, became excited and impatiently spread her open like a present he couldn't wait to unwrap.

She left the car, leaving him snoring in the backseat, and walked up the stairs to her apartment. The dim lights in the hallway outside her apartment made her dizzy and she stumbled a few times before she finally reached her door. When she turned the key in the lock, the sharp sound it made awoke her from the state of confusion she had been trapped in for days. She now knew where she must go.

§

Post-war—1950, Paris

Luke

He felt more foolish and vulnerable after each call he made to Catherine. However fruitless, he felt the need to persuade her to meet with him simply because he felt convinced they were the sole cure to each other's nightmares. While he did think of Marie, he felt a crushing guilt as he dreamed of a future with Catherine by his side.

He thought of the time he first met the two sisters and wondered if his infatuation with Catherine did not take form back then. He was intimidated by her boldness and her loud, unconcealed beauty. On the other hand, his love for Marie stemmed from her innocence and the kindness she exhibited to others. The desire to protect the frail creature paved the way for his attraction to her. Marie was the light he saw when witnessing the horrors of wars as they unraveled: cries of agony, scattered body parts, the terrifying, encroaching darkness that enveloped him day after day on the battlefield. Her face would appear, and he was reminded of an innocence that chased his fears away. She was his savior and his light at the end of a seemingly endless tunnel. Then there was Catherine, the defiance that shone through her eyes, and the unshakable confidence rooted in a sixteen-year old girl who fought her way through countless obstacles.

§

Sitting before his half-finished showing an abstract landscape reminding him of Rouen, he wondered if the intimidation felt towards the young Catherine wasn't cowardice in the face of a growing attraction. He questioned whether he was prepared, as this stage of his life, to take on someone as beautiful and daring. Did he not deserve this? After years of suffering alone, trapped in nightmarish episodes of war, he would finally find someone who understood him. He firmly believed that Catherine would be the source of his sanity and happiness. More determined, he grabbed his pen and hastily tore off a piece of paper from one of the sketches scattered on the floor. He wrote down his request and would wait for her to acquiesce.

§

Post-war—1950, Paris
Catherine

The next few days were spent with little consideration of any calamitous aftermath. Ever since she had parted ways with Henri—the only other person she had shown her unmasked self to—she had fervently built walls to protect herself from being seen for what she truly was: a runaway with no home to return to. After entering into the unscrupulous relationship with Monsieur Lepardieu, it occurred to her that she had sold herself to worldliness and success. But with Luke and the way he regarded her with such admiration and longing, she had begun to feel the possibility of redemption.

There was a rejuvenating relief that came with the realization she had found someone who understood her, and though never vocalized by Luke, she longed to believe she was forgiven for inadvertently putting her family in harm's way. If Luke could forgive her, she could learn to forgive herself. She held on to this belief.

§

After a few weeks had passed, she no longer felt the need to keep him at bay. One evening, after her fifth performance of the month, she invited him to her apartment compelled by a voice much like Marie's to confront their pasts. They sat on her upholstered red velvet couch, one of Monsieur Lepardieu's many gifts, when a voice echoed in the hallway outside.

"Catherine! Catherine, where are you, my dear?"

There was a slurring in the distinctively haughty voice that could belong to no one other than her patron and former lover. Though no longer intimate with her exclusively, Monsieur Lapardieu made frequent and random visits to her apartment, still, in legal terms, one of his many properties throughout the city. He would often visit late into the night in such an unintelligible and inebriated state that it forced her into the role of a mother, undressing him and tucking him into bed. A curiously funny reversal of role, Catherine would smile when she closed the door to the guest room that eventually became his. She didn't mind these visits since the sight of him no longer intimidated her; contrarily, she found his company almost consolatory.

But this evening his visit was deemed an unwelcomed intrusion, and Luke's cold eyes showed little compassion when they found him sprawled on the marble floor, humming a nursery rhyme.

"I'll take him to the next room." Catherine felt embarrassed for her mentor, and she wanted to shield him from Luke's judgemental gaze.

"Can you stand?" The dissonant humming had come to a halt, and loud snoring now resonated through the hallway.

Catherine struggled to lift him up, a man whose weight almost doubled her own. Leaning against the wall, Luke watched as she awkwardly swung the drunken man's arm around her small shoulder. When she realized she was unable to move, he let out a soft laugh. Reluctantly, he approached them and gently shifted Monsieur Lepardieu onto his shoulder, slowly walked him to the room Catherine pointed to. When they shut the door behind them, a deep relief washed over Catherine, and the thought of herself and Luke tucking in Monsieur Lepardieu like irritated parents prompted her to giggle uncontrollably. There was little to do but for Luke to join her, and soon they were falling into each other arms, laughing in hushed voices, bewildered by the incident that just took place.

That same evening, after two bottles of wine shared between them, Catherine drifted off to sleep as she lay comfortably in Luke's arms covered by his coat. For the first time in many years, she felt protected as all her insecurities vanished under the warmth she felt exuding from his body. But nothing could shield her from her recurring nightmares.

She woke up screaming; Luke's arms held her so tightly she had dreamed the enemy was smothering her.

"It's all right, it's all right," he whispered, his breath tickling her ears. She recognized his scent—a musky cologne she had unwittingly become accustomed to. When she reached full consciousness, his face showed a familiar pain and he fought back tears. She wasn't alone in this fight and no longer felt abandoned. No words were exchanged and she settled back into his arms, instinctively knowing they had entered into an agreement. They were in this together now. And they were stronger.

§

Present—1953, Paris
Rita

"No, there are no trees in the far left corner." Rita pointed at the canvas. Her voice took on a patronizing tone that Luke wasn't accustomed to, and his patience was wearing thin.

"Well, wouldn't it look nicer if there were?" he asked teasingly.

"This area was bare—and there was a hill here."

Her fingers dexterously traced the empty background, barely touching the surface, as if treading on sacred ground. There was an outline of Marie, but Rita wanted to have the background in place before Luke moved on to draw her, the protagonist of this work—the woman whose name her fiancée muttered.

Luke sighed and he began to sketch a hill in the area Rita pointed to.

"There was also a church somewhere..." she mumbled to herself.

Present—1953, Paris
Luke

A church. A church on a hill. It was the landscape he dreamt up exclusively for Marie. Rita's voice trailed off and he was back in that night, sketching a similar drawing for Private Friedman. He shook off his musings and stood up, pointing to the exact spot where he drew in the church.

"You mean right here?"

She looked up questioningly, her eyes flashing in recognition. Luke's hand was trembling as it remained where the church had been on the drawing she had lost.

CHAPTER TEN
***

MILLE-FEUILLE À LA VANILLE

Present—1953, Chantilly
Catherine

It took five days of pacing aimlessly in her room, rummaging through many contradicting memories of Friedrich before she was able to bring herself to the address given to her.

Finding the *pâtisserie* wasn't particularly difficult; the distinct sweetness with the faint aroma of vanilla she had tasted that night was unmistakably a signature creation of Mlle LaCroix. But she could be wrong. Perhaps the famous recipe had been passed down, or even stolen after the war. Or, as she hoped and feared, Mlle LaCroix had fled Rouen with Friedrich. That they survived the war would carry both a good and a devastating outcome. Her judgment was clouded and she felt ambivalent about their survival. What would she say? What questions would she ask

Friedrich? Who would she cast her blame to? Her thoughts vacillated among the different circumstances constructed by her imagination, she was almost numb with fear of meeting Friedrich again.

As she had transformed from a young, stubbornly ambitious sixteen-year-old girl to a self-possessed and promising dancer, she explored her memories, trying to make sense of what had happened. Had the nature of their friendship been as ambiguous for Friedrich as it had been for her? Or could his kindness be interpreted as something other than just amicable? She didn't dare venture that far. On the other hand, she blamed him and cursed him in her dreams. The secret alliance they had formed in the Rouen forest may very well have been a trap he had coyly laid out to deceive her and her family, like one would do to lure an unsuspecting prey.

But then why would he have waited so long if that were his intention to begin with? Why did he not kill them the moment he discovered their hiding place after he and Mlle LaCroix stumbled upon her and Marie by their old house? Was this another layer of cruelty she would not have comprehended as a young girl?

§

When the war ended, she and Henri poured over newspaper articles and any source they could find on the Holocaust—a new term for her to grasp. As they dug deeper into the subject, she mourned for those who suffered so violently, and at the same time felt relieved for having escaped the horror by hiding underground. The stories they read from survivors' accounts reaffirmed her earlier belief that something as horrible could have been planted from the start by Friedrich. But her mind was no longer that of a young girl's, and there was no reason behind the crime for which she had accused him. Yet she found it impossible to forgive herself for disclosing her family's escape plan, an event she had always associated with her family's death. She had met Friedrich for the last time and they said their goodbyes silently, as if refusing to acknowledge the moment. She told him they were leaving, innocently and without suspicion of a man, who, in every way, was her enemy.

She now held in her hand the address of the *pâtisserie* famous for its mille-feuilles and macarons à la vanille. Facing the wind, she felt the chill on her uncovered neck. She had forgotten her scarf and the day was cold, but she preferred it this way. If she were to encounter Friedrich, she wanted it to happen in a weather much like their encounter on that winter night when Marie was with her. She closed her eyes as if to chase away her sister's shadow. *This is between him and me. Please, let me do this alone.* She stood still on the train platform as the other passengers passed without noticing her as if she were invisible.

As she walked the streets of Chantilly, charmed by its grand parishes and rows of quaint houses, she momentarily lost sight of the purpose of her trip. Taking her time to stroll the surrounding neighborhood, the thought of giving up the chase and running away was never far from her mind. When she finally found the street, she stopped to ask a group of children playing nearby if they knew where the *pâtisserie* was.

"*Ah, oui, la pâtisserie de Monsieur Fred!*" a small boy of six or seven exclaimed, and a grin appeared on his face. He was obviously acquainted with the sweets, and it saddened her when Philippe's smile came to mind.

They pointed her in the right direction, but her legs were unwilling to cooperate. Their refusal to move came from a force greater than her desire to see him. The truth may not be what she wanted to hear after all. She felt Marie's presence in the wind as it propelled a few leaves past her face, and she understood this was a bridge that must be crossed. Not only for herself, but for her family, who no longer had a voice, and whose resonating presence was still felt everywhere she went. With each new step, her heart felt heavier, as if it were not her own but an added burden she had to carry.

A sweet aroma floated past her, followed by a second curl of sugary scent. She stopped for a moment and breathed in the sweetness and let herself sink into the memories of Rouen. As she continued on towards the *pâtisserie*, she felt calmer than she had expected, not yet caught in the emotional turmoil that would follow.

She approached a small cottage with a signboard that said "*Pâtisserie de Chantilly*," and she peered through the window searching for a familiar face. There were several customers inside, mostly middle-aged women purchasing bread for their families. A teenaged boy stood behind the counter busily packaging orders while his lips moved incessantly. Who was he talking to? She stretched her neck to see if there were any signs of Mlle LaCroix.

A stockily built man appeared at the kitchen door behind the boy. He walked towards the counter and nodded perfunctorily to the customers, all of whom greeted him warmly. When his face came into view, she felt her chest burning and the pain almost threw her to the ground. His face was older, and his eyes had lost some of their cold severity, but they were unmistakably his. He wore his hair longer now, and it was combed in an unruly manner, a stark contrast to the disciplined Friedrich she used to know. She couldn't see him clearly from where she stood, and she could only imagine that the lines near his sorrowful eyes must have deepened with time.

In plain clothes, he didn't look as intimidating and unapproachable; but perhaps it was not how he appeared on the outside, but what had changed within her. Her eyes were dry but her hands unconsciously wiped away the invisible tears she felt were sliding down her cheeks. Then she looked up and saw that it was snowing. Snowflakes descended inconspicuously, their stark whiteness in contrast to the dark cement pavement. She turned back for a last glance at Friedrich, secretly wishing that he would see her, and perhaps confess to her whatever he might have done. But he didn't see her, and she walked away filled with overwhelming sadness and relief. She listened to the sound of her heels crunching against the snow and whispered his name. *Friedrich.*

§

Present—1953, Chantilly
Friedrich

They stood side by side in the kitchen, diligently folding flour as they prepared the dough for the next day, a routine he had come to love. Every now and then he stole a quick glance of Claire, whose small hands rubbed the dough with a force and intensity he found curiously alluring.

He didn't smile often, but at these moments he grinned for no particular reason. As if on cue, whenever he smiled, she would laugh softly, as if this were a language only they could decipher. The night felt peaceful, and he was thankful he had survived the war, if only for this day.

The next morning, as he prepared the storefront with Antoine, their young, part-time help, he glanced out the window. The snow from the night before had accumulated, and even now, the sight reminded him of Catherine. He stopped what he was doing and granted himself a few moments of nostalgia.

"Monsieur Fred, I found this by the door when I came in." Antoine passed in front of him holding a stockpile of bread and casually slid a white envelope across the counter. "Maybe an order from last night?"

Their neighbors would oftentimes write orders for the next day and slide notes under the door. He quite liked the convenient and mysterious nature of this system and gladly accepted orders in the form of a written note.

The envelope was blank, and he shrugged nonchalantly as he pulled out a small folded note inside.

"Meet me at Église Notre-Dame-de-L'Assomption tomorrow morning at eight. I need to know the truth.

Catherine."

He blinked and rubbed his eyes before re-reading the words several times. He became aware of Antoine calling him, asking where the macarons à la vanille should be displayed. His hand clutched the note tightly; still confused by what he had read, he walked back to the kitchen and called out for Claire.

"Where are you?" He was already on his knees, speaking incoherently to himself about something that happened long ago.

§

Present—1953, Paris
Luke

"What did you say your fiancée's name was?"

"I didn't say." Rita sat very still, taken aback by Luke's sudden realization of something he didn't disclose.

"Friedman? Kurt. Kurt, Friedman?" He watched her closely, and his furrowed brow deepened with the flash of recognition in Rita's incredulous eyes.

He began to laugh, but it sounded more like a mocking scoff, and he looked at her in disbelief, like she was a prize he hadn't expected, or even wanted, to win.

"Listen, Rita. You—well, you won't believe this." He ran his fingers through his unruly hair and paused for a moment before continuing. "I knew Kurt. From a few years ago, when we served together—you know, at Milton Hall. We were assigned to the same mission."

"Perhaps," Rita said. "I don't quite remember. And he didn't write to me much when he was there... You—knew Kurt?"

"Yes. Yes, in fact, we were here. In France, for a while anyway. He was wounded when we first came to Normandy. There was a Jewish family that took him in. They were in hiding. It was ... God ... so long ago. It took me—us—a while to get him out. An underground cave, if you can believe it—that was their hiding place. He made it out okay. But, of course, you know that..."

His words flowed like water escaping from a dam, and it was difficult for him to pause and explain the events in a chronological or even a coherent manner.

Rita pieced the story together and could picture Kurt in the events being recounted.

"And Marie?" she interjected, hoping for an answer. Maybe he knew something about her, too. As soon as she had uttered the name, his face showed a profound sadness and she wished she hadn't asked.

"I—I need a drink first. Would you like something?" He hurried towards the shelf where he stored his bottles and searched for something— anything—to hold.

He sat down with a bottle of whisky and two glasses and began to pour the drinks. The bottle collided with the rim of the glass, causing a startling echo in the silent room.

"That drawing you lost—the one that I'm redrawing for you," he said, pointing at the canvas. "That was her. Marie."

He took a sip from his glass and began the story that was the source of his nightmares. His pauses were not to recall forgotten details—these were remembered all too well—but to remind himself to breathe and that it was over, that he was recounting the past and not the present. At times he had to shut his eyes to stop himself from grasping the reincarnated Marie and begging her to recognize him.

§

Present—1953, Paris
Catherine

When she left the note on the door for Friedrich, it was already dark out and the streets were eerily empty. She walked for a few blocks, knowing he must have walked the very same paths, and she imagined that she was trailing his footsteps. With her eyes fixed on her shadow, elongated by the moonlight, she tried to picture how Friedrich lived for the past nine years, what went through his mind as he took his walks at night, and wondered if his memories of the past had faded with time.

§

The train was half-empty, and for that she was thankful. Low murmurs could be heard in the neighboring cars. Occasionally, a child cried but was instantly soothed and all would be well again. Catherine pulled up her the soft fur collar of her coat and soon succumbed to the warmth of the heated cabin and fell asleep. She hadn't had a dreamless sleep for a long time.

A sudden halt shook her awake and she looked out the window. The morning's heavy snowfall had obstructed the train's path to the next station. There was a small commotion in her cabin, but most stayed in their seats, trying to sleep while waiting for the snow to be shoveled away.

Still tired and slightly irritated at being awakened, she closed her eyes and attempted to find her way back into the exclusive, secretive state of repose, where dreams, no matter good or bad, were shut out.

§

Present—1953, Paris
Luke

Rita stirred in her sleep. It felt strange to have someone other than Catherine fall asleep, as she often had, on the couch in the living room. Luke draped a blanket over Rita and listened to her breathe as she soundly slept.

He walked towards the canvas and the half-done work now halted after realizing he was replicating a drawing from nine years ago. After telling Rita what had happened, how the Aumont family had rescued Kurt, and how they had died, he purposely left out his own episode with Marie.

She had listened attentively to every word and had remained silent until he finished.

"Did she... did she look very much like me?" She had asked, knowing fully well what the answer was.

"Yes. Yes she did."

"I see." Her hands stayed neatly folded on her knees, her gaze contemplatively introspective, as though searching for a connection between herself, Marie, and Kurt.

Luke wanted to offer an explanation for the drawing he had given Kurt, but he knew little of Kurt's intentions and had remained quiet while staring into his unfinished canvas. From then on, they had sat in silence, and he began to clean up, closing the oil tubes lest they dry out in the morning—a mistake he often made when absorbed in his work. When he had finished, he returned to the living room and found Rita asleep. He felt uneasy at first, knowing that she would be staying the night, but as night fell, he found a subtle peace and familiarly come over him, knowing there was someone else in the house. He thought of Catherine and how they had kept each other company, though never confronting their past, but somehow dealing with it head on, and together.

He sat in front of the canvas, his hand moving swiftly as he drew from memory the drawing he had sketched for Kurt. When he was done, he took a step back, and looked for any detail he might have missed. Satisfied, he nodded to himself, then to Marie, acknowledging her presence and welcoming her into his reality. *This is home, Marie.*

He opened a bottle of wine and sat facing Rita, who was still asleep. He raised his glass to Marie and watched her eyes fondly staring back into his.

When he heard sounds of footsteps in the living room, he struggled to open his eyes and tear himself away from his dreams. Still in a somewhat drunken state after finishing three bottles of wine, he lay sprawled on his chair with his head on the velvet armrest. A faint silhouette that looked like Catherine walked towards him and placed a note on the shelf by the door. He wanted to greet her, but he was unable to speak or move in his inebriated state. The door slammed as she left.

§

Present—1953, Paris
Catherine

The rain started mid-day without warning and the unexpected downpour took everyone by surprise. When Catherine arrived at the church, she looked down apologetically at the wet marks made by her shoes. She sat down and used her handkerchief to dry her face and hair. Her hair had recently been cut much shorter than usual. When she had caught a glimpse of her reflection in the mirror, she was delighted with her new look and complimented her hairdresser. Her long bangs were curled in a way that gave her a younger, more carefree appearance. Funny what a new hairstyle could do to a woman, she thought, as she strode confidently out of the salon.

But now her hair was flat and heavy from the wetness, and she no longer felt like new and more like something easily discarded. She brushed her hair back with her fingers, probably ruining her new perm in the process, but she had more important things to worry about. She stretched her neck to see if anyone had come in. The pews were empty except for one elderly lady with a scarf over her head, praying fervently to the statue of the Holy Mary. She tried to recall the last time she prayed.

That day, when she ran back towards the cave, following Kurt and Luke into the forest. Yes, she did pray to God that day. She was a selective believer, only religious when she needed to be, skeptical of an Omniscient Being that supposedly watched over them. She had never disclosed her wavering faith to her family and kept her doubts to herself. But that day, she had surrendered every ounce of disbelief bottled up inside of her, pleading to God to bestow mercy on her family. As she ran towards the place she vowed to never call home, she felt something like a dramatic conversion. The faith that she had previously rejected suddenly grew so enormous that she blindly believed that God would listen to her prayers.

The death of her family was the cruelest of burdens that God could have thrown at her. She had lost everything that day, but not her faith. Ironically, she had become more spiritual than she had ever been. Not in a particularly religious way, but simply more aware of the presence of Something or Someone omniscient enough to allow such atrocities to happen, and quite unimaginably cruelly, allow her to survive. The Great Being wanted her to suffer and pay for her guilt. She lived with a constant battle within herself. But in spite of her sufferings, she would demonstrate her ability to achieve her dreams. This rebellious spirit had sustained her until now. Knowing that she fought against a force greater than herself gave her satisfaction, and she continued to overcome her past with every step of her self-made success.

And yet today, she felt different. She felt as though she was preparing herself for an ultimate surrender—that she would finally have to admit she had lost. Perhaps her life was lived not to prove that Someone wrong, but to realize that her strength was not being tested for anyone other than herself. She had come all this way to find out there was no one at the end of the tunnel to defeat. From a few pews away, she heard someone find a seat, and a soft creak came from the old, cypress wood. A few minutes later, she heard the sound of heels against the cool marble floor.

"Catherine?"

The familiar voice startled her. It was not who she expected. The voice rang so clear that she didn't have to turn to know who was standing beside her. Dressed in a dark burgundy red coat, with a white scarf wrapped around her neck, Mlle LaCroix nodded at her as she removed her gloves. Catherine was unable to speak, and she turned back to stare at the statue of the Holy Mary. Mlle LaCroix took a seat behind her.

"Friedrich couldn't come," she said. Her sultry voice still carried the graceful weight that attracted her listeners' undivided attention. "He actually—doesn't know I am here. But I understand that you want an explanation."

She nonchalantly searched for her cigarette and lighter inside her purse. When she put a cigarette between her lips, her other hand pulled her lighter away as if she had become aware of her inappropriate actions.

"*Merde*," she laughed softly to herself, "I had forgotten where I was."

Catherine remained still, her body tense and poised to flee. Where was Friedrich? And why was she here? She was furious with herself and her silly, capricious plan concocted in order to fulfill a reconciliation she didn't deserve.

"It wasn't him, you know."

Reluctantly, Catherine tilted her head, anticipating what Mlle LaCroix would utter next.

Seeing that Catherine was waiting for her to continue, Mlle LaCroix paused briefly. She closed her eyes and clasped both hands together. Then she let out a long sigh as if blowing smoke from a cigarette.

"I wrote an anonymous note, so that no one could trace it back to me or Friedrich." Her large brown eyes were expressionless as she recounted what she did.

"When I went into town, I passed by the hospital, knowing where this one commanding officer would be. Friedrich told me about how he got wounded a few days earlier—and so I went into his room and left the note near his bed while he was still sleeping. He must have read it the next morning and sent out the search order." She stared coldly at the back of Catherine's neck.

Someone shifted in their seat, and a loud creak echoed through the church. Catherine felt unable to move. Blood rushed to her head, which she supported between her hands. She didn't want to hear this confession from the one person she hadn't anticipated to be the culprit.

"It was me." After a brief pause, as if to graciously allow Catherine the time to take this information in, she continued. There was no trace of guilt or remorse in Mlle LaCroix's voice. It was just something that needed to be said.

"Friedrich—did he ..." Catherine felt shame at the sound of her weakened voice. It was as though it was she who had committed the unthinkable crime.

"Yes. Yes, I told Friedrich about it," Mlle LaCroix said as she played with her untouched cigarette. "But that was years after it had happened. He understood why I did it, of course. Yes, I believe he did understand." Her voice was calm and assertive as she nodded to herself. She wasn't a criminal. And this wasn't a confession but rather the delivery of an answer to a question she had been asked.

Catherine kept her head down and stared at her own shoes. She felt powerless and her chest hurt when she breathed.

"And just so you understand," Mlle LeCroix continued, "he shot Marie because of what the other soldiers were planning to do to her." There was a short pause in her voice, giving Marie a moment of silence. "He is a kind man. Far kinder than I will ever be."

There was little Catherine could do to prevent a sob escaping her. She thought of Marie's last moments and wished that she had been there to protect her. Like the time when they encountered those boys. That time when Friedrich first saved them.

"He couldn't come today, because he didn't want you to know, I suppose," Mlle LaCroix paused again. This time, she inhaled deeply before she resumed to speak. "But I thought you should know that it wasn't him who betrayed your family." Having dutifully delivered her message, Mlle LeCroix put her gloves back on and stood up again, stopping in front of Catherine.

Her tall, voluptuous figure had remained unchanged from what Catherine remembered. But she couldn't bring herself to look at the woman she had admired and loved as a child. Mlle LaCroix stretched out her hand, as if wanting to soothe her with a familiar touch like she had done when putting extra sweets in the bag for her. But Catherine could only pull away.

Before Mlle LaCroix left, she let her gaze linger on Catherine's face.

Catherine felt her cheeks burning and she wondered if the woman who had betrayed her family had ever felt remorse for what she did. And what of all her previous compassion and kindness that she showed them?

"I love him too, you know."

Unable to respond, Catherine blinked several times before she heard those words echoing through her mind. By the time she turned back, Mlle LaCroix had gone, and she sat eye to eye with Luke, a few pews behind her. He looked tired and older. She briefly felt that connection again— the desire to fight together that had first unified them. They had never mentioned what happened, and while they both tiptoed around the looming danger, they had loved each other passionately in a way that only they could understand. Today, she needed him here. She couldn't have withstood the truth on her own, and although she had given no reason in her note about the purpose of her invitation, she trusted that he would come and that he would understand.

He sat staring at her silently. Had she wronged him by crossing the unspoken boundaries that had protected their relationship for so long? But it was already broken, and there was nothing left to protect. It was a battle they had fought together but each in their own way. Was she wrong? Her eyes pleaded with him.

He stood up and for a moment she thought he was going to say something. She sensed a deep yearning to reconcile as they searched their hearts for such a possibility, now that they had faced their evils.

§

Present—1953, Paris
Luke

He had heard every word. The church was solemnly quiet, as it should be, and the confession from a woman he had never seen before reverberated throughout the religious space. He hadn't understood why Catherine had left a note instructing him to meet her here. Knowing her headstrong ways, he couldn't help but admire her strength, her ability to persevere. Maybe he also wanted this—maybe it wasn't over.

When he first read the note, he sat and studied the neat, cursive writing that spelled out her request. He read the words several times over. Her beautiful face with its elf-like features had made her irresistible to many, and he was no exception. But there was something more to her. She possessed an admirable perseverance that had guided her through these years. He better than anyone knew what she had suffered. But as he faced her now, the beautiful, bold, and undefeated Catherine, he despised her for her strength. He was led here to have his heart cut out in front of him, to relive the pain all over again, hearing a stranger's voice denouncing a harrowing crime that he had believed was his from the beginning. He couldn't forgive her for trespassing beyond the sacred boundary they had created to protect themselves.

He saw her clearly now, her eyes pleading for him to understand that the truth should set them free, that neither of them were the reason her family was no longer alive. Should he yield? Was this a chance for them to reconcile their pasts and be cast free from their demons? As he blinked, he felt he had just now realized the toll and weight of the past he had succumbed to still lurked close by, waiting for a chance to swallow him whole. He retreated from the alluring prospect.

Defeated once again, he turned away from Catherine and left.

CHAPTER ELEVEN

HOME

Present—1953, Paris
Rita

When her mother had called the night before, she made no mention of Kurt in their brief conversation. But Rita understood he was well from the way her mother had purposely omitted any news relating to him. It was time to go home. She accepted her unavoidable return with less zeal than anticipated. When she hung up the phone, she began to pack. She had prepared a whole day to organize her things but only later realized the futility of setting aside time for the task. There was really nothing much to pack. Only two months, she thought. Had it really been only that long?

Even though she found the answer she had been searching for, she felt disheartened to be leaving Paris. She had yet to gather sufficient courage and reason to go back. What frightened her most was the gap he had deliberately left between them and one that he had forbidden her to cross. While they had grown apart, she was uncertain whether she wouldn't crumble like a fallen leaf if their being together ceased to exist.

Having finished packing much earlier than expected, she made a cup of tea and went out on the balcony to give this place one last chance. She tried to picture the events that Luke told her about, hoping to make sense of it all. With her tea in hand, she sat and looked out at the view of the city, engrossed by the calm skies dispensing blends of gold, orange, and yellow across the rooftops. Captivated by the changing colors, her mind drifted from the past and she allowed herself to become immersed in a world where earlier mistakes didn't have a foothold. She dreamed of a place and time where everything was made anew, with no room for the past.

§

Present—1953, Paris
Luke

He walked up the stairs and it dawned on him that he had never been to Rita's apartment before. She had always visited him at his home. Rightfully so, since she was his muse, and that was what they had agreed on. But as he stood waiting for her to answer the doorbell, he felt like a child again, waiting anxiously for a friend to arrive. A sense of nostalgia swept over him, despite the lack of history with Rita. He thought about the past few weeks, and how they had spent hours together, sometimes talking, but mostly observing each other in silence. Remembering those moments made them somewhat precious. She had come here to find something, an answer to a question, and he believed that she found it. Although it might not be quite what she was searching for; and nothing that explained or justified Kurt's changed behavior since the war, it did at least account for some of the changes.

Somewhere between the sadness he felt for Rita and a vague awareness of self-pity, he gave thought to his own predicament. What had he gained from knowing the truth of that day—the terrible day he found

Claude, Lucille, and Marie shot dead. What had changed? Had the truth given way to any relief, and was he even expecting a degree of redemption upon discovering it? There must be something at the end of a road filled with self-inflicted guilt. What had he been waiting for?

"Hello."

Rita opened the door with a large brown suitcase in her hand. The leather exterior was worn, but she didn't look like an experienced traveler. It must be Kurt's. And she was going back to him. At the thought of their reunion, he smiled broadly at the sight of this young woman who had something to look forward to.

§

Present—1953, Paris
Friedrich

He read every word, until he had memorized them, and then he read them again subconsciously aloud. When he heard chirping outside, and the sunlight discreetly greeting him from the half-opened window, he realized he had not slept at all. It was time to work, but he had little strength to begin his day of kneading flour and hauling trays of bread. He stared blankly at the paper that lay on the table; there were not enough words for him to further decode the intention of her invitation. He read instead the pamphlet for the ballet that featured Catherine Aumont, which was included enclosed together with a single ticket to her performance.

§

When Claire had returned home the day before, she told him everything. Usually an animated converser, she did not elaborate on the details. She did not describe to him what Catherine wore, whether her blond hair hung loosely above her shoulders as he remembered, or whether her eyes were angry or sad after hearing the truth. Did she cry? Was there any room for forgiveness? But the rare, sullen look in Claire's eyes made him withdraw all the questions he had longed to ask.

In a monotone voice, she told him she had met with Catherine and that the truth was now known. Her manner of indifference surprised

214

him, but her hands, which she casually folded on the table, were visibly trembling. She described the encounter with ease, but it must have been difficult for her. When she finished, he did not demand more details but instead stood up, patted her gently on the shoulder, and went about his work. He entered the kitchen sluggishly and began kneading dough. The movements of his fists were swift and harsh, and he was surprised at how much the action relieved him.

Later that day, a small envelop was delivered to their shop, addressed to him. He had been out delivering orders in town at the time. When Claire brought it to him, it remained unopened, but she knew who it came from and what it contained. She stood by and watched in silence as he reluctantly opened it, feeling a boyish excitement that he kept suppressed. He slowly unfolded the letter and saw the familiar handwriting; he felt contentment and wanted to sigh. Strongly aware of Claire's presence, he kept his face as blank as he could, and showed her the letter and the ticket. She laid them on the table and held him with a steady, accusing gaze.

"Will you go?" She sounded unaffected, but her expression was cool as she glanced at the ticket. There was only one, and she felt a sting that she hadn't felt in a long time. So accustomed to adoration, she had forgotten the feeling of being slighted.

"I'm not sure." He stood up and let his strong arms support his body weight as he bent over the letter. "I have more work to do. I'll think about it."

As he walked away, he refolded the letter with the ticket and tucked them inside his pocket.

Then she saw it: a subtle and seemingly insignificant gesture, but nonetheless she witnessed it. He patted his pocket, almost thoughtlessly so, but it was reminiscent of something familiar to her. Yes, he would pat her gently on the head whenever she would return to her apartment in Rouen after a long day at the *pâtisserie*. Or he caressed her cheeks adoringly with her fingers when they would awake together in her bed. That was love. And Friedrich loved her. And Catherine.

§

Present—1953, Paris
Catherine

Her hands shook as she applied her stage make-up. She sat in front of her dressing table in a dark-colored silk robe with patterns of overlapping purple and brown butterflies. She adjusted the collar and felt the silken material brushing against her neck. Unsettled about tonight's performance, she searched for something to adjust in her reflection. A loose strand of hair had deliberately separated itself, and whenever she moved, it would tickle her cheek. Reluctantly, she tucked it behind her left ear and then quickly moved it back. No one in the audience would notice the difference. They didn't know her when she was younger, that this was how she usually wore her hair if it were up. Just like Marie. But Friedrich did. Would he come? Tonight, she wore dark red lipstick, a choice not hers but the stage director's. But he wouldn't know the difference. She impulsively wiped off the lip color with the back of her hand and repainted her lips with a faint shade of pink. Her fingers played with the loose strand of hair and left it where it should be.

§

Present—1953, Paris
Friedrich

The theatre was filled with avid ballet fans, their voices high and animated as they could hardly contain their excitement for the long-awaited performance. Friedrich kept his head low while his eyes scanned the room. He had never been approached with suspicion but was constantly on guard for officers who may be looking for him. A war criminal—he winced at the thought of his legacy. For the past nine years, he had worked at burying the condemning thoughts of the crimes he had committed and never confronted. Claire had shown an unwavering support and had never voiced her fear of their being discovered, nor did she blame him for lost freedom when she chose to spend her life with him.

At times, he would feel moved by her strength and her ability to go on living without the burdens of the past. Only seldom would he feel that something within her was amiss, particularly when she appeared to be impossibly unaffected by what they had lived through. And he loved her. He wasn't very articulate and rarely expressed his affection with words, but he believed that she knew, and this muted understanding kept him hopeful. Their life, as complex and full of sadness and cruelty as he knew it for so long, had meaning. Perhaps they had been brought together in the war to find peace and solace through each other.

He believed this wholeheartedly until she fell asleep before he did. And when he lay awake in the silence, Catherine's face would come to mind. However hard he tried to justify his survival, the reasoning he had confidently built and believed in would still dissolve into nothing, and he once again would feel defeated.

Tonight, as he stood alone in a room filled with strangers, he felt wedged in between two cliffs about to smash together. He didn't know whether to climb to the top or let himself suffocate, a punishing fate he thought he deserved. The room had become unbearably warm, and he rushed towards the door that led outside in an attempt to breathe fresh air lest he collapse in the lobby. As his hands grasped the door handle, the start of the performance was announced. He turned back hesitantly and as he watched the crowd scurrying towards the theatre entrance, he began to breathe normally again. He took his ticket out of his pocket joined the columns of people moving into the auditorium.

When he found his seat, he was glad there was no one to the right or left of him. He let his arm stretch out comfortably over his own armrest and waited for the curtains to open with an overwhelming anticipation. He had never seen a complete ballet before tonight.

As the music began, his eyes searched for the orchestra that was absent from the stage. Unfamiliar with classical music, he felt surprisingly calmed by the harmony of the strings, his ears detecting the occasional piano sound. It was a whole new world, his hands relaxed with a new kind of peace anchoring deep within him. For a few enchanting moments, he let himself forget the reason why he was there.

When he caught his first glimpse of Catherine emerging from the corps de ballet, his hands were clenched, and the peace that had descended upon him vanished and was replaced with the familiar fear of being discovered. But she couldn't see him from where she was. Tense but no longer fearful, he watched her arms fold and unfold rhythmically to the music. He had never seen her dance before but had imagined it countless times. None of his dreams did her performance justice. She tiptoed on clouds, her steps light and graceful. Transfixed by each movement, a faint silhouette of the young Catherine materialized, and that look of fierce determination he had so loved about her left him unable to distinguish one Catherine from the other.

Memories rushed back, and he allowed them to take over his crowded mind. He closed his eyes briefly and saw himself standing in the Rouen forest, with his arms crossed behind his back, a posture he often found himself in when he felt anxious. The familiar figure approached him and he adjusted his coat collar as if he were meeting someone of considerable importance. But it was only Catherine, a young Jewish girl he had no obligations to except for his wandering heart. It quickened when he met her gaze, always curious and firm; her eyes older than her years.

He watched her incredulously, the only perfect symbol of happiness he had ever known, and realized that the truest reflection of him had been left in that forest. Unsure, unguarded, and vulnerable, he believed he had found himself during the war when he confidently took up his position as commander of his platoon. But it was all a clever pretense set up by someone else to reassure him of his new and indispensable role in a war that was not his to begin with. He had been fooled, and his epiphany threw him into a violent anguish he hadn't experienced before. Who had he sacrificed his life for, and whose lives had he in turn sacrificed for a cause that cost him the only happiness he had known and never indulged in? The questions lingered in his mind as he watched Catherine with an intensity he could interpret only as love, and he waited for her eyes to meet with his.

§

Present—1953, Paris

Catherine

Her body moved unconsciously. With endless and grueling practice, she could have danced flawlessly with her eyes closed. On this night, she relied on instinctive memory of movement as her mind drifted and her eyes scanned the audience for someone she knew from long ago. *What would he be thinking if he were here? Does he know of the guilt I've suffered? And love—does he know that I once loved him before I even understood that it was love?* She thought she saw flashes of his face, although blurred, like the last time she saw him at the *pâtisserie*. Her memory of Friedrich had always been unclear, and she was never able to remember his features, or how he looked when he smiled. Still, she would recognize the sound of his footsteps from the heavy military boots he wore, and his low, disciplinarian voice that suppressed an abundance of warmth she knew he possessed. She stared boldly into the audience, hoping that her eyes would find him. Desperation drove her performance; her sweat was not simply from the physical toll of the dance but from the draining away of all the things she had never said to him. *I forgive you. And I forgive myself.*

§

Present—1953, Paris
Friedrich

Her movements displayed perfection, not in a technical sense since he was ignorant of the rules of dance. But she had conquered and mastered everything that life had thrown at her, turning each obstacle into something daringly beautiful. He had avoided life and its challenges at every turn, his cowardice, cleverly disguised in the form of survival. He had fled with Claire and lived a life in refuge. What did that give him? Another day to live in shame.

He had lived as a coward since the day he lied about Nikolaus' death— a young man who had served him so faithfully and blindly and whom he had executed for supposed insubordination. Unlike other days, when he would cast away thoughts of the young soldier, he now let unbearable guilt and self-condemnation consume him..

Catherine seemed to be calling him from the stage. She was the evidence that not all hope was lost. He did do some good in the end, did he not? Could it be possible that fate had placed him in Rouen, with the plan for him to to save one as beautiful as she? He lingered in his seat, savoring the sight of her, until it was time to go. There was still a chance for happiness. Claire was waiting for him. He stood up, murmuring apologies as he hurried past the seated spectators, tripping over their feet. He ignored the accusing glances and walked up the aisle towards the exit. Catherine would understand his abrupt departure. His stopped at the door and turned to face the stage and watch her once more leap gloriously into the air like a bird discovering its wings. He heard himself whisper her name aloud, and it gave him strength enough to muster the courage to walk out to another possibility at happiness and a second chance at life.

§

Present—1953, Paris
Catherine

She leapt into mid-air. Guillaume caught her without fail, and they both exhaled a breath of relief. No matter how long they had practiced, she always feared not being caught in time. They danced away from each other in a sequence of pirouettes. She couldn't be sure if she had seen a shadow moving towards the exit. For her next pas de bourrée, she had to turn away from the audience and forcibly reminded herself not to turn around. It wasn't time yet. She looked at Guillaume standing across from her, facing the audience, and she wondered if she could see Friedrich's reflection in his eyes. Her partner reached for her with his outstretched hand and pulled her into his arms—a lover's embrace. The thought of Friedrich being here stubbornly lingered in her mind.

Impulsively, she pulled away from Guillaume's embrace and turned around abruptly. Her heart was pounding, and she feared that the sound of the misstep her slipper made was like a cymbal for everyone to hear. All would unmistakably know what a coward she was. Had she heard the sound of Friedrich's heavy footsteps echoing throughout the hall? She saw the door close behind him. He left her as stealthily as she had felt his presence.

At Guillaume's cue, she continued to dance, seemingly unaffected by a fleeting encounter with the man whose unassuming compassion had shaped her childhood. She would likely never see him again but maybe this was the best way to reconcile their pasts and the pain they both had suffered. *Goodbye.* She raised chin high and smiled faintly. The door to her past had closed and she leapt boldly into the air.

§

Present—1953, Chantilly
Friedrich

When he arrived home, he sensed something was amiss—an unfamiliar feeling of bereavement and loss. As he walked down the hallway to their bedroom, he felt her absence and his steps quickened.

In the seconds before opening the door, he dreaded what he would find. She was gone, not from their home, but from his life altogether.

She had hanged herself with their white linen bedsheet, her hair neatly braided into a bun. She wore the same white-laced dress she had bought for their wedding that never took place. He calmly untied her from deliberated bondage and lowered her stiff body onto their bed, gently placing her arms on her chest. She lay, sphinxlike, as if she were keeping a vow sworn to secrecy. She still looked beautiful, and he wondered when she would wake again and ask how his day had been, her brightly inquisitive eyes looking at him with adoration.

He sat by the bed until daybreak when his thoughts cleared. She had chosen to end it this way. He got up and pulled the covers over her so that the cold would not wake her as it usually did in the morning, then headed for the door. Quietly, he left their home and made an anonymous call to the morgue. As he walked away from this place where he and Claire ventured unto a new beginning, he realized that it was time for him to close this chapter. Because he too, had made his choice.

§

Present—1953, Paris
Luke

He didn't realize how long he had sat by the bar after his dinner with Lenny. When sunlight warmed his back, he felt compelled to get up and leave. But where would he go? The night had passed as quickly as it always did when he was struck by waves of anguish and recollections of the past. This time, Catherine was the culprit.

Only a few days before, he was the willing, self-condemned perpetrator of a crime. The unquestionable fact remained that his complacency had ultimately made Catherine an orphan and had left him grieving the loss of his one chance at happiness with Marie. But after hearing the confession of a French woman he had never met, he found himself furiously angry rather than relieved.

He left the church and Catherine, who had stayed behind in tears. He was unworthy of standing before her, someone he had once deserted after leaving her with Kurt the day he found himself desolate and stripped of his future with Marie. He had not a single drop of kindness left to spare, no compassion he was able to salvage from the emptiness that over him. He blamed her and cursed her for fleeing without bothering to ask her the reason for her escape.

After years of learning to cope with nightmares and shadows of the past, their paths inadvertently crossed and fate had given him a chance to make things right. He had rejected that chance by deserting her a second time—perhaps at the time she needed him most. Remorse had managed to sink him to a depth he hadn't thought possible.

He walked the familiar path home and winced at the thought of his desolate house. He had adjusted to the loneliness for as long as he could remember, but after several weeks with Rita as his companion, he felt deprived now of something important. He dragged his feet and as he strolled by the newspaper stand for a pack of cigarettes, a newspaper headline on display caught his eye. "Former German Commander of the SS Surrenders."

He anxiously flipped through the pages to find a face he might recognize. There was a photograph of an older man, lines defining his face, his eyes firm, not downcast or guilty like those of a criminal. Had he seen this face on the day that Marie and her family were viciously killed?

He had looked through hundreds of pictures of German officers on trial, but now his memories were obscured by different faces overlapping one another. He wanted to feel the anger rise, the familiar pang of suffering to take hold so that he could redirect his anguish to a stranger once his enemy. But there was nothing. He stood with his hands clutching the newspaper and restlessly scanned the page for random information, something—anything—that would provoke him.

He found the damning evidence he had been searching for in a sentence under the headline.

"Unnamed witness with new information suggests Commandant's involvement in hiding Jewish family in Rouen."

He read it again and again until his mind could no longer see the words clearly. The memory of the Nazi SS insignia, torn at the seams but still very much intact and lying in Catherine's jewelry box, cut into his thoughts. The young Catherine reappeared in his mind, her shoulder slanted by the weight of the bag she carried filled with rare items even he had not seen in the weeks since landing in France. There were thick slices of ham, apples, strawberry jam, and potatoes. Someone had helped her and her family survive all those months when they had hidden underground. *It was him.* Anger lay rooted in his chest and rose in his lungs. This was the oxygen he was meant to breathe. His life depended on dwelling in this consuming anger.

Present—1953, Paris
Luke

"You testified for him?"

His voice must have startled her; there was fear in her eyes. Catherine glistened in sweat from dancing. Her left arm was arched over her head when he swung open the door of her practice room. Without mentioning the Commander, she knew who he was referring to. **He detested the closeness that existed between her and this man who murdered countless families before he impetuously decided to save one.**

"What kind of a sick relationship did you have with this man?"

She wanted to say something but no words would come out of her mouth, and she couldn't bring herself to explain the friendship she had had with the man she barely knew. What could she possibly say in their defense?

"Did you love him?" He spoke with such disgust and disdain that she was hesitant to answer.

"I—I don't know." Her voice trembled with an uncertainty that made him want to push her against the wall with his bare hands.

Why was she not sure? It was a notion of love that she concocted in a sixteen-year-old mind possessing little discernment. She had been so young. He stood before her now, a man who once temporarily halted her nightmares and one she also had loved but with more conviction. She began to falter.

"God, Luke—you don't understand. I was so young—there are, were, things that you can't know at that age. And—it wasn't like that."

She paused for a moment, and her eyes shone with a softer light.

"He fed us. He came every week with food and assurance we wouldn't starve. He saved us."

He saved us. Yes, something that Luke had failed to do. He couldn't help but cringe at the last three words uttered from her lips. And how fitting it was to remind him now of his failure.

"So what, you decided to repay him with kindness now? You stood as a witness that he saved *you*, while he watched so many others die?"

The silence between them lasted long enough to contemplate his question. He stood in front her with trembling hands at his sides. His reflection, along with Catherine's, looked back at them from the mirror that ran across the length of the wall. He saw himself for what he was: shaken, anguished, and foolish. The guilt of not being able to do anything but drown in his anger had made him a pitiful example of a man destroyed by hate.

"I'm just telling the truth, Luke." She stood her ground. The great Catherine wasn't going to let his outburst of anger defeat her.

He loved her more than he knew. He was envious of the grip this man had on her since and dumbfounded by her determination to help him, an ex-Nazi Commander. He admired and loved her for her strength, her conviction to tell the truth. But he hated her now for the same reasons and resented her actions.

She took a cautious step towards him. Her eyes withheld a truth that neither of them would admit to: that they were finally able to cross forbidden ground, to expose the unscrupulous past they both shared. Perhaps this would be a new beginning. a chance for them to face their fears together.

After an extended silence, she brushed aside the stubborn strand of hair that lingered over her left cheek before she spoke again. She took a step closer, and before she knew it, she had her hand in his, and could feel his grip tightening around hers.

"Luke—I…" Her voice trailed off when he pulled away from her.

"The truth!" He had scoffed at the idea of Friedrich's sentence being reduced in light of her testimonial. "He doesn't deserve the truth."

§

Present—1953, London
Rita

She stood by the door for some time before entering, stunned to find Kurt in this room. She had dreamed about his death so many times while she was away, constantly fearful that he would disappear forever. But now, as she watched him sleep, she felt somewhat unprepared for the confrontation when he woke. She positioned herself at the wall across from his bed. This space would do, and she pulled out a large rolled-up canvas from her bag.

§

Present—1953, London
Kurt

When he woke, he thought he was in a different place; a familiar and painfully nostalgic place. He blinked a few times to be sure. It was the same landscape that foretold when his dreams would take a twisted turn and transform into nightmares. But now, staring at the pine trees of the Rouen forest, he felt at peace.

225

She appeared, unannounced and with the same grace he remembered. *Rita.* She stood before the canvas, facing him with a faint smile that curled the edges of her soft lips. She was standing exactly where Marie was supposed to be drawn in. Why was was she even there amidst the trees of the Rouen forest? Then she blinked and was no longer part of the painting.

"How—how did you…"

She smiled at him faintly and she slowly walked towards him, her hands tightly clutched together.

"It's alright," she nodded as if she knew his inmost thoughts, "I know."

Together with Rita, with whom he could build a future and a home to fill with children of their own, he was seeing his worst nightmares appear. But could he still achieve his dream now? How was he to face her? His shoulders trembled, and no words could escape his lips.

She sat on his bed and reached for his hands.

"I have a story you won't believe." Her eyes were smiling and she took both his hands in her own, gently assuaging his fears with a calming certainty that told him everything was going to be alright.

§

Present—1953, Paris
Luke

He watched the prisoner intently, trying to decipher which part of his face looked more incriminating. The arched eyebrows? The coldness in his eyes? He had confronted many Nazi soldiers before, even a few SS Unit Commanders, but he never got used to looking them in the eye, knowing the person he sat across from was guilty of crimes that no sentence could ever measure up to.

There were other people sitting nearby, but the room was silent and somber, much like the hospital ward he visited during the war in Bastogne. The white plaster on the wall was wearing off and dark blotches appeared near the cracks. It was a forgotten place, filled with people whose crimes were not so readily forgotten.

Friedrich seemed out of place. The others all wore a similarly heavy, saddened expression that he interpreted as regret. But he appeared to be unaffected, not in the least fazed that his hands were bound by cuffs, or that his freedom meant nothing in a confined area monitored by guards. He maintained his stern gaze and remained as silent as a statue. He must have been accustomed to being cold and expressionless while ordering families to be massacred, schools and villages burned. Even in a place like this, he retained an authoritative composure.

Luke laughed inwardly, but he felt his eyes burning into his enemy. After so long, he was still his enemy.

"I wanted to see if I remembered you." Luke heard himself speak as if disconnected from his voice. "I was there on that day—when you and your men killed her family."

Friedrich remained stolid at the mention of his crime. His eyes held a detached look.

"Catherine thinks you saved them." Luke said, shuffling in his seat. He felt remorseful at how he had left things with her, but this was not his crime.

"I don't think that's true." He stared at Friedrich, wanting to undermine his composure and witness the same guilt that he so acutely felt.

"I think she saved *you*. That you used her as a kind of twisted redemption for your own despicable crimes."

Friedrich returned his gaze with an unreadable expression. Was it contrition? Shame?

"I never meant to hurt her family."

His voice was softer than Luke imagined. "What about the hundreds other families that died at your hands? What about them?"

He felt consumed by outrage and self-righteousness and reminded himself that there were guards in the room.

Friedrich deliberately let the silence linger. His jaws clenched as he pursed his lips. He didn't have to answer him. Perhaps he had no answer to this question.

Luke recognized the futility of their meeting. He had wanted to seize on some degree of clarity, a kind of release from the obfuscated image of a man he understood as important to Catherine, a man who had radically wavered between the boundaries of good and evil.

"Catherine…" Friedrich's voice trailed off as he spoke her name. He cleared his throat before he began again. "Catherine spoke of someone who was rescuing them…" His blue eyes took on a rare tenderness. "Was that you?"

Luke felt transported back to the day he had failed to deliver his promise. Yes, he was there to rescue them but to no avail.

"It doesn't matter now. I couldn't save them." He looked out the window beyond where Friedrich sat.

He could hear the bullet rounds. He tried to muffle the sound but his mind was imprisoned by the past. He was so eager to make things right, to save them. The harrowing images of Claude, Lucille, and Marie's bodies flashed before his eyes. Defeated, he lowered his gaze. The tips of Friedrich's boots were worn away. He wouldn't be shining them again. Now Luke wished he were sitting on the other side of the table, that he were the one paying for this crime.

"She survived." There was a certainty in Friedrich's voice—a finality that perhaps was meant to encourage them both. He tilted his head and attempted to meet Luke's averted gaze.

"Yes. Yes, she did." Luke nodded. He had already stayed too long. He didn't want to be caught up in a past he had been trying to bury for nine years. Grabbing his jacket from the back of his chair, he stood up to leave.

"And you found her again." The fine lines between Friedrich's furrowed brows began to soften.

Luke didn't answer right away. He thought about how their paths had crossed again after the war. How she had resurfaced that night in the theater, bringing an uncommon joyfulness back into his life. He hadn't found her; instead, fate had untangled all the improbabilities and linked their paths again. He had a second chance at happiness, did he not?

"Has she changed?" Friedrich asked.

Luke turned back to face him, the ex-Nazi who had killed so many without a second thought. Here was the man who had defied his orders and saved a Jewish family in hiding; a soldier in a war that had broken them both.

"No, I don't believe she has." This was what Friedrich wanted to hear. Whatever image of Catherine he lived for, he would savor. So he would be given that much—the satisfaction of something beautiful he had treasured through time. For Marie, for the torture he spared her, and for Catherine.

As Luke moved towards for the door, opened grudgingly by the guard, he heard Friedrich shifting in his seat. Looking back over his shoulder, he saw a faint smile appear—a look of peace. Did Friedrich deserve it? He wasn't sure, but he felt grateful that this was his last glimpse of the man who had kept Catherine alive.

§

Present—1953, Paris
Luke

When he woke, there was little motivation to start the day or to paint. He turned his head towards his canvas, just the way he had left it the night before, and glanced at his brushes, the dry paint latching on like a curse. More sleep was an alluring option, but hunger stirred and his stomach roared in protest. He struggled to get up, feeling dizzy as his tired arms lifted him from the couch.

He walked towards the kitchen and caught a glimpse of a pile of unopened mail. Reaching for it, he began to read each piece, carelessly discarding the uninvited mail. A familiar name caught his attention: Rita Friedman. Wasn't her last name Collins? He ripped the letter open nearly tearing in half the picture inside the envelope. As if unraveling a precious gift, he removed the photograph slowly. The young soldier who had fought by his side looked into the camera. He wore a simple suit, his hair neatly brushed to the side. Rita's arm intertwined with his. The picture had captured Kurt and Rita's wedding day. Patterns of intricate lace covered Rita's wedding dress, and he envisioned her cheeks blushing as the photographer took the picture. He smiled at the thought of Rita reunited with Kurt, and he wished them every conceivable happiness.

The telephone rang, interrupting his wandering thoughts, and he placed the photograph on his canvas. Maybe they would be his next project.

"Hello?" He still sounded half-awake, and cleared his throat before speaking.

"Monsieur Newman?" An older, raspy voice said.

"Yes. Can I help you?"

"I was wondering if we could meet to discuss the price of one of your works I've long admired. I believe the name is *La Ballerine Perdue*."

"It's not for sale." Luke sighed impatiently. There had been countless generous offers in the past, but never one close to being accepted.

"I see. Then I suppose I'll have to commission you to draw one of her."

He recognized that voice now—Lapardieu. He should have known the haughtiness from the start. "Have you seen her recently, by any chance?"

"No, I haven't. I thought she was at the school."

It irked him that Monsieur Lepardieu demanded a portrait of Catherine, like he had any rightful ownership over her.

"She said she went home. But—" he laughed, "I just realized I had no idea where her home is. Do you know?"

H could it as though it were yesterday. The tall rows of snow-laden pine trees. The underground cave that held the people he loved. Marie. Catherine. The deafening sound of bullets being shot in the air. Catherine running. He shook his head and shuddered as though these images were overpowering him.

"Yes. Yes, I think I do."

Monsieur Lepardieu went on about his misgivings on Catherine's odd behavior lately, and Luke dove into the variety of possible reasons that would stop him from going after her. He last saw her in the Rouen forest, breathless and imploring him to help, and he had shut her out when he failed. The dismayed face of the sixteen-year old Catherine stuck in his mind. The thought of losing her family had left her shaken and unable to speak coherently.

She cried in her sleep remembering the terror that came at night. And now she was going back to the place that had tormented her for so many years.

Luke suddenly knew what he must do—it had been so simple all along. He dropped the phone and shuffled through the pile of clothing that lay on his couch. Throwing on his coat, he ran out to do what he should have done nine years ago when everyone Catherine held dear had vanished and he had left her to fend for herself.

§

Wartime—1943, Rouen
Marie

When her sister climbed back down carrying a worn-out basket full of bread, ham, packed jams, and even a piece of meat carefully wrapped in paper, she thought she had stumbled into a dream. She rushed to Catherine and patted her face and arms to make sure she hadn't been assaulted or otherwise harmed by the German commander who had followed them to the cave the night before.

She looked into Catherine's eyes and saw a faint change. There was renewed hope, for he did not come to kill their family, but instead, was helping them. And she detected a glimmer that made her appear older and wiser.

"Catherine, are you all right?" She gently squeezed her sister's arm.

"Oh, yes, I'm fine," she replied, emptying the basket of its goods while her eyes wandered elsewhere.

Marie recognized the look of infatuation the day she met Luke, a young American soldier who vowed to take her away. She came to understand her sister's distraction, her daydreaming, and the discreet smiles she would try but fail to conceal. She dared to dream for herself and her sister. One day they would find their own happiness, and she prayed that Catherine would be fiercely loved, as she loved her.

§

Present—1953, Rouen
Catherine

It was a long way home. Catherine sat alone in the cabin, her fingers twirling the ends of her woolen scarf. She looked out the window and listened to the calming rhythm of the train. After her last performance, she had announced that she would take a few days off. With no reason given, it was assumed she was tired, and friends and colleagues wished her a speedy recovery as they looked forward to her next performances lined up for the year.

Monsieur Lepardieu had been agreeable. She smiled as she recalled his patronizing tone.

"Catherine, chérie, of course you must take time and go home. Go and find your inspiration before you return to me."

How right he was. She was traveling hundreds of miles back to the hometown she hadn't seen since she left. Inspiration was not something sought on this journey, but something closer to reconciliation. Only a few nights ago, she stayed awake and tried to recount the memories of her family. She had never had a chance to dance for them.

"Dance for us," Maman would often plead even while knowing her most stubborn child would not perform without a proper stage. She would gently pat Catherine's head as she carried on with her errands, humming as she went. Her daughter would dance onstage one day, and she would be the proudest parent in all of Rouen.

Catherine would tiptoe into the living area of the cave and practice while everyone slept. Her imagination provided the music, and the steps were sometimes improvised and not always from memory. She had caught Marie staring at her one night as she spun repeatedly on the soil ground, secretly appreciating the audience that she had lacked. And every so often, late at night when she couldn't sleep, Papa would sit by himself, sadly pondering their future underground. He would sigh quietly, and when he saw her, his crestfallen face would melt into a reassuring smile and he would gesture for her to join him. They would sit and talk of the things they would do after they left the cave. He would joke with her and ask her to buy him expensive cars when she became famous.

"Of course, as many as you wish!" She would smile and take on the same sardonic tone. He was more supportive of her dreams than anyone.

When the train stopped, she was one of the first passengers to get off.

The station was newly built, but she recognized the setting immediately. Nothing much had changed. She breathed in the fresh, pine-infused air and felt energized. It was as though she had never left. The half-day's journey to the Rouen forest felt like only a few minutes had passed.

As she neared the familiar pathway home, her pace quickened. She lifted her small suitcase into her arms and began to run. Like the day she desperately ran from everything here, except that now she was returning home.

§

When she reached the entrance, her hands brushed away the loose dirt from the wooden plank that had served as a door. She allowed herself to sink into the melancholy and nostalgia that came over her. *Don't run away, Catherine.* She hung on to her determination as though were her last chance at life. Pushing aside the wooden plank, she slowly made her way down. The ladder had been kicked away from the ground, and she tried not to think about what took place that day. It wasn't a steep jump, but she let herself down carefully, not wanting to damage any part of this home. How much she had hated it before, but now it was something precious.

Her feet touched the ground and she felt unable to stand. Her legs weakened and she found herself sitting on the ground, unable to do anything but look around the hollow cave. She was a deserter coming home and now incapable of stopping her tears. As she wrapped her arms around her knees and lowered her head, a familiar book caught her eye. Marie's biology book lay opened to the page that showcased the intricate anatomy of the heart. She reached for the book and dug it out from under a pile of dust. Wiping away lingering dirt, she imagined she was curating a most important artifact from the war. Her tears stopped. Holding the book brought evidence to the life her family had lived underground, and to her subsequent life that had not been so wasted.

It was still a cave—but it wasn't empty. There were traces of life everywhere. The remainder of Marie's books lay scattered throughout the living room where German soldiers had forced everyone out. Her sister had never been careless about the alphabetical arrangement of her books.

Papa's stack of old newspapers, read repeatedly with supreme diligence as though meticulously preparing a lecture on the past, were still neatly stacked under the dining table. He would be pleased to see them as he last left them. She caressed Maman's scarf left on the table then used it to tie up her hair as she had done when no one was looking.

She mustered the strength to stand. This was surely her second chance to give the performance that she had so determinedly refused her family.

She journeyed back in time and heard the music in her head again, the only accompaniment to guide her steps. She began her demi pointe as she prepared to glide over the familiar ground with pas de bourrée.

This was not like the grand ballet performances she was so used to rehearsing for, but it was a dance she had learned as child and had never mastered because of her underground confinement. She struggled to remember the steps, which were oddly more difficult than any masterpiece she had performed. She felt the weight of war in her arms and legs, and her heart felt burdened by insufferable grief, but she strove to continue. *Maman ... Papa ... Marie ... Philippe ...*

With each pirouette she danced, she whispered a prayer for each of them.

§

Present—1953, Rouen
Luke

It was just as he remembered. He strolled down the familiar road to where he last saw Marie, and his chest tightened.

He had boarded the train to Rouen with a cluttered mind, but he allowed himself to be cradled to sleep by the train's pulsing beat. It was a deep sleep with only a few indistinct images among a scattering of memories. Unlike his previous dreams, he didn't see the faces of Kurt, François, Claude, Lucille, or Marie. But one silhouette appeared clearly from the dense mist that was the setting of his dream. *Catherine.* He reached out to caress her cheeks as he had done in the beginning, and when he touched her, her eyes shone with familiar warmth and love.

As the train pulled into the station, he woke with an urgency to see her. He jumped off before it had come to a halt, and he ran. He ran as fast as he could towards the place that contained the nightmares that had shackled his mind. He needed to get to her even while knowing what waited ahead. This obstacle must be overcome in spite of the inescapable pain at the sight of all that would remind him of the past. If they were to confront it together, they would finally be free.

He ran along the familiar path and dared to dream that he was free from what had gone before. He ran towards a long-awaited freedom.

The End

ACKNOWLEDGEMENTS

To my first readers, Carrie, Deb, Kar, Josephine and Hiukei, a huge thank you for taking the time to read my first draft and for providing me with countless insightful and honest feedbacks, and for all your encouragement.

My wonderful, ever so patient editor, Irene, thank you for the many Skype sessions and e-mails and for working with me in East Africa Time. Thank you for your invaluable guidance and kindness.

To Jodie, for the time you spent discussing the many characters and plotlines of Freeing Shadows. You are, without a doubt, my best listener and advisor, as you tirelessly helped me weave my ideas into a book. Thank you for supporting my thoughts, critiquing my wild imagination, and laughing through my epic mistakes together.

Aug, thank you for valiantly taking over the numerous work emails—for not minding to work more hours as I kept on writing.

To my parents, for always inspiring me with your stories and love . . . This book is a testament to what you have taught me: that Love trumps all evil and that Love never fails.

To Sam, my rock and mpenzi—thank you for your love and for supporting me to do what I love (and for lulling Emma to sleep while I wrote). This one is for you and Emma.

Made in the USA
San Bernardino, CA
12 March 2017